Nosy Neighbours
Nieschieaje Nohbasch

Available from Evertype

By Jack Thiessen

Dee Erläwnisse von Alice em Wundalaund
(*Alice* in Mennonite Low German, 2012)

Neighbours: Stories in Mennonite Low German and English
Nohbasch: Jeschichte opp Plautdietsch enn Enjlisch
(Jack Thiessen 2014)

Other short story collections

The Partisan and other Stories (Gabriel Rosenstock,
tr. Mícheál Ó hAodha & Gabriel Rosenstock 2014)

The Book of Poison (Panu Petteri Höglund & S. Albert Kivinen,
tr. Colin Parmer & Tino Warinowski 2014)

The Burning Woman and other stories (Frank Roger 2012)

Nosy Neighbours

Stories in Mennonite Low German and English

Nieschieaje Nohbasch

Jeschichte opp Plautdietsch enn Enjlisch

Jack Thiessen

evertype

2015

Published by Evertype, 73 Woodgrove, Ballyfin Road, Portlaoise, Co. Laois, Ireland. www.evertype.com.

First edition 2015.

A catalogue record for this book is available from the British Library.

ISBN-10 1-78201-108-0
ISBN-13 978-1-78201-108-8

Set in Minion Pro and Imprint MT Shadow by Michael Everson.

Cover: Michael Everson.
Cover photograph by Amy J. Graber of a "Farmer's Delight" quilt made by her mother, Julia Graber, juliagraber.blogspot.com.

Printed by: LightningSource.

Nosy Neighbours

Nieschieaje Nohbasch

Ennhault

Contents

Dedicated to
Alex Kasser who decorated Life
J.W.A. who defined Perfection

Nosy Neighbours
Nieschieaje Nohbasch

"Saj mol, Thiesse, ess de Ead rund enn dreit dee sich oplatzt doch?"

Schusta Boaje ess Kanädja, enn hee weet daut, enn wann hee daut vejäte well, doohne de Russlenda, soo's mien Voda, ooda uck mien Onkel Wellem ahm daut schwind biefaule lohte.

Wie fuahre noh Boajess, wiels dem siene twee Hocklinja enn een Bollkaulf sich aul dreemol ons enne Alfalfaweid enn uck oppe Howastap vebiesat haude, enn sich den Buck stiew enn rund enn ditj volljepanzt haude. "Soohnt" saje de Foarmasch, "send schlajchte Veehmanneare" enn motte oppjesettelt woare.

Wie kaume bie Boajes aun. Boaje kaum ute Däah rut, enn schobbt sich, enn meend, "Na Goodnowend, Nohbasch enn huage Jast, Thiesses. Schod, wann wie jewisst hauden, daut wie soohn huagen russlendschen Besuch tjrieen wudden, haud ons Jeaten eenen extra Hos jeschoten, enn wie hauden Junt jearn toom Owendkost enjeloden. Oba daut ess vebie, enn etj kaun mie blooß noch den Scheenschmack schobben."

OHO!, docht etj mie. Diss Boaje ess vleijcht mau een Kanädja, oba siene Uahre hoole meea auls blooß siene Hoah oppen Kopp enn Uat enn Städ.

Enn dann: "Woamet kaun etj deehnen, Ohmtje Thiesse?"

"Wie habe," säd Voda, "eene gaunze Schwitt framdet Jungveeh bie ons emm tjilenen Tun hinjrem Staul enn-jepaunjt, enn wulle mau weete, aus dee hiea bie Junt Tus send?"

"Tell me, Thiessen, is the earth round and, by any chance, does it spin?"

Schuster Bergen was a Canadian born Mennonite, meaning lesser voltage and he knew it, and if chose to forget it my father would remind him of it, quickly and *pro bono*, or Uncle William would do so with similar dispatch.

We were on a travel mission to the Bergens since their heifers and a bull calf had had more than ample feeds in our alfalfa pasture and also munched our oats in an adjacent plot, and all of Thiessen property and propriety. Such behaviour amounted to unacceptable bovine manners, calling for settlement.

We arrived at the Bergens. Schuster Bergen emerged from his hovel, scratching himself randomly. "Well, a pleasant good evening to my neighbours and high society, the Thiessens. Too bad, had we known that you, Russlander, classy and mannered, would honor us with visitation, our George would have shot an additional bush rabbit for dinner and we would have bade you to table. But such repast is past and all I can now do is to administer a grateful scratch in happy morsel well ingested."

Oho! I thought to myself. This Schuster may well be but a humble Kanädier but his ears serve wider purpose than merely keeping his hair in place.

And then, "What service may I offer?"

"We have a whole squadron of strange cattle in a little enclosure fenced up behind our stable and all I want to know

"Eene Schwitt?" sajt Boaje, "sooväl hab wie noch niemols nich jehaut. Daut motten dann Jeat Niefeld, dem Rußlenda, enn Jun nohdra Nohda siene sennen."

"Na," sajcht Voda, "Etj hab dee Bussels nich selwst jetalt, oba meea aul twee Zäjel sach etj dann doch derjch den Stacheldrohttun enn mien Paunjstaul weppre."

Boaje wisst sich, soo's jesajcht woat. Hee dreid sich eene Schmeatj, enn dann noch eene, enn meend fein schmeissijch, "Ohmtje Thiesse, daut ess mie dann doch eene Eah, daut Jie noh ons mett jun oppjewatjten Benjel Hauns jekohmen send. Noch eene jratre Eah wudd mie sennen, wann Jie mett mie toop een Trubbtje schmeatje wudden, enn dann uck noch een Kroostje Strufetjoaschenwien too Enj schmatjen wudden."

Daut haud siene Fru, Taunte Boajsche, vestohne, enn reatjt Voda een Kroostje Choke-Cherry Wien, den Voda biem Cigarette schmeatje drunk.

Dann stald Schusta Boaje sien lintjet Been opp dem Nowel vonne Trailareif, krautzt sich unjre Metz, enn säd gaunz feintjess; "Etj kaun mie väastallen, daut ons Bollkaulf soo nieschierijch auls daut aul emma ess, sich mol bie Junt ommtjitje wull, omm too seehnen, auls daut mett dee russlendsche Harrlijchtjeit wertjlijch waut opp sich haft. Oba, wann hee sich wertjlijch vebiestat haben sull, dann mott etj ahm bätre Mannearen biebrinjen, ahm scheen masten, enn emm Hoawst schlachten, enn Junt mol eenen scheenen Kaulfsbroden brinjen."

Etj betjitjt mie dit Schachspell vom Jespräch, docht aune Sinndachschool, enn Salomon, enn schobbt mie uck noh de Oat vonne jratre Ohmtjes aum Ooah.

Daut Jespräch wea oba noch nich too Enj.

Etj kunn seehne, daut Ohmtje Schusta sich de jeistje Meiwe opptjremple deed, eea hee wieda vetald: "Waut etj aul emma eenen jeleaden Russlenda froagen wull, tjemmt mie nu too Pauß: Saj mol Thiesse, ess de Ead wertjlich rund, enn dreid

is whether they are normally at home in your farm?" answered our father.

"A whole squadron?" answered Schuster Bergen. "I have never had so many. They surely must belong to George Neufeld, the Russlander, your neighbour closer to your estate."

"How many?" said our father, "I personally did not count the thieving little munching monsters but I for sure did see more than two tails switching behind the barbed wire enclosure of my impound."

Then Schuster switched gears, so to speak. He rolled himself a careful cigarette and then another one with equal attention before addressing the issue in a Low German, classy and unconventionally conventional. "Mr Thiessen, I have to collect myself a bit before expressing delight that you and your jaunty Johnny, have come for a visit. You would pay me further honor if you were to accept a little tobacco drum-let rolled with respectful care as befits my guest. You can honor me further still by accepting a cruse of choke-cherry wine and drinking it to the lease."

Mrs Bergen obviously heard her husband's offer and a goblet of cherry wine already was in our father's hand, which he accepted with the grace dispensed, while smoking an Old Chum of home-rolled manufacture.

Then Schuster Bergen placed a careful leg on the navel of our trailer tire, gave his hair line under an engineer's cap of unknown age, a civilized scratch and then pronounced, in a tone and quality of language, damn near made in church, "I can well imagine that our bull calf, as curious as it has been from birth, was intent on seeing for itself what Russian-Mennonite glories have to offer. However, and if it indeed committed an indiscretion as implied, then I have to teach it better manners, and feed and fatten it so that it will be the fatted calf of Biblical repute by late autumn after which it will

5

dee sich woomäjlich sogoa? Word Junt soowaut noch enn Rußlaund vetalt?"

"Meist soo ess'et," säd Voda, mett een haulf einsteinschen Schmusta, enn kaum sich doabie bediedend wijchtja väa auls Tus wann Mutta ahm von ähre Breeda aune Peetaborja Universität vetald.

"Daut well mie uck stemmen,"meend Schusta Boaje. "Aulso mett mien Bollkaulf hab wie daut soo eenjamohten jeräjelt. Oba ons bliewen noch dee Hocklinja äwrijch, enn etj mott mie, bie Die Thiesse, auls gooda Nohba fe dee Leesung bedanken. Daut ess aulatoop gaunz eenfach: Dee Ead ess dochwoll rund, enn see dreid sich uck, wann uck measchtens de Nacht. Aulso send miene Hocklinja de Nacht eenfach rutjestelpt, enn kaumen bie Junt emm Howafletj too lidjen!"

"Dankscheen, seea, enn kohmt mol wada! Audé!"

be butchered and a fine roast of veal will be the Thiessen's in due time."

I marveled at the chess game played by such polished amateurs before me and in my fantasy I was in Sunday School with King Solomon on the agenda and I risked a little scratch myself on the ear, and in the manner of the grown-ups.

The discourse of the men before me was not yet over. I had a strong sense of Mister Schuster rolling up his mental shirt sleeves before resuming his discourse, "Something which I have always wanted to ask an educated Russlander, will finally, I hope, find answer. Tell me, Neighbour Thiessen, is the earth really round and could it possibly be true that it is, also, indeed spinning from time to time? Was there talk of such unheard of things already in Russia?"

"That's pretty much as claimed," said our father, with a half Einsteinian smirk, while feeling considerably more important than at home, where mother talked about her brothers educated at the St. Petersburg University.

"I have lately come to agree with such monstrous thoughts myself," suggested Schuster Bergen. "We have pretty well resolved the matter with my bull-calf, I would think. Now there is the case of my missing heifers to be resolved, but before we do so, I would like to express my appreciation to you, Mr Neighbour Thiessen, for convincing solution to serious ponder. Obviously, the answer to a riddle of long standing is: The earth on which we dwell is obviously round, and, not only that, it also spins, even if mostly at night. And just as obviously, my heifers were unceremoniously dumped from behind my barn right into your field of oats, where you found them scattered about, dizzy but intact!'

"Thank you so much, and come again, soon! Goodbye!"

Taunte Jreeta stoawt

Auls Groottaunte Jreeta nohm Tweeden Tjrijch noh Kanada kaum, reatjend wie mett een Huptje Onjletjch, daut wie, wäaweet vleijcht aul morje too Grauf droage wudde. "See ess seea oolt enn jebräajlijch," säd Taunte Auna, "enn ahr schmatjcht meist goanuscht meea. Butadem haft see soo väl em Tjrijch erläwt, daut see goanijch meea läwe well!"

Daut wisst wie aules, auls wie ons emm Septamba 1949 sinndoagsch auntrocke, enn Frindschauft, oba besondasch Voda siene Taunte Jreeta, aum C. P. R. Station aufhohlde. Wie fuahre goot veatijch Miel de Stund noh Winnipeg opptoo, enn Voda enn Mutta spekeleade, woor'et Taunte Jreeta seehne wudd. See weare sijch eenijch: gohne wudd see mau affens tjenne enn äte vleijcht soo's een Spautz. "Schod, see wea emma eene jestuckte Fru von hundattachentijch Pund, enn doabie nijch fatt, enn nu woat see oolt enn vedreajcht senne enn Poggelada aum Jesejcht enn Henj habe. Schod!"

Wie weare aum C.P.R. Station aunjekohme, enn fruage, auls de Zuch boold aunkohme sull. Wie haude noch nijch utjefroacht, auls von hinjrem steenanen Stenda mie eene Fru toohoole tjreajch, enn mie aunfong too posse enn too dretjche, daut mie de Loft knaup word. Doa wea see! Taunte Jreeta haud ons jeseehne enn sijch vestoake, enn ons beluht, dee Zuch wea tiedijch nennjepulld. "Woo tjannst Du mie?" wull etj weete, "Du hast mie doch verhäa niemols jeseehne?" "Aune Näs, Jung, du hast doch een Thiesses Rissel." Well, docht etj, stoawe woa wie woll aula, oba disse läwendje Buschtje woat disse Nacht noch äwastohne. Meist soo wear'et

8

Aunt Margaret's Demise

When we heard that Great-Aunt Margaret was coming over from Russia, after the Second World War, we envisioned her as a little heap of misfortune we might be carrying—who knew—to her grave within the year. "Yes, she'll be old and frail by now," said Aunt Anna. "She's bound to have lost her appetite. After what she went through during the war, poor thing, I wouldn't be the least surprised. She's probably already lost her will to live."

That September in 1949 we got dressed in our Sunday best and all drove down to the C. P. R. station in Winnipeg to pick her up. All the way from Gruenthal to Winnipeg, father and mother speculated about how she would look. They both agreed she'd barely be able to walk, that she'd eat less than a sparrow. How sad, how very very sad. She had always been such a substantial woman, one hundred and eighty pounds and no fat at all; to have to see her now, all withered, her face wrinkled as frog's leather, not to mention her hands. It was a terrible shame.

We had only just reached the station and were about to ask whether the train was on time or what, when a woman charged out from behind a stone pillar, grabbed me in a wrestler's clutch and began hugging and kissing the dickens out of me. It was Aunt Margaret! She had seen us, had hidden behind a pillar, and had prepared an ambush. The train had come in earlier that day.

"But how did you know who I was? You've never seen me before," I wanted to know.

"Your nose, my boy, your unmistakable nose! You have the Thiessen trunk!"

dann uck. Wie weare affens Tus aunjekohme, auls Taunte Jreeta säd: "Etj hab noch een poah Stund Tiet opp disse Welt. Tjinja, send jie uck aula reed too stoawe, ooda jehea jie noch nijch too de Breedajemeend?" "Holy Doodle!" doch etj mie, enn jintjch em Staul auffoodre.

Auls etj tridj kaum, saut Taunte Jreta hinjrem Desch enn nu sach etj, daut wie woahrhauftijch Frindschauft weare; see haud eene Schiew verr sijch mett eenem gaunzen Kulla Roakworscht, een Hupe Silltjees, Schwoatemoag fief Zoll emm Quadroht, eene Japps voll Zipple, enn een Kuffel voll Äditjch. Enn nu fong see aun too vetalle: see vetald von Witte enn Roode, von Russe enn von Schwoatasch, von Frindschauft enn von Kirchlijche, von Doot enn Diewels, von Schindasch enn Molotschna. See vetald soo läwendijch, daut mie aunfog too grusle, enn too flautre, enn etj veschluckt mie, enn kaum daut mett'em Odme goanijch noh. Auls see vetald, woo see eenem hasseljen Russ eent mett'em Fortjestäl äwajeresst haud enn doabie biem Vetalle uthohld, stelpt etj vom Stool. Wie jinje toom easchten Mol em Läwe noh twalw schlope; Taunte Jreeta läd emma wada mett'e Vetal loos, wiels, säd see, vleijcht ess dit de latzte Nacht hiea emm Jaumadohl. "Oba, wann nijch, Leena, dann koak morje Borsch enn moakst een Gaunsebrode enn vleijcht eenen jestuckten Hohn mett Bobbat. Enn Peeta, du hast vleijcht emm Spitja noch een Schruwglaus mett Kwaus." Donn nauhm Taunte Jreeta jrodsoo ute Buddel utem Atjschaup twee Schluck ooda meea Aulpentjreita—oba goode Schluck, wiels etj seeh noh vondoag äahren Haulsaupel goot siene fief Zoll han enn häa weppe auls see de Buddel toodoak jintjch. Donn kroop wie enne Bocht, trocke ons de Zube ut, enn reiwde.

Nääjchsten Dach wea Sinndach. Auls etj vom Besorje nennkaum, läd Taunte Jreeta mette Vetall loos. "Joh," see haud goot jeschlope, enn bät haud see Liefschniedinj jehaut,

I stood back a little and sized up my "frail old aunt".

"I'm not so sure about us, but *she'll* certainly last the night," I decided.

Meanwhile Aunt Margaret wasn't taking any chances.

As soon as we'd arrived home she sat us down and pinned us with a stem look. "Now listen, all of you: I may have only a few hours left in this world, and I want to reassure myself. Are you all properly prepared for His Coming, or don't you belong to the Mennonite Brethren Church yet?" I hurried out to the barn to do chores.

When I returned Aunt Margaret was sitting at the table, and if I'd had any doubts before about our being closely related, those doubts immediately evaporated. The huge plate before her was heaped with no less than a full ring of smoked farmer's sausage, a mound of headcheese, at least five cubic inches of collared pork, and a whole cupful of vinegar.

And then she started to talk—and Lord God in heaven, this aunt was some talker. She told us all about the Whites and the Reds, the Russians and the Blacks, of relatives and half-believers, of heretics and the Molotschna. She talked so animatedly and so rousingly, I kept finding myself forgetting to breathe; when she described how she'd let one particularly bad Russian have it with a fork handle and then demonstrated the blow with a powerful sweep of her arm, she knocked me clean off my chair.

For the first time in our lives we went to bed after twelve o'clock that night, Aunt Margaret still talking furiously, because after all, there was always the chance it might be her last night in this vale of tears. "But if it isn't, Lena, then please cook me some borscht tomorrow, and roast a good goose, and maybe a fat rooster, and don't forget the stuffing! Oh and Peter-could you see your way clear to bringing in a sealer of *kwas* from the granary?" Having thus assured herself of the next day's provisions, she headed for the corner cupboard and attacked a bottle of *Alpenkraeuter* with such enthusiasm, the

11

enn uck jedretjcht haudet aune Milz, oba sonst haud ahr nuscht nijch jeschohd. "Wann wie enn Russlaund han enn wada soohn Vebietsel auls jistre zeowends jehaud haude, haude de Russe tjeen Kommunismus meea. Oba von Bassemkrut jeft daut mau denne Supp, enn wann eena mett schwackem Oarm de Russebenjels tooschetjch holp, worde dee boold wada ooltnäsijch!"

"Du, Hauns," säd see too mie, "komm mol häa, sitt'et mie noh stoawe?" "Daut weet etj nijch, eajentlijch nijch, wiels du best nijch jäl omme Uage, enn uck sesst jeit'et doch noch mett dienem Aupetit." "Du meenst de Väakost jistre?" "Joh," säd etj. Too Meddach wudd see mau weinijch äte, bloos waut een bätje meea veschlohne wudd, enn donn sijch opp'et Ooah laje.

Noh de Tjoatj sad wie ons aum Desch han; Jast weare jekohme enn Frindschauft; Taunte Jreeta haud de Lied aul fiefentwintijch Joah nijch jeseehne, oba see tjitjcht noh Näse enn noh Jedohnte, see head sijch dee Stemm aun enn säd: "Du best Jeat sien Tweeda," ooda "Du best Sarah äähre Cousiene," enn "Du best Peeta Ditje Dochta, dien Voda wea doch dee aufjefolna Predja!" "Joh, enn du best de Hiebatsche äah Hoawstjitjel, wie dochte aul, daut wudd een Utstelpsel jäwe, enn dochte aul aun aufdoktre, oba du best doch noch een staumjet Wief jeworde." "Lied, etj saj, jie sent hiea aula een bät hoat jeworde, enne Tjoatj hield tjeena!" Oba de gaunze Tiet äwa aut see, veea Schiew Borsch veschwunge, Hohns- schintjess enn eene haulwe Gauns weese boold äähre blanke Knoakess, jekoakta Schintje veschwung uck schelwawies, enn de Plumesteena noh too uadeele wea uck eene haulwe Komm Plumemoos bie Taunte Jreeta too de latzte Ruh jekohme. Doabie vegaut see daut Vetalle nijch; de Lied hielde enn lachte, roade enn säde: "Woo ess'et bloos mäajlijch!" enn muake den Tjnippsbiedel op.

sight of her vigorously bobbing Adam's apple remains vividly in my memory to this day. Then we finally all went to bed.

Next day was Sunday. When I got in from the barn Aunt Margaret was already in the midst of another tale. Yes yes, she had slept quite well, she had had a bit of discomfort what with her spleen acting up again, probably from all the excitement—but other than that she felt just fine. "Oh yes, if back in Russia we'd had a little lunch like the one we had last night, they wouldn't have had the Communism over there, I guarantee you that. But you can't cook a decent soup from broomweed, and if you don't give the Russian boys a good solid wallop very morning they're snooty again by the afternoon."

"Listen Hans," she said to me then. "Do I look to you as If I'm going to die very soon?"

"No," I said with some conviction. "You're not yellow around the eyes yet. And besides," I said, "your appetite is still pretty good."

"You mean that little snack we had last night?"

"Uh-huh," I said.

"Ach so," she said.

After church we sat down at the table; the house had filled with relatives and visitors. Aunt Margaret hadn't seen any of these people in twenty-five years but she looked at their noses, compared their gestures, listened to their voices and then delivered her verdicts: "You're George's second child!" and "You must be Sarah's cousin!" or "You would be Peter Dyck's daughter; wasn't your father the disgraced minister?" To Connie Hiebert she said: "Ah yes, you are Mrs Hiebert's autumn chicken, the late child. We thought your mother would have a miscarriage and there was all sorts of talk of doctoring around with you, but now look at you—a good solid woman... yes yes... but tell me, what is it with you people in this country, you seem to have become a little thick-skinned; I didn't see a soul crying in church this morning!"

Did I forget to mention that during all this she was munching and swallowing as if there might be no tomorrow?

Taunte Jreeta fuah boold noh B. C., doa wea nijch soo väl Frost enne Ead, doa kunn eena "billewanneea stoawe." Enn wie saute enn Jrienthol emma reed hantoofoahre. "Anyday," säd see opp dietsch, "kunn eena toom latzten Mol stoawe. Wäa äwrem Ozean foahre kaun, dee kaun uck stoawe," säd see enn freid sijch doabie, enn scheffeld noch eenmol de Schiew voll. "Enn du, Hauns, vespratjchst du mie, daut du tjemmst, wann etj daut latzte Schateltje utjeläpeld hab? Joh? Daut's goot. Komm mol een bätje nohda. Saj mol, du best doch soo jelead," säd see nu aul drettien Joah lohta enn B. C. "Meenst du, de doodja Mensch ess bie sienem Bejrafnis irjendwoo een bät doabie?" "Kaun senne," säd etj. "Meen etj uck; enn wiels daut soo ess, bruck etj Nieet toom Tjleed." Wie fuahre enn kofte Poajchem enn Sied fe eenen schwoaten Jumper enn eene witte Blus; Taunte Jreeta leet fuats eene Schniedasche kohme mett Nohtle enn Scheea. Nu word aufejmäte enn donn fuats bosijch jeprunt. Doabie musst etj Eadbäare, Himbäare, enn eene Arbus hohle; Taunte Jreeta hungat wada verre latzte lange Foaht...

Wie haude jejäte, enn de Tjleeda toom Soatjch weare foadijch; unje Schwoat, bowe Witt. See sad sijch een äah nieet Autfit han, foljd de Henj enn hield: "Mie grult nu doch, meist gaunz reed too senne, oba mett eenentachentijch Joah kunn'a vondoag de Nacht bie mie aunputtre. Blifst du noch bett morje? Eajentlijch haud etj noch een bät doaraun jedocht, mie enn Kanada too befriee, waut meenst du, Hauns?" "O" säd etj, "enn Dietschlaund ess een restja Onkel uck eentletzijch, de oola Adenauer!"

"Sposs nijch soo groff, Hauns," säd see, "du weetst dee ess kathoolisch!"

"Sorry," säd etj.

Aum näjchsten Dach sag wie ons wada. Taunte Jreeta schoawd aum Freestitjsdesch soo enn, daut mett jiedem Aufbietsel de Penschonscheck tjlanda word. Nä, see wea noch

Oh yes: four bowls of borscht that evaporated like water under an August sun; a pile of rooster legs and half a goose which reappeared in short order as a neat pile of gleaming bones; slice after slice of cooked ham, and from the heap of plum pits you could see that at least half a tureen of fruit soup had found its final resting place in the depths of Aunt Margaret. But all the while she kept talking, exhorting, proselytizing; people laughed and they cried and they exclaimed: "What a world, what a world!" Some were so moved, they even opened their billfolds.

Aunt Margaret soon left for British Columbia—the ground wasn't as hard there in the winter; you could die there any time you wanted—leaving us sitting in Gruenthal, set to go to B.C. at a moment's notice. "Because I could die any day now," she assured us. "Oh yes, it could happen any day now. Anyone who can cross the ocean can also die." And she heaped up her plate.

Thirteen years later I visited her in B.C. And again I sat by her side as she ate, and she told me stories. And then she leaned over to me confidentially and said: "Listen Hans, will you promise me that when I've spooned out my last little dish, you'll come to my funeral? You will? That's good. And now tell me, Hans, you are so educated now, give me your opinion. Do you think a dead person can... well, you know... attend her own funeral?"

"Probably," I hazarded.

"Well, that's exactly the way I see it too! And because of that, I need new material for a dress!"

We immediately climbed into my car and drove off to a wholesaler to buy cotton and silk for a black jumper and a white blouse. As soon as we got back Aunt Margaret phoned for a seamstress, who arrived half an hour later with scissors and needles. There was a great deal of measuring and cutting and fussing, and then the old Singer began to hum its age-old tune. And while all this was going on I was sent out to buy strawberries, raspberries and a watermelon; just the

15

nich gaunz wajch, onn doabie haud see doch aul "daut Ticket enne Fupp." Oba ahr haud jedreemt, see wea aul em Himmel, enn doajäjen kaum ahr daut hiea oppe Ead aules mau seea fleiw väa.

Aune 1967 em Farjoah—Taunte Jreeta wea 93 Joah voll—auls alewäaje daut Läwe loos jintjch enn bute Hei jemoakt word, kaum uck bie Taunte Jreeta Eena mett de Sans nenn. See stiepad sijch toom latzten Mol. See haud sijch jrohts noch eenmol vebäte: Schintjefleesch, Tjieltje enn Moos. Wada tjneep'et hiea enn doa. Enn see läd sijch han, oba see bleef ditmol lidje. Donn muak wie daut Fensta op, enn leehte äähren Jeist rut enn wajch...

Taunte Jreeta haud veea Jumpasch enn fief Bluse biem Bejrafnis-Praktisse derjchjedroacht, oba nu wear'et vebie. Biem Bejrafnis lach see emm Soatjch enn frinteld een bätje. Medden enne Predijcht musst etj mie haustijch ommdreie. Yessiree, etj jleew uck noch vondoag, daut Taunte Jreeta uck een bätje doabie wea. Jie uck?

contemplation of her long last voyage had made Aunt Margaret very hungry.

When we had finished eating and her funeral clothes were ready—white on top, black beneath—she sat down in her new wardrobe, folded her hands and cried a little. "I'm a bit afraid, now that I'm ready; when you're 81 years old, that final knock at your little door can come at any moment. Will you stay with me until tomorrow? Actually, I'd always thought I might get married in Canada, but I don't suppose anything will come of it. What do you think, Hans?"

"Well, I'll tell you," I said, "I know of a perky old bachelor in Germany who's available, old Adenauer you know, if that's any help…"

"Stop those rude remarks," she admonished sternly. "You know perfectly well he's a Catholic."

"I'm sorry," I apologized.

The next morning, at breakfast, Aunt Margaret ate so heartily that her pension cheque crumbled with every bite. No, she wasn't gone yet, she informed me, though she had her ticket in her pocket. But while I'd tossed on the living-room sofa she'd been dreaming she'd gone to heaven, and it had been so wonderful, she told me, she was finding things on earth a little flat this morning.

It wasn't until the spring of 1967, when she was 93, that Aunt Margaret finally gave in to heaven's blandishments. She had just finished a little lunch—cooked ham, noodles, onions and cold fruit soup—when a bit of pain here, a little pinch there, convinced her to "lay her ear on her mattress" for a few minutes. This time she didn't rise again. And when it was all over, we opened the window and set her spirit free.

Aunt Margaret had worn out four jumpers and five blouses practising for her funeral. Now she lay in her coffin and smiled a bit. In the middle of the sermon I turned around and had another good look at her. Yes, I believe to this day she was enjoying herself. And she didn't look the least bit hungry.

Fruesunjabetjze
enn eene Goldmedaulj

Wie schriewe daut Joah 1936, den easchten Juli, aulso dee Kanada-Dach. Wie, enn doamett meen etj ons Voda, haud jrods von J. R. Friesen en Steinbach eene meist gaunz niee Koah, een Ford, den aule Menniste donn, enn nu een *Fuurd* nanne, jekofft; ons Fuurd haud acht Zylinda enn wea soo straum auls eene fresche Brut.

De Koah wea greiw, ritjt noh Luxus enn blentjad soo's Nippa-Wota. Wiels ons Voda eene License auls Traktorist von Elloag, enne Ukraine haud, enn disse License fe aule Tiede golt, aulso bette "Eewijchtjeit" wea wie reed toom loosfoahre.

Onse Koah haud tjeen Schlätel, oba uck tjeene aundre Koah; aule dree-entwintijch enn gaunz Kanada haude donn tjeen Schlätel.

Dee Grootstaudt Wienipetj wea ons Reiseziel enn onse stohtsche Limousiene, enn uck daut Eaton's Stooah, aulso Lauftje, wiels too dee Tiet wea Wienipetj enn Eaton's soo meea eent enn dautselwje, soo's Steinbach enn eene haulf Dutz Tjoatje, dautselwje wea enn send.

Wie Tjinja saute oppe hinjaschte Sett. Tjinja gauf'ett veea. Peeta, sass, boold säwen, etj wea jrods fief jeworde, Auna jintj bosijch oppe veea loos, enn Neetatje, ons Baby saut bie Mutta väre, oppe Schoot ooda aune Brost, see wull boold een haulwet Joah oolt woare.

Unjawäjess, wiels de Dach soo scheen auls Wiehnachte emm Somma wea, sunge de Ellre "Ich bête an die Macht der

18

Bloomers and a Gold Medal

The year of record is 1936 in the month of July. Day One: Canada Day. We, meaning our father, had just purchased from J. R. Friesen in Steinbach an almost brand new Ford (which Mennonites then as now called *Fuurd*) an eight-cylinder model.

The car was grey, smelled as new as luxury and sparkled like the waters of the Dnieper. Since our father had a licence as a *Traktorist* from Kitschkass, Ukraine, with expiry date "Eternity" we were fit and ready to go.

That Ford V8 had no key, neither did any other vehicle on the road.

The metropolis of Winnipeg was our aim and destination in our streamlined limousine, and also Eaton's, since at the time Winnipeg and Eaton's were pretty well synonymous, like Steinbach and a half a dozen churches were the same, then as now.

We children sat on the back seat of our stately car. There were four children to be counted. Peter six, soon to be seven, I had just turned five on the tachometer of time, Annie was bating four in two weeks, while Baby Agnes sat with mother in front, either in her arms or mostly at her breast; she was rapidly going on half a year.

En route, because it was a day lived for, our parents sang "Ich bete an die Macht der Liebe" in Russian; things were that celebratory in our Fuurd between Gnadenfeld and Winnie-petj that memorable day.

Liebe" opp Rusch; daut jintj aun dem Dach soo fiealijch too tweschen Jnodefeld enn Wienipetj!

Onse Ellre vesproake ons jiedem een Ice Criem enne groote Staudt, woa Obraum Driedja oabeid, enn nohäa wudd een jiedra eenen haulwen Doughnut tjriee; soohne spondoble Harrlijchtjeite garantiede schmocket Benehme oppe hinjaschte Sett enn uck wiedahans.

Onse Mutta haud ons jrods de Miela mett Ice Criem beschmät mett äah Schalduak bie Silver Dairy's aufjewescht, enn wie fuahre värewajch aulso noh Eaton's opptoo. Nohm Post Orda, doa, woa eena sich ver een Katalooh hansatte, sich de Woare betjitje, befeehle, bestalle, betohle enn noh Hus foahre kunn.

Wie koffte Droagbenja fe Voda, wiels siene noch ut Rußlaund weare, enn dee stiepade sich, siene Betjze lenja too droage; see weare meed, utjeratjt, enn utjefrenst. Uck fong ons Voda aul een tjlienet Schemedauntje too droage, oba daut wea nich daut Thema aun dem Dach.

Wiels Frulied too dee Tiet tjeena lange Betjze druage, haude see Bloomers, aulso Bloomasch aun, enn de druage see, jieden Dach, Somma enn Winta, wiels dee macklich enn woam weare, enn wiels daut soo enne Bibel stund, daut daut soo mußt. Soohne Bloomasch bedatjte aules vom Bucknowel bett aune Tjnees, enn dee Jäjende doatweschen, hab etj mie vetalle lohte. Dee weare woam enn ditj utjefoodat, enn weare roosa enne Foaw; blooß roosaroot, enn doamett soo goot! Sie weare wind-dijcht enn mollijch, enn kaume enn eene Jreese; dee Bloomasch ratjte sich je noh dem Jewijcht ooda Ella. Soo's aul aunjediet, enn uck aul meist utjesproake, Maunstjleedie soo's lange Betjze weare too dee Tiet fe de Frulied, soo selden auls een nich unjajeduckta Brooda bie de Doop, ooda een Foatjel ohne Tjrinjel aum Zoagel.

Wie koffte twee Poah fe onse Mutta, enn stoppte dee enn eene Tut, enn doa selle see uck opp vereascht bliewe.

Our parents promised us an ice cream each at a dairy in the Big City, where Abe Driedger worked, and later at Eaton's we would be rewarded with half a doughnut each; such generous promises guaranteed good behaviour on the rear seat and beyond.

Our mother had just wiped our mouths clean of ice cream evidence with her apron at Silver Dairy's and we were already fully on our way to Eaton's. To the Mail Order, where you could order from the Catalogue whatever you wanted, scrutinize the potential, pay for it, and go home.

We bought suspenders for our father, because his were still from Russia and they were reluctant to further put up with his pants; they were tired, droopy and frayed. Also, our father was beginning to carry a bit of a belly of pot, but such was not on the agenda of the day.

Since womenfolk in those days wore no long pants, bloomers were the dress item of choice and of necessity, and by Biblical decree. Bloomers were formidable and warm underpants, covering knees to belly button and mounds in-between, I was told. Also, they were fleece lined and came in colour rosy-red only. Windproof and cosy, one size fitted all.

As implied and almost stated, men's wear, like long pants for women at the time were rarer than a Mennonite Brethren not ducked under during baptism, or a pig without a twirl in its tail.

Mother bought two pair but these stayed in the shopping bag for the time being.

We were now set to go after the shopping invasion and a happy lot we were. We had an ice cream and half a doughnut each in our bellies, gratitude in our heart and a Fuurd smile on our every face and now set out on the far, far distance home, where our dog Karo was waiting.

I had almost forgotten to mention that our father also took along our neighbour, his factotum Abraham Wiebe. "You

Nu weare wie reed toom foahre nohdem wie Eaton's soo meea ladijch enn utjekofft haude; wie weare aulatoop soo schaftijch auls een Topptje Mies. Jieda haud een Ice-Criem enn een haulwen Doughnut em Buck, Dankboatjeit emm Hoat, enn een Furdschmusta oppem Jesejcht, enn nu wea wie reed, dee lange, lange Reis noh Hus auntootrede, woa ons Hund Karoo opp ons wacht.

Etj haud meist vejäte too erwähne, daut ons Voda uck onsen Nohba enn sien Faktotum Obraum Wiebe mettjenohme haud. "Eena kaun niemols nich weete," meend ons Voda, "leewa eenmol too väl, auls tweemol too weinijch!"

"Dochwoll tjeen Chance unjawäjess eenen sturren Chocholl too traffe, ooda een rietschen Machnowtze enn disse Jäjend, oba wäa haud uck mett een Tjleenjemeenda enne Beeatätj jerätjent?"

Obraum Wiebe lach dobbelt tweschne Hinjasett enn dee ladje Kohma enne Koah gaunz hinje. Oba hee wea een Russlenda, dee bie ons han enn wada utschauft, enn jieden Dach bie de Draschtiet, enn onbedinjt den gaunzen Dachäwa aum Tjätjedesch bie ons saut.

Wiels miene Nieschiea aul emma jrata wea auls etj, enn miene Ooltnäsijchtjeit doppelt soo groot, enn miene Bibeltjantnisse forscha auls eene Tabun Prädjasch von eene haulwe Dutz gaunz moderne Tjoatje enn Steinbach, fruag etj Ohmtje Wiebe soo meea ut Spoß: "Kunne sich Ähre easchte Väaellre noch aun dee Eenzelheite von Noah siene Artj dentje?"

Wiels Wiebe soo meea aules wißt, enn sich daut Äwaje utdocht, krautzt hee sich den Stobbel aune Backe enn aune Tjeewe, eea hee mie mett'e Woahrheit kaum, Woahrheit enn siene eajne Dentj-Backkomm enjereaht. "Etj kaun mie nich kratjt perseenlich doaraun dentje, oba aune Nippa-Eewasch wea doavon aulnoch foaken de Red, sooväl ess mie sejcha!"

never know," said our father, "better one too many than twice too little."

"Hardly a chance to meet up with some troublesome Chocholls, meddling Cossacks or murdering Machnowtse, in these parts, but then again who expected to meet a *Kleingemeindler* in a beer parlour?"

Abraham Wiebe lay doubled up between the rear seat and empty space called the rumble area at the time. But he was a Russlander, who worked at our place now and then, and certainly for days on end during threshing, and definitely every day at our kitchen table.

Because my inquisitiveness was always bigger than I, and my smart-assed-ness twice as big, and my biblical knowledge greater than a church load of Springs People, I once asked Mr Abraham Wiebe just for the fun and hell of it, "Did your very earliest primeval forebears still remember details of Noah's Ark?"

Since Wiebe knew pretty well everything and invented the rest, he scratched his gill stubble before coming out with the truth, home-made, "I don't personally remember, but there was talk of it on the Dnieper banks, for sure."

As of that day I knew that Abraham Wiebe, while having an altogether different name was distantly related to our father; they shared distance memories and were capable of correcting most records retroactively. Both were ministerial material and we knew it.

Whatever: Then, as now, Ste. Anne's Road is the route which will take you from Winniepetj to Jrienthol. And to Gnadenfeld, as well, like today.

And then as now, Ste. Anne's Road in St. Vital will take you very close to the Red River. Our father must have known this. And when our father saw a larger body of water like today, he could not be contained: then it was fishing or swimming time. That was the DNA dictate of a hundred thousand Mennonites

23

Von dem Dach aun, wißt etj daut Wiebe, obzwoa hee een gaunz aundren Nohme haud, mett ons Voda wietleftijch Frindschauft wea; see kunne sich aun aules dentje, enn brochte too Staund aul daut Äwaje rejchtijch too stalle, gaunz nohdem ahn daut paußt. Enn beid haude kunnt Prädjasch woare, daut wea mie uck dietlijch!

Oba, woo uck emma...donn enn uck nu, feahd dee Ste. Anne's-Wajch von Wienipetj noh Jrienthol. Enn uck wieda noh Jnodefeld; donn enn uck noch vondoag.

Enn donn, enn uck noch vondoag, feaht dee Ste. Anne's Road gaunz dijcht aum Red River uck Riefa, ooda Rie vebie. Daut mußt ons Voda jewißt habe. Enn wann ons Voda, een grootet Wota sach, soo's vondoag, wea hee nich too hoole: dann mußt hee fesche ooda schwame. Daut wea sien DNA, enn uck dee DNA von hundat Dusend Menniste, dee ahn de Nippa sienatiet enjeimpft haud, eene Kollektivpsyche von een grooten, joh jewaultjen Stroohm, saje de jegrommde Mensche doatoo.

Fesche ooda schwame...vondoag wull Voda schwame. Omm onse Mutta bie de Helljedagstemmung too hoole, fung Voda aun solo, "Ich weiß einen Strom too sinje," oba auls hee den Riefa sach, vewaundeld sich daut Leed enn Wota; hee klunjd oppe Brams, enn hee haud sich uck aul dee niee Droagbenja aufjeschlowe, enn haud uck aul een Foot butre Koaredäah. Onse Mutta tjand onsen Voda, enn hilt sich de Henj verre Uage, enn räd meist soo's een Jebed: "Oba Peeta Du wurscht doch nich, nä?"

Oba Voda wudd. Nohdem see opp Rusch een bätje Han enn Häa jeret haude, jestund Voda, daut hee eene Lomm fe twintijch Zent doa oppe Städ liehe, enn dee Obraum Wiebe aune Sied bie ahm biem Schwame roodre wudd.

Aules wea nu reed, enn Voda haud sich uck aul dee Betjze, Einwegstraße, soo's se saje, aufjestreept, enn hee haud uck aul twintijch Zent fe de Bejleitlomm boa betohlt, auls een Polizist,

injected in them by the Dnieper, the definitive River of a collective psyche.

Fish or swim…today our father elected to swim. To keep our mother in the spirit of the day father had uncharacteristically launched into a solo rendition of the mighty hymn "I know of a stream", but when he saw the river, the song turned to water; he stepped on the brakes, and had already slipped off his new suspenders while half out of the car door.

Our mother knew our father and her hands were before her eyes as she rocked her head left and right and left again while pronouncing, "Oba, Peter, you wouldn't, would you!"

But Peter would. After a bit of muffled but spirited back and forth, father conceded that he would hire a boat for twenty cents which was rent-able by the water and which Abraham Wiebe would row alongside.

Everything was set to go and father was already stripping off his pants of no return, since he had paid twenty cents in full for the row-boat, when a policeman, also in a Fuurd, pulled up from behind. Mother jerked off her apron in a jiffy which father used to hide his private parts, similar to the original apron of fig leaves; also, he said the apron would keep the snoopy a safe distance from his Atlas physique.

The man of the law engaged in some serious conversation with our father; a serious conversation with our father happened twice in his lifetime, maybe just once. "Here in Canada, we swim not like in the Bible or in Rushia" was the long and short of it. Verbatim, I heard it.

They reached an accord of commonality.

The hired boat fully paid for tipped the scale.

What had to happen to satisfy the law? Father slipped back into his upper and lower long johns, all in one piece, buttoned up his hind door, called flap and to further and fully accommodate the Morality Squad he pulled a pair of mother's

uck enn een Furd, platzlijch hinje oppduckt. Mutta tetjt äah Schalduak auf, enn Voda bedatjt siene Privautsache doamett, kratjt soo's Adam enn Eva em Paradies mett een Fiejeblaut auls de leewa Gott Polizist späld, wann uck nich em Furd, ween's soo jleew etj.

Voda meend uck noch soo bieaun, hee "kunn sich mett dem Schalduak dee Nieschieje bäta vom Liew hoohle. Wann eena soo straum jebut ess auls etj, mott eene mett Biekrupasch rätjne," meend hee.

Dee Jesatzmaun enn mien Voda hilde earnste Unjared; soohnt pessead ons Voda tweemol enn sien Läwe, vleijcht eenmol! "Hiea enn Canada schwam wie nich soo auls enne Bibel ooda enn Rußlaund," war der lange Rede kurzer Sinn. Kratjt soo head etj daut!

See eenigte sich; daut Voda dieret Jeld fe de Lomm betohlt haud späld doabie de entscheidende Roll.

Waut mußt Voda aulso nu doohne, omm dem Jesatz too befrädje? Hee schloof sich de lange enn bowe Unjabetjze, aules enn eenem Stetj wada aun, tjneept sich de Hinjaluck too, oba wiels dem Moralpolizist daut noch emma nich jenuag wea, trock hee ut Mutta ähre Tut een poah von ähre lange niee Unjabetjze, roosa-root äwa sien Privautissimo, enn dann wea hee reed, gaunz reed dee Red Rie unjatoonehme.

Wann nich aules gaunz kratjt jeflauscht haud, soo's jeweehnlich, wudd etj nich hiea sette, enn disse Jeschijcht mett eene Woahrheitguarantie, soo's jeweehnlich, oppje- schräwe, enn utjestallt habe.

Bett sien Stoawesdach, bestund Voda doaropp, daut hee den Red aun dem Dach enn eene Rekordtiet jeschwomme haud, wann uck mett leztje Zube aunjetrocke. Enn ahm stund eene Goldmedaulj too!

Etj mott ahm Rajcht jäwe!

brand new rosy bloomers over his private parts for extra measure and then he was set to go.

If things would not have worked out perfectly, as always, I would not be here to report the incident with the customary warrantee of truth.

To his dying day father insisted that he deserved a gold medal for having swum the Red River back and forth in record time with the handicap of apparel. I agree.

Oppem Pioneer Tjoatjhoff
enn Steinbach

Disse Jeschijcht fong oppem steinbachschen Tjoatjhoff, den Pioneer Tjoatjhoff aul twalw Joah tridj aun. Donn wea en Steinbach noch aules aulatoop een bät dolla em tjlienen enn doamett uck moakhauftja. Wann eena nohm Lauftje fuah, kunn eena de Hunj, auls Ljuba, Mister ooda Reeschtje ranne lohte, enn daut deed etj dann uck jieda Wäatjch, aule dree.

Ljuba ess een Beagel enn haft eene schoapere Näs auls eene darpsche Pludamoazh. Mister haft nijch gaunz soohne schoape Näs, ess doafäa oba ooltnäsijch, enn Reeschtje ess bloos langnäsijch, enn sesst nuscht nijch. Daut etj Reeschtje uck foaken een Glommskopp nann blifft enne Hunjsfamielje, enn doamett soo goot.

Wann etj aune wastne Sied vom Lauftje, aulso vonne Extra Foods oppem Parkplautz stohne bleef, freide sijch de Hunj aul drall, daut see mol wada oppe Schneediene späle kunne, enn dee uck een bät bunt enn jäl foawe kunne. Boold foll mie oba opp, daut de kortbeenje Ljuba nijch bloos väl opp dree Been too bestalle haud, oba daut ahr daut väl dolla auls de aundre Hunj nohm Tjoatjhoff trock, enn daut see daut doa mett ähre schoape Beagelnäs seea drock haud. Ähre Näs weppad doabie dolla auls een Lammazoagel, enn see piepad enn kolbätjad ve luta Oppreajung. Enn emma wada jintjch see noh dree Städe oppem Tjoatjhoff enn läd sijch doa han enn säld sijch enn reef sijch doa enn, enn freid sijch auls een Hund, woohna jrods eene Worscht jetjräje haud.

Etj kunn mien Wunda nijch lohte, bett eene ella-achtje Taunte daut doa uck oppfoll, enn mie vetald, daut enn Russ-laund uck aul mol soo waut sondaboaret pesseat wea. "Jun

On the Pioneer Cemetery
in Steinbach

This tale commenced twelve years ago in Steinbach on the Pioneer Cemetery in Steinbach. At that time things in Steinbach were a bit slower, simpler, more humble, certainly more manageable and therefore more credible; life was easier. If going to the store is what one had in mind, all three of my dogs, Ljuba, Mister and Reeschtje went along for the ride and attendant business, once a week.

Ljuba is a Beagle with a sharper nose than the village gossip. Mister's nose is not quite as reliable but he compensates for such lesser gift by being cocky, while Reeschtje is as unpretentious as solid virtue is meant to be. I have been known to call Reeschtje a blockhead but that is an in-dog family joke, and not to be narrated beyond canine family confidence.

Whenever I park on the west side of Extra Foods, all three dogs squirm with delight since I allow them to run free on the snow drifts and banks and to colour the snow as they please with their built in crayons; their colours of choice are mainly tinges of yellow. It was not long before I noticed that the short of leg Ljuba Beagle hound negotiated less business on three legs than the other dogs, but was more interested in the cemetery, the churchyard, scant distance away. While there, she rummaged around busily, following a scent, obeying the bidding of her nose. Her nostrils then wiggled like a lamb's tail while issuing testimonies of things more believed in than seen, while grunting, then braying like her farmyard rivals and even crowing like a peacock when zeroing in on the object of inner dictate. Soon her persistent constant was seeking out three exact spots on the cemetery on which she rolled and twisted

Hund Ljuba," säd see too mie, "kaun daut ritjche, daut doa deep unjre Ead eenje Doodess em Grauf vewese, enn daut ritjcht ahr scheen," meend see.

Toom Jletjch saut etj nijch opp een Stoohl, sesst wea etj vom Stoohl jestelpt, soo seea vefeahd etj mie äwa disse Nohrejcht doa medden oppem Tjoatjhoff, oppem Frädhoff. Oba etj jleewd ahr daut dann doch. Oba etj säd doatoo vereascht tjeen Wuat; etj sie een stella Maun.

Twee Wätjch lohta säld Ljuba sijch wada opp dem Tjoatjhoff, enn deeselwje Fru, noch ut Russlaund, betjitjcht sijch daut Spektoakel, enn wundad sijch uck mett een haulf scheewen Kopp. Ljuba socht sijch uck aulwada dee dree Städes ut, enn wetjeld sijch doa drall fe luta Vejneajung. Etj fruag dee Taunte—eene Taunte Leppsche wea daut—waut daut woll too bediede haud, oba see säd bloos: "Etj hop, daut ess nijch daut, waut etj jleew daut ess. Oba wann daut soo ess, dann well etj leewa nijch doaräwe räde. Butadem tjanne See, Mista Thiesse, doch den Al Reima, enn dee mucht daut dochwoll weete, woo sijch daut mett june Ljuba enn dee besondere Städe opp sijch haft."

Wiels etj ut Taunte Leppsche nuscht nijch wiedret rut-tjreajch, säd etj opp vereascht nuscht nijch, oba enn miene Fantasie dreide de Reemschiewe von mien Pedaumtje aul nedroat enne Rund. Enn etj laus, enn etj forscht, enn etj fruag een poah Prädjasch von Fräjoah, enn uck een poah kathoolische Tjoatjevodasch, enn lieseltjes jintjch mie een Lijcht opp, enn boold haud etj uck miene Theorie soo langsom oppjestalt. Aum measchten holp mie doabie dee heilja Voda, uck Pohp jenannt, dee Pious, woohna enn Rom emm tweeden Welttjrijch oppem Throon saut, enn soo väl Domms enn Iebel sijch utdocht enn uck deed auls Goodet, wann nijch sogoa meea.

Enn auls diss Pappa Pious storf, gauf daut eene schratjelje Äwarauschung, wiels? Enne tjristelje Tjreise ess daut enne gaunze Welt bekaunt, daut wann een gooda Mensch stoawt, dee Leijch gaunz langsom vewest, ooda aunjchmol äwahaupt nijch. Toom Biespell habe se mien Grootonkel, den

with atavistic delight. Ljuba's delight was on par with any dog having secretly taken off with a chunk of Mennonite farmer sausage.

I could barely contain my surprised bewilderment at this behaviour, a mixture of delight and secrecy on her part, and not about to be shared. Cemeteries are not the customary site of happy frolicking in the Anabaptist tradition, and so I alternated from somber dignity to empathetic delight in Ljuba's merriment, obvious, and the only sentiment she willingly shared.

While I was pondering the ways of my hound, an elderly lady chanced by. She, of gentle reserve and even a hint of benign wisdom, took an interest in Ljuba's church garden rooting while discreetly remembering similar canine behaviour in Russia way back then, "Your dog Ljuba," she gently suggested in unobtrusive fashion, "has caught a whiff of something deeply buried and I am fairly sure it's a corpse mouldering that so much delights her Beagle schnozz. "

Lucky I was not sitting on a chair because it would have rolled me off, such was my surprise at hearing her observation there on the cemetery, on the Pioneer *Frädhoff*, the "Peace Yard" as we call it in the original. Since I was not prepared to come to terms with such revelations, I dismissed her observations by simply refusing to believe her. Contrary to inclination, I said nothing; I am a man of few words, so I keep telling myself for however long it takes.

Two weeks later on a bright late March afternoon, Ljuba was again rolling in the churchyard. The same lady as before was taking a walk; she paused to reflect on the spectacle of Ljuba's creation with abated wonderment, and a reflective listing to port of a well coiffured head. As if programmed, Ljuba again sought out the exact three spots on which to concentrate her rolling delight. I mobilized my courage and suggested to Mrs Loepp, for such was her name, if she would please volunteer the essence of her ponder.

She replied with concerned discretion, "I hope it is not what I fear it is. But if is indeed so, I would prefer not to talk about it. Moreover, Mr Thiessen, I am fairly sure you know old Peter

Missjoonoa enn Dokta Pappa Johaun Thiesse aune 1953 enn Bandung enn Indonesien begrowt. Aune 1968 musst dee jewaultje Gruft mett Pappa Thiessen doabenne noh een hejchren Uat velajcht woare, enn auls se daut deede, nauhm daut Wunda von aule Bedeelijchde tjeen Enj. Pappa Thiesse lach doa em Grauf enn haud buta eenen noch lenjren Boat enn lange Finjanäjel sijch nijch een bestje ve-endat. Hee schleep sondasorj wieda, enn wea nuscht nijch vewest. Tjeen Dripps!

Wann soowaut eenem Pohp pesseat, dann sajcht de Reemische Tjoatjch, soohnen kaun eena heilijch spreatje, wiels Gott soo stoatj enn ahm wohnt. Lacht wann jie welle, oba etj jleew daut, wiels etj hab dusend Bilda enn Photo-graphiee von mien Grootonkel em Soatjch jeseehne, enn hee schleep soo deep, daut tjeena nijch docht, daut hee opplatzt doch doot wea!

Waut oba den hasseljen Pohp Pious pessead ess meist nijch uttoodentjche. Knaup lach hee em Vaticum feierlich opp-jebeajt, dann fung dee Donna soo grulijch noh Ohs aun too stintje, daut haulf Rom bedieseld, enn de aundre Halft sijch krank kotzt. Joh, enn dee väle Dusende haude sijch mau affens de Miela vom Kotze enn uck de Näse vom Jestank jewescht, dann foll dem haulfheiljen Donna uck aul siene total schwoat jewordne Näs, gaunz vefuhlt, auf.

Joh, enn aul daut wisst etj auls etj mol wada medden em Winta noh Steinbach toop mett miene Hunj oppen Pioneer Tjoatjhoff jintjch. Ljuba dreid sijch mol wada total drall, enn säld sijch enn stankad ve Vejneaje, enn freid sijch ut aule Lajcha. Oba ditmol tjitjcht etj gaunz jeneiw han, enn waut sage miene Uage? Aulewäje leet Ljuba sijch daut goot gohne, oba oppem Grauf von eenem Leewe, eenen Goosse, enn eenen Friese doa fieahd see een Jenote, daut sijch sogoa de leewa Gott freid, soo scheen!

Joh, oba dann jintjch miene Forschung loos, enn etj schreef mie aules opp, wiels etj mie docht, daut doa wiet unjre Ead dochwoll dree Beesewijchta lage, enn wiels see dochwoll gaunz groote Halunke jewast weare, enn seea ritjch oba uck

32

Reimer, the village sage, and he probably knows what to make of Ljuba's interest with the spots of fascination of her scent."

It was obvious that Mrs Loepp had said all she intended to reveal on the topic and so I held my peace, but the pulleys in my imagination were starting to gain momentum. And so I read, and I researched and consulted some ministers of the word from days gone by, including some fathers of the pulpit of Jesuit persuasion; then slowly a light, dim but distinct, started to dawn in me and a theory gained contours. My notions assumed form by remembering the pontiff, Pope Pious, to be explicit, who occupied the papal throne in Rome during World War II, and who entertained more mischief, if not downright evil, than good during his tenure.

When this Pious Pappa died, his death issued startlement of exceptional range. It is well known throughout Christendom that if a good man departs, his body sinks into mouldering state very slowly, sometimes not at all. Let a granduncle, the medic missionary Doctor Johann Thiessen buried, 1953 in Bandung, Indonesia serve as an example. In 1968 his grave had to be relocated to higher ground; when this was undertaken there was no end to the surprise awaiting all involved. Pappa Thiessen lay in his coffin in a great vault, and aside from a longer beard and fingernails, he had not changed or mouldered an iota. He slept in perfect repose, with death and time having withered him not at all.

If such phenomenon transpires in the Holy Roman Church, then a giant step towards declaring permanent sainthood to the deceased holy man is a given, because God obviously dwells so powerfully in the departed. Snicker, all you will, but I happen to believe this implicitly because I have seen a thousand photographs of my grand uncle in his coffin, and I have spoken to half as many who witnessed this incident. Both pictures and people persuasively communicated that he had appeared so deep in restful repose that no one present believed that he had passed away.

On the other hand, what happened to that dastardly Pope Pious is almost beyond credibility. He had barely been placed

seea hunjsch, stunke see nu soo auls aule Diewel noh Ohs, enn onse Ljuba ähre Näs vetald ahr enn mie daut.

Aulso fruag etj Al Reima gaunz kratjcht ut, enn waut hee mie dann gaunz langsom enn seea väasejchtijch vetald, eajentlijch fuscheld, bestätijcht aules waut Ljuba ähre Näs sijch doa oppem Pioneer Tjoatjhoff fe ahr enn mie ennjereaht haud.

Joh, oba waut Al Reima mie noch aules doabie vetald, woa etj een aundat Mol vetalle. Vondoag nijch, wiels mie grult noch väl, väl too seea, oba wann etj perseenlijch uck wiedahans noch soo scheen ritjche woa auls Ljuba mie daut auntoovestohne jefft, dann tjemmt dee gaunze steinbachsche Woahrheit vom Pioneer Frädhoff rut. Hoolt junt faust!

to lie in state in the Vatican then this unholy scoundrel started stinking, dispatching half of Rome into fainting spells while the other half became sick to their souls. Thousands had barely wiped the puke off their faces and the stench from their nasal orifices when the pope's nose, literally black from rot, rolled from his face.

All this was well known to me when I took to the Pioneer Cemetery in Steinbach repeatedly in the middle of the winter of 1998 with Ljuba, Mister and Reeschtje. Ljuba squirmed with delight in 360 degree arcs on her back and kicked happily but vigorously at the many enemies of Beagles' imaginations; her every orifice exuding pure joy. However, today I was in a totally watchful mode and I paid explicit attention to the exact site of Ljuba's moiling. Ljuba delighted all over the holy acres, but on the graves of one Löwen, a Goosen and a Friesen her antics assumed celebratory status of such order that everyone suddenly present knew that even God took delight in the spontaneous celebration of death gone to the dogs.

My research assumed feverish pitch and I recorded every detail, safely assuming that there in Steinbach lay buried three heinous scoundrels, who had been as avaricious as the Protestant work ethic in their day, then very wealthy during their much acclaimed lives but equally as ruthless, with all still paying the price by stinking like the devil through many feet of earth for years, indeed decades on end. The smile on Ljuba's every feature revealed that she knew! By DOG, did she know!

Knowing all this, I approached Old Peter Reimer, the village bard, and what he then very slowly, most deliberately and even more carefully narrated by way of a concealed whisper, documented every detail of Ljuba's finely tuned nose at work on the Pioneer Cemetery in Steinbach, Manitoba.

There are more items that came to light during the palaver of the man in the know, but my fear is still too great to tell it all. But with Ljuba's nodding consent all this will be revealed in the fullness of time, and then the truth in matters of the Pioneer Cemetery in Steinbach will be a matter of public record and overdue conversational material in pew and pulpit alike.

Een Knockout

Auls etj tjlien wea, etj meen noch tjlanda, haud jiedet Voagel
enn jiedet Tiea bie ons Tus oppem Hoff eenen Nohme,
enn doamett uck eene Seel. Oba soohne Nohmensjäwarie
schiend mie dann doch een bätje probleematisch, wiels Peeta
Netjels haude alf Heehna, enn jiede Hahn haud eenen Nohme,
oba Heehna enn Seele pausste mie donn nich toop, enn uck
vondoag nich.

Oba soo wear'ett. Wie haude drettien Tjeaj, enn jiede Kooh
haud eenen Nohme, enn bie de Nohbasch, wea daut uck nich
aundasch. Een Nohme, plus eene Seel, enn dann wisst een
jiedra, em Darp enn uck sestwoo, soo's enne Nohbaschauft,
enn enneTjoatj, woo'rett senne musst; daut wisst sogoa dee
leewa Gott.

Nohba Oola Johaun Wiens, dee vonne '42 measchtens mett
sien tjlienen Trakta spezeare fuah, wiels hee too kortsejchtijch
fe sien tjlienen Laustwoage toom foahre wea, haud uck Tjeaj,
enn uck Mamaschka, dee meea Maltj gauf, auls enn een
tjlienen Amma nennpausst.

Joh, Mamashka wea eene groote Holsteenkooh, dee soo väl
Maltj gauf, daut see den Moonat-Maltj-Scheck—omm 15%
gaunz auleen aunhoof.

Emm Fahrjoah aune 1942 storf Taunte Wiensche; see haud
aul Joahrelang aun Parkinson's jeläde, enn ähre Henj tetjade
emma. Miene Mutta enn Taunte Wiensche weare sich goot,
enn see spezeade aul noch foaken toop, han enn häa. Wann
Wiense spezeare kaume, reisde see emma enn een
Deemokraut; daut wea een Fadawoage mett Pulsta-Sette,

The Full Count

When I was little, I mean even littler, every bird and animal on our yard had a name and, thusly, a soul. However, such nomenclature seemed problematic to me because the Peter Nickels had eleven hens and each had a name but hens and souls did not square with me, then or now.

But that's the way things were. We had thirteen cows and each one also had a name; things were no different at our neighbours. A name, plus a soul, and then everyone knew the state of things in the village, in the wider neighbourhood, in church with even God being in the know.

Neighbour Old Johan Wiens, who as of '42 went visiting mainly on his little Farmall tractor, because he was too short-sighted to drive his pickup, also had cows, including Mamaschka, which produced more milk than a small pail could hold.

Yes, Mamaschka was a big Holstein cow who produced so much milk on her own that she raised the monthly milk check by 15% single-handedly.

In the spring of 1942 Mrs Wiens died; she had suffered from Parkinson's for many years and her hands were always shaking. My mother and Mrs Wiens were the best of friends and they rather frequently visited back and forth. When the Wienses came for a visit they always travelled by democrat, a three star buggy with upholstered seats, because Mrs Wiens came from the Molosch; moreover, she was a stately lady even if she had come from Timbuktu. Our mother and Mrs Wiens represented a perfect fit.

wiels Taunte Wiensche kaum vonne Molosch; butadem wea see eene rejchtje Daum, uck wann see von Timbuktu jekohme wea. Onse Mutta enn Taunte Wiensch pausste toop.

Wiense brochte emma waut mett, wann see spezeare kaume, auls Ente Eia, ooda Himbeere, ooda Olbassem emm Somma, enn emma weare de tjliene Jeschentje schmock vepackt. Wie nauhme noh ahn Reatjaworscht ooda Schwoate-moag mett.

Auls dee goode Taunte storf, hield wie aulatoop. Onkel Wiens leet uck noh, enne Bewäjunge enn enne Jedohnte, enn siene Henj lage nu lenja oppe siene Tjnees, uck wann see nich meed weare.

Oba hee haud Tjinja Tus, enn uck eenen Hoff mett Tjeaj, soo's aul erwaehnt, dee bestalt enn besorjt woare musste.

Noh eene tjliene Truapause, fong daut Läwe wada aul-doagsch aun, enn dee Oola Johaun Wiens rolld siene Papparosie noch emma noh de rusche Oat, aulso hee beletjt daut Papiea vonne rajchte noh de lintje Sied, enn dann kroop hee wada opp sien tjlienen Trakta, kortsejchtijch, enn fuah loos, während siene Jungess entweda oppe Pead reede, ooda oppem tjlienen Laustwoage loosläde; besondasch dee tjliena Wiense Johaun, Johnny jenannt, jung oba iewrijch, enn sich jearn manke Langbeenje opphilt.

Daut ess eenfach mol soo: Wann Mensch groote Trua erläwt habe, enn wann dee dunkle Woltj vetrocke ess, dann nemmt daut Läwe mett een extra Schulps wada too. Meist soo's een tjlienet Wunda: dann tjriee Mensche wada niee Idee, kohme opp fresche Biefall, enn kohme äwadäl sogoa mett Koaschheit enne Been; soo uck bie Wiense. Enn soo pessead daut, daut aum veatienden Juni, aune '42, de Wiensetjinja ähre Tjeaj een poah Heifortje voll fresche Lucerne ennem Koohtun nennschmeete, enn mett eene extra Moht fe Mamaschka.

The Wienses brought along something whenever they came visiting, be it duck eggs, or raspberries and currants in summer, and always tidily made up. We took along farmer's sausage or collared pork in return.

We all cried together when the good lady departed. Mr Wiens slowed down a bit in movement and demeanor and placed his hands on his knees often, even if they needed no rest. But he had children at home and a yard with cows, as mentioned, to look after. Life, after a brief pause, shortly assumed pace and rhythm and Johan Wiens again rolled his smokes in the Russian manner; he wetted the cigarette paper from right to left, then he mounted his Farmall, bumped along, vision impaired, on his tractor, while his boys were either riding horses, driving around in their pickup, and that more often than not; it was particularly Johnny Wiens, very young but mighty eager, who was frequently to be seen where the long of leg gender congregated.

It is simply fact: after people have experienced deep grief, and the dark cloud of grief passes by, life asserts itself in slightly extra measure. It almost amounts to a little wonder that people then get new ideas, draw new hope, even courage, and surface with an extra bounce; so it was with the Wienses.

So it happened that on the 14th of June 1942 the Wiens kids threw a few forkfuls of fresh mowed alfalfa over the barbed wire fence enclosure for the cows to forage, with an extra helping for Mamaschka.

The children were simply too innocently young to know what then may happen. And did happen. Mamaschka started bloating fearfully and the children, realizing the animal's terrible distress, gave her water to drink. Death was not long in coming; her inner organs burst and she keeled over and died. When Old Frank Wiens witnessed this barnyard tragedy, he immediately took off on his Farmall and headed for the Ungers who already had a telephone, and called Dr

39

Dee Tjinja wear eenfach too onschuldijch jung, omm too weete, waut dann pesseare kunn. Enn uck deed. Mamaschka donst schratjlijch opp, enn auls dee Tjinja sage, daut dee Kooh groote Noot liede deed, gauwe see ahr Wota too supe. Dee Doot leeht nich lang opp sich wachte; de ennere Organe plausste, enn see stelpt omm, enn wea doot. Auls Oola Johaun Wiens disse Tragödie sach, sad hee sich fuats opp siene Trakta, enn fuah auf noh Ungasch, siene Nohbasch, woohne aul een Telephoon haude, enn hee roopt Dokta Johaun Tjäla enn Steinbach aun; dee dee eensja Veehdokta wiet enn breet wea.

Dokta Johaun Tjäla wea dee basta Veehdokta, uck wann'et een Dutz von dee Sort jejäwt haud. Hee wisst nich blooß, woa dee interne Organe bie een Tiea weare, oba hee wisst uck gaunz jeneiw, waut enn woo dee unjanaunda mett sich too doohne haude, ohne daut aules studeat too habe. Daut wea ahm soo enn, sien Talent, soo's de Musitj bie aundre Mensche.

Butadem wea Johaun Tjäla nich blooß een gooda Veehdokta, oba uck een butajeweehnlijch sympatischa Mensch, wiels etj ahm noch perseenlijch erläwt hab mett de groote Weisheit, vonne Tjinjauage. Hee wea groot enn forsch, enn wertjlijch intelligent, enn kunn Resseriete soo's irjendeena utem Oolen Testament, enn dee tjand etj uck aula. Enn, kratjt soo's Jesus, trock hee tjliene Tjinja aun, wiels hee dee goot wea, enn see ahm; daut wisst wie. Enn uck see.

Wann Mensche vondoag-den-dach vonne Dokta Johaun Tjälaschfamielje vetalle, woare fuats eene Dutz ooda meea Jeschijchte oppjedescht, soo's ute Pistool jeschote. Enn wann Akademika sogoa vondoag doaropp bestohne, daut Al Reima mett disse bunte Tjälasch-Tabun Frindschauft ess, dann sulle oppjewatjte Tjapp daut ruhijch auls Bibelwoahrheit jleiwe.

Oba nu schwind tridj noh Mamaschka, dee toovääl Lucerne jefräte haft. Auls Dokta Tjäla mett siene Essexkoah bosijch oppen Wiensehoff aunjerätet kaum, wea daut aul too loht.

Johan Kehler in Steinbach, who was the only veterinarian far and wide.

Doctor Johan Kehler was the best veterinarian, even if there had been a dozen of the sort. Not only did he instinctively know where the inner organs of an animal were located and how they functioned but he knew the inner interplay of such without necessarily having seen or studied them. People call such constitution a gift. That is the make-up of the so gifted, it was said, like the talent of music.

Moreover, Johan Kehler was not only a good veterinarian, he was also an exceptionally sympathetic person and I know this because I personally experienced him with the infinite wisdom of childhood reliability. He was big and stout and strong and highly intelligent, and as good a story teller as anyone in the Old Testament; I knew them all. Also, like Jesus, he attracted children, because he loved them; we knew that.

If people nowadays talk about Dr Johan Kehler and his brothers, a dozen and more stories vie for competitive telling like a shot from a starter's pistol. If academics claim even today that Al Reimer is related to this merry band, then such telling is to be taken literally.

But back, and on the double, back to Mamaschka who has ingested an over abundance of alfalfa.

When Doctor Kehler arrived in his Essex car on the Wiens's yard as fast as possible, it was already too late. Dr Kehler immediately produced his thin stabbing knife, and placed it at the left edge of the left hand just outside the finger line; his hand surrounding the left hip bone of the cow, then delivering a sharp thrust. A great cloud of alfalfa gas shot out and Mamaschka imploded but the harm had been done. Mamaschka's innards had been ruptured by the great pressure of bloating and she had died a miserable, horribly painful death.

Dokta Tjäla haud een schoapet, spetzet Massa enne Haund, woohnt hee väasejchtijch, doa woa de lintje Finjasch Haund woare, enn dee den Hoftknoake vonne Kooh ommfoohte, aunläd, enn eenmol kort toosteatje deed. Eene groote Woltj Lucernedonst fluag platzlijch rut, enn Mamaschka schorrd ennalijch toop, oba dee Schode bennalijch wea jedohne. Aul dee ennere Organe bie de Kooh weare derjch daut Oppdonste jeplautzt, enn see wea mett schratjele Noot tjrepieat!

Tjenn Jie enn June Fantasie von dee Trua ver ons een Bild aufnehme? Wann joh, dann wudd opp dem Bild Dokta Tjäla too seehne senne, dee bie de Kooh steiht, sien Hoot enne Haund, enn mett een trujet Jesejcht, enn mett Respatjt fe daut Läwe em Gaunzen, enn aun siene Sied, Oola Johaun Wiens, enn Kopp tjarta, mett een scheewet Jesejcht vom Hiele, vetrocke; enn dann kohme de Wiense-Tjinja: Väare de tjliena Frankie, veatien Joah oolt, mett siene eewijch roode Näs, dann Marga, eene Brell oppe schoape Näs, ähre Perischtjie-Leppe, dann dee bedajchtje Ellie, dann Miejche, soo's eene Mutta-Maria mett Lamma, enn dann Johnny 12, dee uck biem Trure aun Post-Woatjentiens Agnes docht, ooda aune Brunemädtjes siede vom jrientholschen Park.

Wie haude ons aul eea enn disse Jeschijcht vetalle lohte, daut nieet Läwe maunjchmol noh groote Trua opptjiemt, enn daut, mett een Schmusta oppe Jedohnte, aulahaund aun-tjemmt.

Dit wea uck bie onse Wiensenohbasch de Faul. Wiels daut tjeen Bild vom näjchsten Kapitel jefft, mott Jie junt mett miene Vetall bejnäje, wiels daut miene Oppgow auls Vetalla ess, aulewäje doabie too senne, enn Biekrupa too späle, enn von dee Unjabrätjunge too berejchte soo's miene Ennbild-ungskrauft mie daut väasajcht. Enn wann Jie mie daut nich jleewe welle, dann froagt ruhijch Al Reimer, een Plemmenitj von Dokta Tjäla, enn dann weet Jie!

Can you, in your imagination manage to take a picture of this sad scene before us? If so, you would see on the picture Doctor Kehler, standing by the cow, with hat in hand demonstrating genuine sorrow, respect for departed life and compassion, and next to him Old Frank Wiens a head shorter, with a slight twist on his face from weeping, and then come the Wiens children: in front, Little Frankie, aged 14 with his invariably red nose, then Marga, glasses on her sharp nose and with pierogi-like tight, no-nonsense lips, then Elly, reflective, then Mary, like a Mother Mary with lambs, and then Johnny 12, who even during sadness thought of Post Warkentin's Agnes and the Braun Girls from the South of Grünthal Pack.

We were earlier informed in this story that new life sometimes sprouts after great sadness, and that things then arrive with a new smile on their many features.

This also held true of our Wiens neighbours. No photograph exists of the next scene of the second act and that is why you will have to make do with my telling of the tale, since in my consignment as a raconteur it is my duty to be omnipresent and to eavesdrop, and, if need be, to imagine the interludes and report on them as my fancy dictates. And if you choose not to believe me, than please ask Al Reimer, a nephew of Dr Kehler's and then you'll know.

Ohmtje Wiens wiped away the last tears of Mamaschka's death and asked, "Doctor Kehler, how much do I owe you?"

Dr Johan Kehler embraced Ohmtje Johan Wiens and then they shed a few, final tears before replying,

"Free of charge, but would you allow me to cut off Mamaschka's udder and take it along as a keepsake?"

"Gladly."

Three minutes later the big udder lay on the rumble seat of Kehler's car and he drove home.

Ohmtje Wiens wescht sich de latzte Trohne von Mamaschka äah Doot auf, enn fruag: "Waut sie etj schuldijch?"

Dokta Tjätla foot Ohmtje Wiens omm, enn dann kaume ahn beid noch eenmol Trohne, eea hee säd: "Daut's omsonst, oba wurscht Du mie de Erlaubnis jäwe, Mamaschka äah Ieda auftooschniede, enn daut auls Souvenir mett toonehme?

"Jearn."

Dree Minute lohta lach daut groote Ieda enne Rumpel-kohma vonne Tjälaschkoah, enn hee fuah noh Hus.

Dokta Johaun Tjäla wea een fromma, oba tjeen puri-taunscha Mensch; hee wea een begowda, earnsta Maun, huag intelligent, oba oppe aundre Sied von dit Goldkepietje wea een Resserieta von Gott siene groote Jnod too seehne, enn wann disse twee toopknaulde, soo's dee "Big Bang", fluage schepferische Funke, enn doawäjen, boold hundat Joah lohta, wann von de Tjälasch de Red ess, brädre Mensche uck noch vondoag dutzendwies loos, enn schlohne sich doabie oppem Hinjarenj.

Unjawäjess, auls Johaun Tjäla wada enn siene jeweehnlijche Fohtung nennjejleppt wea, hild hee bie de Bush Farm Road stell, trock sich siene jratzte Overauls aun, enn stopt sich daut Koohieda enne Buckjäjend vonne Schlaubbetjze nenn. Ahm wea too Senn jekohme, een bät Spoß too driewe, von dee Oat, dee doatoo biedroage, daut de Steinbacha, soo's aul erwähnt, uck noch vondoag jearn dee Famielje em Dentjch habe. Butadem wea daut Sinnowend zeowentz, enn morje, aum Sinndach aulso, fong dee Earnst vom Läwe wada opp earnst aun.

Auls Tjäla Tus aunkaum haud hee sien "Veealoopa" soo's hee den nannd, reed. Hee kroop ute Koah, enn leet eene vonne Mamaschka ähre Strijcha, uck Tett jenannt, gaunz lostijch väre ute Betjze bommle. Tjäla haud de Koahredäah noch nich toojemoakt, auls de Obraum Leewesche schreajch:

44

Dr Johan Kehler was a pious, but not puritanical man; he was a gifted, serious fellow of high intelligence, but on the flipside of that Kehler coin, was to be found one of the raconteurs of Gods' immense grace, and whenever those two attributes met Big Bang on, strange creativities ensued, and that is why, even today, a hundred years later or so, talk of the Kehler clan leads to laughter and ass-slapping merriment.

En route, when Johan Kehler had regained his usual composure, he stopped at the corner of the Bush Farm Road, slipped into his largest size coveralls, and stuffed the named udder into the belly region of his vestment. He had in mind to exercise a little fun this Saturday evening prior to the seriousness of the pending Steinbach Sabbath. A little mischief had to be, for otherwise, as mentioned, people would not still be equating hilariousness with the Kehler clan.

When Kehler arrived home he had his Four Shooter, as he termed it, at the ready. He stepped out of his car and had one of Mamaschka's teats jauntily dangling from up front. Kehler had not yet closed his car door when the neighbour's wife, Mrs Abraham Loewen, screamed, "Kehler, goodness grief, what kind of accident has befallen you? Shame on you!"

"Well, what now?" said Kehler. "Are you referring to this little radish?" and while saying so, he took his butcher knife and cut off that very radish, or digit or cow teat or even tit and threw it at Mrs Loewen's feet.

Mrs Loewen was still open-mouthed when she fell down full length busily fainting while dropping.

Shuster Bergen was witness to all this from the other side of the street and came eagerly ambling along. Kehler had reloaded in the meantime with Digit Number Two cockily dangling from his fly.

"Kehler, you are but a Chortiezer, but this time things are going too far, have you no shame?"

"Oba, Tjäla, Harre Gomms! Waut ess Die fe een schratjeljet Onjletj pessead? Schäm Die!"

"Na, waut's nu aulwada?" säd Tjäla, "Meenst Du dit tjliene Radiestje?" enn noch biem Räde, nauhm hee sien Schlacht-massa, enn schneet daut Radiestje, ooda Strijch, ooda Tett auf, enn schmeet daut de Leewesche verre Feet.

Taunte Leewesche haud noch daut Mul op, auls see delenjd hanfoll, enn biem Handrasche uck aul pienijch beschwiemd.

Schusta Boaje haud aul dit vonne aundre Sied Gauß mettje-träje, enn hee kaum uck aul bosijch aunjeschibbelt. Tjäla haud enne Tweschentiet aulwada nohjelohd, enn nu stuak aul Strijch Numma Twee gaunz fideel ute Betjze.

"Tjäla, Du best mau een prosta Chortietza, oba dit jeiht doch too wiet; hast Du tjeen Schomp?"

"Na, wauts dann nu aulada loos?" fruag Tjäla, "deit disse onschuldje Postanack Die toofallijch steare? Hiea, kaunst dee habe!" Enn mett een Schwung mett sien Schlachtmassa schneet hee daut Postanacktje auf, enn schmeet dem Schusta daut verre Feet. Boaje beschwiemd toom easchten Mol enn sien Läwe, enn lach nu soo's 'ne macke Pogg oppem Fahr-joaschgraus.

Wann Menniste emm vollen Iewa eene earnste Sach räjle welle ooda motte, räde see von "oppsettle" enn daut meent, daut de Sach soo earnst ess, daut eena daut Wuat sogoa emm plautdietschen Weadabuak finje kaun. Dit bediet, daut de Polizei jeroopt woat, omm Onschlijtboaret too räjle, enn daut ess uck kratjt waut Butscha Reima, twee Hiesa wieda enne Nohbaschauft, deed.

Dokta Tjäla haud noch een Äwabliezel von eene Schmusta oppe Tjeew, enn haud jrods nohjeloht, auls de RCMP von beid Siede opp ahm tookaume, auls hee breetbeensch ver sien Essex stund.

"Mista Tjäla, dit Mol gohne Ähre Schoose too wiet!"

"Well, what's the fuss now?" asked Kehler, "does this innocent little parsnip offend you, by any chance? Here, you can have it." And with one sweep he cut it off and dropped it at Bergen's feet. Bergen fainted and lay still as a limpid frog on the grass of verdant spring.

Whenever conscientious objecting Mennonites intend to resolve serious matters, they talk about "settling up"; you will even find this term in a respectable Mennonite dictionary. Settling up means to get the police involved by phoning them to resolve the irresolvable, and this is exactly what Butcher Reimer, two yards down had already done.

Doctor Kehler still had remnants of laughter on his jowls and had just reloaded when the Mounties approached him from both sides, while he was standing, straddled-legged by his Essex.

"Mr Kehler, this time your pranks have gone too far."

"What you mean, Mounties?"asked Kehler.

"Your member sticking out in public is indecent exposure," they replied while reaching for the handcuffs.

"You mean this little milk pistol which is hanging out, but not sticking out?" and already had teat number three in his hand which he sabered off the udder with a neat gesture, before tossing it towards the Mountie's royal boots.

The two men of the law fell as if shot.

Four people now lay unconscious on the lawn in the immediacy of the Kehler neighbourhood and the peace of the evening could finally descend to envelope all of Steinbach.

Only that Doctor Kehler had one digit left to offer a further nosy customer; he was not yet inside his house when his wife screamed, "Oba Johaun, this goes much too far, much too far, this is much beyond the pale, oba, oba, I say."

"Well, what is now loose?" said Kehler and cut off the fourth tit. Mrs Kehler, his Frau, imploded like a paper bag filled with water.

"Waut haft daut too bediede, Ohmtje Mounties?" fruag Tjäla.

"Jun Jied, enne Effentlijchtjeit rutsteatje, ess een moralischet Vebrätje," auntwuade see, enn hohlde aul de Henjspaunsels äwadäl.

"Jie meene disse Maltjpistool, dee rut henjt oba nich rutstatjt?" enn hee haud nu uck aul Strijch Numma Dree enne Haund, dee hee aufgnuweld enn donn mett een extra Schliesa dee Polizei ver ähre tjennitjlijche Steewle schmeet. Dee Manna vom Jesatz folle omm auls aunjeschote.

Veea Mensche lage nu besennungsloos oppem Rose enn Tjäla siene enje Nohbaschauft, enn nu kunn dee Owendsfräd endlich äwa daut fromme Steinbach kohme.

Dokta Tjäla haud blooß noch een Strijch äwrijch fe een latzten nieschiejen Kund; hee wea noch nich gaunz enn sien Hus benne auls siene Fru ut ludem Hauls gaulmd, "Oba Johaun, dit jeit too wiet, oba väl too wiet; dit jriest ut, oba väl too seea, oba, oba, etj saj!"

"Na, oba waut ess nu loos?" säd Tjäla, enn schneet de veade Tett auf. Dee Tjälasche schorrd toop, soo's ne Papieatut voll Wota.

Nu spood sich Ohmtje Tjäla oba seea; hee jintj noh de Hinjadääh, enn eea noch meea Trubbel oppjeduckt kohme kunn, schmeet hee daut Ieda enne Dranktonn hinjre Dääh. Auls daut Ieda noch unjawäjess, aulso derjche Loft fluag, sach Tjäla daut noch eene Tett aum Ieda hong.

Donn erläwd uck Dokta Johaun Tjäla sienen easchten Knockout enn sienem Läwe.

Now Ohmtje Kehler hurried up; he went to the back door and before any more trouble could come calling, he quickly threw the udder into the garbage bin behind the back door. While the udder was still air bound, Kehler noticed that a remaining tit was still hanging on. It was then that Doctor Kehler himself went down for the full count.

Wäa ess dee niea
heilja Voda äjentlich?

Auls etj jistre toop mett dusend Milljoone too sach, daut mett eenmol witta Ruak utem heiljen Owe emm Vatikan rutjeschohte kaum, bedieselde väle, de measchte bäde, aundre hielde, enn noch aundre säde: "Well'we ons freie, nu jeiht daut noch bäta auls verhäa loos."

Etj wea ditmol nich eena von aul dee, wiels etj vom Stoohl stelpt, enn wann eena mett meist twee-enntachtentich Joah vom Stoohl drascht, ess daut nich soo's Fräjoah. Eena stund opp, wescht sich de Betjze, measchtens von bute auf, enn jintj maltje. Enn dee Heehna besorje, enn dem Kohta vepriejle. Enn dann Eadschocke brode.

Waut wea? Bie heilje Sache, saul eena bie de Woahrheit bliewe, enn daut foll mie aul emma leijcht. Daut weet Jie. Oba woaromm etj mie soo morschijch vefeahd wea, wiels auls dee niea heilja Voda oppe Väaleew enn Rom oppdukt, kaum mie dee Maunsmensch bekaunt väa; etj haud den aul verhäa mol jeseehne, kaum mie soo väa. Etj tjitjt nochmol han, enn säd opp ludes: "Yesiree, daut ess'a!" Enn daut weara!

Daut kaum aulatoop soo's dit. Etj sie mau tweemol enn Buenos Aries jewast, enn uck jewese. Etj stund em Hilton Hotel, woa eena omsonst Prosciutto mett Kukkeruzzmehl— Tweeback äte kaun, soo väl auls eena well. Enn etj wull!

Tweehundat Meeta siede von dem Hotel, jefft daut een Restaurant mett Nohme Moska Blanca, aulso dee Witte

And who really is
the new Holy Father?

When together with a thousand million others I yesterday saw a plume of white smoke billowing forth from the Holy Stove of the Vatican, a multitude of fellow pilgrims fainted, others prayed, many wept, and all said, "Let us take heart, things will now be better than ever before."

As for me? I did not share in any of these sentiments, simply because I dropped clean out of my chair, and dropping from a chair at almost eighty two is not as in the sprightliness of chronological spring. During the down and up of youth you simply got up, stroked your pants into shape, mostly externally, and went milking. Then you took care of the chickens, administered the necessary drubbing on the tomcat, and repaired to the kitchen to fry potatoes.

What happened, you may well ask. When narrating or discussing matters of holy purport adherence to the truth is mandatory; this was never an issue for me. My readers know this. But why I was so seriously startled was simply the fact that when the Holy Father appeared on the balcony in Rome, he seemed familiar to me; I had seen this fellow before was my more than distinct impression. I took another good look and then said for all to hear, meaning all my three dogs and tomcat, "You betcha, that's him!" And it was him and he.

This is how it all came to be. I have been in Buenos Aires only twice. While there, I stayed in the Hilton Hotel where

Moschtje. Doahan jintj etj toom Owenkost mett mien Frind, omm mie dee Tjeewe mett dem basten Rindfleesch, woohnt'et enne Welt jefft, volltooprommle.

Daut jletjt mie.

Uck drunk wie eene Buddel Wien, vleijcht sogoa twee. Daut mott doa soo. Aules jintj jlei too, bett etj aum Nohbadesch head, daut sich mehrere Manna tjibbelde. Wiels etj auls Mennist opp Fräd hool, stead mie ähre Zankarie. Oba wiels etj Moot em Hoaten hab, enn uck enne Oarms, enn enne Knoakes sowesoo, wann'et senne mott, bestald etj bie dee Bedeenung eene haulwe Buddel Wien fe dee dolle Hohns, omm ahn Eintracht bietoobrinje. Oba see bleewe biem Tjibble.

Wiels mie daut dann doch too oajch word, säd etj opp Plautietsch, enn miene Frädungsstemm: "Jungess, Jie steare mie. Etj sie een plautdietscha Tjrist vom mennischen Model, oba etj kaun uck, wann'et senne mott, oolttestamentlijch woare.

Enn nu heat opp, wie send hiea emmahan enn eene Ätstow, enn nich enne Tjoatj, woa daut Jachte dolla mood ess!"

Stalt Junt mol väa, waut dann pessead! Dee dolle Hohns aum Nohbadesch, dee sich zankte weare Mennoniete! "Wäa haud daut jedocht?" säd mien Voda dreemol den Dach Tus. Enn etj ditmol uck.

"Jenuag" soo's Taunte Kloßsche Tus emma säd, daut jintj doa aum Desch, emm Moska Blanka enn Buenos Aires, em scheenen Argentinien, groff enn sogoa doll too. Oba, oba!

Waut wea, enn wäa weare dee dolle Hohns? Etj schäm mie meist, oba wie welle doch bie de Woahrheit bliewe. Aulsoo: Dee Leidhaumel wea tjeen aundra auls Peeta Ditjch vom MCC, een langa, haulwa Kohlkopp, enn mett stiewe, bleiwe Uage, enn mett forschem Wesen, enn doatoo uck noch Vegetarier, dem eena aulso mett een Filet Mignon nich soo

prosciutto with corn flour rolls come free, as many as you like. And I liked many.

Two hundred meters south of the hotel, a restaurant called Moska Blanca, meaning the White Midge, offers excellent food and an enviable reputation. My friend and I decided to have dinner there, and treat the inner man to the best beef on the globe. We managed well.

Also, we drank a bottle of the house wine, possibly two. Everything went smoothly until we heard that at a neighbouring table several men were engaged in serious quarrel. Since I am a peace loving Mennonite, their quarreling did not sit well with me. However, and since I am a resourceful pilgrim and have the mental gumption as an equivalent to considerable horsepower in my biceps, and prefer peace to occupy my space, I ordered half a bottle of wine for those in heated discussion to allow accord to prevail. My gesture failed, they further engaged in discord.

Since their animated bickering was too much for me, I called upon my voice of peace to boldly announce in my mother tongue, "Boys, I find your lack of Christian peace disturbing. I am a Mennonite Low German Christian Model, but, if need be, I can wax Old Testament like. And now let peace prevail; we are, after all, in a restaurant, and not in a church where quarreling is more the order of the day."

Just imagine, what then happened! The feuding roosters at the next table were Mennonites! "Who would have thought that?" is what my old man said three times a day, back in a former day on the farm.

"Enough said," is what Mrs Jake Klassen used to say regularly in my back home days; let us get on with it; after all, there was a heated discussion going on at an ample table in the White Midge restaurant in Buenos Aires, Argentina; heated indeed, bordering on anger! Oh my!

leijcht bandje kunn; hee wea iewrijch, enn opp sien Stetjch bedocht.

Daut dee Sach eene earnste wea, kunn eena sich dentje, wiels sesst haude se den grooten Oppriema nich von Frankfurt jehohlt, omm hiea soo wiet auf eenen Vebiestaden Hott aum Diestel too leahre. Soohnt kost Jeld!

De aundra Kurrhohn wea een Moatien Dertjse, een groota, forscha Priejel, dee Henj soo groot auls eene Jeträjdscheffel haud, enn mett dem nich too sposse wea. Hee wea hiea enne Staudt de Eppaschta vom MCC, enn bieaun uck noch Prädja.

Dee Dredde, den see sich aum Desch väanauhme, wea een Jeat, aulsoo Jorge, Boaje.

Diss Boaje wea enn eea deemootja Pilja, oba een bät aufjefolle, soo's sich daut rutstald, enn dem see doa bie mie aum Nohbadesch beoabeide deede.

Daut stald sich rut, daut see aul eenje Doag vebrocht haude, dem Jeat Boaje een bät meea Iewa auls Prädja, enn MCC Vetreda mank daut veloarne Toakel hiea enne Grootstaudt bietoobrinje. Uck stald sich rut, daut diss Jeat M. Boaje, tjeen rietenda Evangelist wea, enn daut hee sich manke Kathoolitje enn Buenos Aries eenfach een bät too seea tusijch jemoakt haud. Dee hiesje Mensche jefolle ahm, enn ääh mässja Läwensgang soowesoo. Enn dee Mensche hiea enne Grootstaudt hilde opp ahm. Vleijcht too seea, je noh Uagemoht vonne Seel.

Mien Frind enn etj aute ruhijch soo wieda, enn leehte ons daut goot gohne. Eea wie twee de Staudt veleehte, kaum daut dann oba noch doatoo, daut wie mett dem Jeat Boaje Adrasse uttuschte, enn ons vleijcht sogoa mol wada traffe kunne.

Wiels Ditjch enn Dertjze mien Frind enn mie von Heareseehne tjannde, haude see ons oppjejäwt; wie weare Sindasch, eenfach too wiet vom sejchren Eewa jerutscht. Em deepen Wota, oba onbetjeat, meende see.

What was, and who were these angry roosters? I felt a tad embarrassed at all this but the truth must prevail. The bell-wether was none other than Peter Dyck of MCC fame and stature; tall, semi-bald, with piercing blue eyes, a man of stout essence of faith, and further, a vegetarian who could not be pushed into the traces of peace with a filet mignon; he was in aroused frame of mind and soul.

It was obvious that the matter under discussion was serious for otherwise the Great Resolver himself would not have been flown in from distant Frankfurt, Germany, to read those here involved the Riot Act. Such measures cost real money, a Mennonite consideration.

The other feuding rooster was one Martin Doerksen, a huge fellow with dukes the size of a shit shovel, whose sense of humour was but sparse. He was the head MCC honcho in this city and also a preacher of note.

The third party whom the Christian men of means were lassoing in this very evening was one George, aka Jorge Bergen. Bergen was a humble pilgrim, but given to back-sliding as it turned out, and he was now being worked over at the neighbouring table.

It shortly was to become obvious that the animated discussion I witnessed was now into Day Three. During all this time, the men of persuasion had tried to light a fire of greater heat under George Bergen's tail of faith so that he, as a minister and MCC rep. bring more of the lost and fallen in this great city to the fold of the saved and secured. Also, I learned that George Bergen was no fire and brimstone evangelist; fact was, that he had simply become a bit too much at home among the Catholics of Buenos Aires, such of tranquilo disposition. The local people suited him, he loved them and their more leisurely pace. Also, the inhabitants of this cosmopolitan city took kindly to him. Possibly too much and too well, depending on the measure of the inner eye.

55

Soo's daut maunjchmol emm Läwe tjemmt, ooda kohme saul, kaum etj sass Wätj lohta, nohdem etj enn gaunz Paraguay plautdietsche Jeschijchte vetalt haud, tridj noh Buenos Aries. Dee Prosciutto, dee Pampasteaks, enn de Wien kroagde mie tridj, enn vleijcht uck een bät dee besonnene enn ruhje Oat vom Jeat Boaje.

Etj stund wada em Hilton Hotel, enn roopt Boaje aun, enn looht ahm toom Äte enn. Wie aute goot enn lang, enn vetalde ons oba noch bäta enn lenja.

Jeat Boaje läd aum dredden Owend vollet Betjanntnis auf: Hee haud sich entschlohte ohne Peeta Ditjch, enn ohne Moatien Dertjze, enn ohne daut MCC wieda too piljere, enn haud sich de kathoolische Tjoatj aunjeschlohte. Tridj jegohne, wear'a!

Sien Nohme word donn Jorge Mario Bergoglia. Oba von jistre aun heet hee Pohp Francis, dee niea heilja Voda.

My friend and I completed our leisurely dinner and had a good time of it, and in the city. Before we departed, we even exchanged addresses with George Bergen; on the off-chance that we might meet again, sometime, somewhere.

Since the trouble-shooters, Dyck and Derksen knew my friend and me via heresy, they had given up on us. We were sinners, drifting too far from shore.

As it happened, or was meant to happen, I returned to Buenos Aires some six weeks later after I had told my Low German stories all over Paraguay. The prosciutto, the pampas steaks and the red wine called me back, and possibly also, the reflective and peaceful presence of George Bergen.

I again assumed quarters in the Hilton Hotel and called Bergen and invited him to dinner. We dined long and well and talked even better and longer this time around.

On the third evening, George Bergen, divested himself; he delivered a full confession. He had decided to come clean and to pilgrim on without Peter Dyck and without Martin Bergen, and without the MCC, aka Mennonite Central Committee made in Akron, Ohio, USA, and had re-joined the Catholic Church. Returned to the former fold after five hundred odd years.

He changed his name to Jorge Mario Bergoglia. But as of yesterday he is known as Pope Francis, the new Holy Father!

Peter-the-Grate

Too de Tiet aus de latzte Generation von'ne baste mennische Models, woone Gott jemols em kenaudschen Goade stohne leet, oppwosse—enne Dartjajoahre nämlich enne Oostresarw—gauf'ett büta Tiet enn Boschhose enn Raupheehna bloß noch een Dintj omsonst: de Eatons Kataloo. Jo, wann de Kataloo mette Post tweemol em Joah aunkaum, donn jintj'ett doll. Donn word betjitjt, jeblädat enn bewundat. Oba seea!

Opp Jantsied wear'ett doabie meist too eenem Mennischen Playboy Club jekohme, weens soo säd Niestädja. Hee säd, de Siede mett de Frües-Unjawausch em Kataloo weare bie de bloomenoatsche Jungess noch populära aus de dietsche Fiebel. De Jungess doa em Darp nauhme den Kataloo oppem Staulebähn enopp, vestoake sich doa em Hei, enn worde doa Tjenstla enn Axeperts, hand made.

Kaun senne. Etj jleew ahm daut, wiels uck bie Jrienthol 'eromm wea wie meist soo wiet.

Woo populäa dee Kataloo wea, weet etj uck nich kratjcht, enn uck woll tjeen aundra nich. Waut etj oba weet ess, daut sogoa bie Prädja Ennse de Bibel sich twee Wäatjlang em Atjschaup vepüste kunn, wann de Kataloo kaum. Enn bie mienem Voda noch bediedent lenja. Etj meen de Bibel.

Bestale deede de measchte Mensche meist aules ütem Kataloo, oba mau enne Fantasie. Waut se wertjlich bestalde, wea hejchstens waut too Wiehnachte, enn donn fe Ma een poah Bloomasch—fleece jelaint—enn fe Pa een Sautz lange Combinations, enn beid size: Stout!

Etj haud boold jesajcht, bie Voda hild de Bibel bediedent lenja aus twee Wäatj opp eemol Vacation. Enn daut wea nich

Peter-the-Grate

At the time when the last generation of the best Mennonite models God ever permitted to bear fruit in the Canadian garden grew up—in the Thirties in the East Reserve—we had, in addition to lots of free time and bush-rabbits and Prairie chickens, only one other item which was free: the Eaton's catalogue. Yep, when that catalogue arrived twice a year by mail the speed of things picked up. People gathered around to look at it, to inspect, to leaf through it and to express surprise.

In Jantsied (the other side of the Red River) the catalogue almost led to a Mennonite Playboy Club, at least Neustädter said so. He said that the pages with the ladies' lingerie in the catalogue were even more popular than German grammars among the Blumenort boys. The boys of that village took the catalogue to the barn loft, hid in the hay and took matters into their own hands.

It could be true. I am prepared to believe him because around Grünthal things developed much the same. Now just how popular the catalogue was, I don't really know and probably no one else does either. What I do know for sure however, is that even at Preacher Ennses the Bible had two weeks holidays in the corner cupboard when the catalogue arrived. And in my father's case quite a bit longer. I mean the Bible.

People ordered most everything from the catalogue but only in their imagination. What they really ordered was only an item or two at Christmas—a pair of bloomers (fleece-

uzhend wäjnen Kataloo, daut wea emma soo. Voda laus nich daut Oole Testament, he wea daut Oole Testament, enn soo lang aus hee doabenne den mennischen Gott späle kunn, enn Rosmack hoole, enn daunze enn diewele, enn schriee enn bloare, enn de Mensche de Näse enn hanenwada uck de Täne omsonst behaundle kunn, enn daut Hinjarenj soweso, oba dann uck wada leewtolig enn spoßig senne kunn, wea daut soo's daut mußt.

Oba aul daut mau soo aum Raund. Aune Sassendartig blädad Voda emma oppe selwje Städ em Kataloo 'romm, enn donn egol wada. Daut foll uck Mutta opp, enn see säd mett eemol: "Heea, wann de Kataloo eene Bibel wea, weascht Dü aul meist een Schreftjeleahda, enn een Bibelforscha soweso. Leahscht Dü aum Enj ütem Kataloo Englisch?" Voda säd nuscht nich, hee fuah noh Jrienthol nobre, wundad sich, oajad sich, vetald sich mett sich selwst bett'a doll word, speaj linjsch enn rajsch üt, schmeet siene Schlubb äwrem Holt-klompe, enn blädad donn wada em Kataloo, bett hee siene Städ jefunge haud.

"Waut betjitjcht hee sich?" ess de Froag. Bitte leiser.

Daut'et aune Sassendartig soo heet aus enne Hal word enn so dreajch aus enne Sahara, jefoll Voda seea schlajcht. Hee wea measchtens bossig, enn wann nich bossig, dann neewadrig. "Nich mol jescheiden Trubbel buschelt daut dit Joah!" meend hee eemol, aus etj daut head.

Na joh, vondoagschen-Dach saje se von soone Mensche, see send tweschen eenen Steen enn eene hoade Städ, ooda Koofoot; oba Voda wea soo mea tweschen de Groow enn dem Mesthüpe.

Oba soo langsom word sogoa mie daut dietlich, waut vonne Sort Warm mien Voda haud, enn woo ahm dee ploagde enn piesackte. Wiels: Aune Fiewendartig haud een McCullough von'ne Wille Hundat sich de Ranch jekofft, woone aun ons Laund aunsteete deed, enn dee siede enn siedooste äwrem Tün enne Nobaschauft von ons lach. Enn disse Ranch wea jrata, soo weens säd Voda, aus Jehaun Cornies siene Schopfenz enn Rußlaund. Aus daut soo wea, weet etj nich;

lined) for mom and a pair of long combinations for pa and both in size stout.

Did I almost say that the Bible enjoyed quite a bit more than two weeks vacation? I probably did and this was not necessarily because of the catalogue. My Pa did not read the Old Testament, he was the Old Testament and as long as he could play the Mennonite God in it and raise hell and dance and devil and yell and scream and could work over noses and teeth free of charge and asses to boot, and occasionally become loving and reflective and humorous, everything was as it ought to be.

But all that only on the edge of things. In 1936 Pa was always leafing around in the same spot in the catalogue. Even mom noticed this and she suddenly said, "Listen, if the catalogue were a Bible, you would almost be a scribe, if not a scholar of the Holy Script. Tell me, are you learning English from the catalogue?" Pa said nothing at all, he just hitched up the horses and went to Grünthal to make the rounds and then he was surprised and got mad and talked to himself till he got even madder, then he spat left and right and threw his cap over the woodpile and then he resumed leafing in the catalogue until he had again located chapter and verse.

You're probably asking, well what was he looking at? Well, just take it easy for a bit, okay? That it was as hot as hell in '36 and as dry as in the Sahara did not sit at all well with Pa. He was bossy most of the time and if not bossy, then mad and if not mad then ill-tempered. "One can't even reap a proper crop of decent trouble!" he said once when I overheard him.

Well, today they say of such people they are between a rock and a hard place but our Pa was between the gutter and the manure pile. But gradually even I came to understand what kind of worms were bothering the old man and how they plagued and pestered him.

waut etj oba weet, ess daut McCulloughasch ähre schwoate Angus bie ons kaume Howa enn Aulfaulfa fräte. Kroope eefach derjchen Stacheldroht, enn muake sich daut bie ons tüsig: fraute, schnerzte, enn läde sich han enn schleepe uck enn.

Well, daut wea eene goode haulwe Miel auf, oba aus Voda enn Mutta aum Sinndach fuahre de Stap enn de Fletja sich too betjitje, toobd Voda mett eemol loos, aus wann he Biswarm haud, enn hee wea platzlich pienja aus een nerweesa Hummingbird. Hee schreajch: "Biet ahm aum Zoagel enn aum Pungel, Mopps. Jeff ahm!," enn joag mett Hund toop daut Veeh tridj, daut'et stoof enn stritzt.

Aus Voda den oolen McCullough noch denselwjen Dach troff, räde see measchtens body language. Enn derjche Däah, wiels "Miester Kullah" ve Voda schnett haud. Voda räd, wann'a doll wea, emma lüda enn lüda enn iewaja, kratjcht soo's Swaggerts Jamie biem prädje. Bloß daut Voda staut 'ne Bibel eene Füst enne Henj haud, enn Rusch räd. Oba Mensche engrüle? Daut kunne se beid jlitje goot!

Na joh! Waut doa wertjlich wea, enn woa etj uck aul derhinja jekohme wea, wea dit: Voda wea eemol enn Winnipeg jewast, enn he haud doa jeseehne, daut bie fiewendartig Grod Kold een Poliesmaun emm Pelz so sondasorj romm jintj "aus wann'a aum Nippa em Juli enne Unjabetjse rommdwauld."

Voda siene Fantasie haud von dissem jestuckten Jesautzmaun enn sien Biffelpelz medden em Winta een Bild aufjenohme, enn dit Bild word'a nich meea loos. Uck emm Somma nich. Enn aus Voda sach, dautet soon Pelz fe $36.98 emm Eatons Kataloo too bestalle gauf, kaum siene Fantasiedaumpmehl nich meea too Rüh.

Enn he jintj foaken doahan, ooda de Mehl trock ahm doahan—waut uck emma, jenoag, dee leeht ahm nich mea loos. Enn toom easchten Mol enn sienem Läwe freid Voda sich oppen Winta; ahm wudd woam senne, enn daut mucht doch mett'em Schinda toogohne, wann hee sich nich boold dem Biffelpelz äwastreepe wudd.

In '35 one McCullough from nowhere or the "Wild Hundred" had bought a ranch adjoining our land which lay to the south and east of the fence of our farm. This ranch was larger, at least Pa said so, than Johann Cornies' sheep ranch in Russia.

Whether this was true or not, I don't know but what I do know is that McCullough's black Angus came to visit and to eat our oats and alfalfa. They simply crawled through the barbed wire fence and made themselves at home; they ate, they shat, grazed some more and then laid down and even snoozed.

Well, all that was happening a good half a mile away but when on Sunday, Pa and Ma took off to inspect the fields, Pa immediately had a fit as if warble flies were pestering him and he suddenly became as active as a hummingbird. He bawled, "Go for his stem and his grapes, Mopps! Let him have it, make the juice fly! And now for his carrot!" and then he chased the bull and cows back at such a speed that you could see the dust and green squirts fly.

When Pa met Old McCullough later that day, they talked mainly body language through the door because "Miester Kullah" was afraid of our Pa. Pa spoke always louder and louder when he got mad, just like Swaggert's Jimmy when preaching. Only that Pa had a fist in his hands instead of the Bible. But scare the hell out of people? They were both damn good at it.

Na joh! What there was really to it all and what even I had managed to understand goes as follows—Pa had once been in Winnipeg and there he had seen a policeman walking around at thirty-five below as casually "as if he were sitting in the sun in shorts by the Dnieper in July."

In his imagination Pa had taken a picture of this stocky man of the law wearing a buffalo coat in the middle of the winter and this picture simply refused to leave him. Even in summer

"Bai gosh enn bai golly," meend'a, enn uck noch een bät "Holy Doodle,": size 44 bett 46. Enn dann mol seehne, waut de Winta enn uck de Jrienthola von ahm hoole wudde. Hee wudd derjch den Winta enn derjch Jrienthol gohne, soo's daut Volk Israel derjch daut Roode Maeah. (Voda säd derjch daut Schwoate Mäah, wiels daut haud hee jeseehne, enn "daut wea je woll doch deepa enn breeda aus daut Roode" meend'a, "enn wäa weet, mett daut Roode Mäah, eena kaun de Mensche nich aules jleewe, nich mol de Jüde."

Na joh, oba hee mußt doch noch lenja opp sien Biffelpelz wachte, aus hee jedocht haud. Wiels? Na, $36.98 wea too dee Tiet een unjaheia groota Hüpe Jeld. Enn uck wiels? Joh, wiels emm nächsten Somma, aus Voda toop mett Miester Kullah sien Veeh toop too Jeld kohme wull, schreef de Wadagott 1936. Enn daut wea je dann uck de Somma aus'ett soo heet enn dreajch wea, daut'ett Veeh eefach too marood enn too meed enn too mack enn too medassa wea, om bie ons daut Jreenfooda too sample. Aulso frooa Voda noch eenen Winta, oba donn jintj'ett loos! Oba seea!

Oh joh, eene groote Pelzmetz kofft hee sich em selwjen Winta: eene mett ditjet Fall von benne enn von büte. Wann Voda von de Pelzmetz räd, enn hee dee de Mensche wees, säd hee emma: "Äwrem Hund send wie aul, äwrem Zoagel mott wie noch. Oppjoah!"

"Waut meenst Dü doamett, Thiesse? Wua west Dü han?" fruage de Lied. Oba Voda jniesad bloß een bät enn säd: "Gedepp!" enn fuah loos. Mette Pead, soo's aule aundre.

Oba? Joh, aum 2 August aune Säwendartig wear'ett soo wiet. Aun dem Morje weare bie ons emm Howa enn ennem Aulfaulfa vearefeatig schwoate Tjeaj enn Bolles, enn Tjalwa. Dee fraute enn freide sich enne Wad bie ons oppem Fletj enn oppe Stap, enn uck doatweschen. Oba Voda leeht dee toch, enn säd nuscht. Etj docht mie aul: "Ess'a blind, ooda reis wie morje tridj nohm Nippa, ooda ess'a schaubig? Ooda haft hee mol wada waut vea?"

Aum 3 August Klock tien zemorjess wort etj, enn uck de schwoate Angus von Miester Kullah enn, waut Voda aules

time. When Pa saw that it gave such a buffalo coat for $36.98 to order from the Eaton's catalogue, his mind gave him no peace.

For the first time since coming to Canada, Pa actually looked forward to the winter; he would be warm and even if everything went to the devil, Pa was going to have a blanket of buffalo on his back before long. Damn it!

"By gosh and by golly," he said and even a bit of "Holy doodle, size 44 to 46." And then let's just see what the winter and the Grünthalers would think of him. He would walk through the winter and through Grünthal like the people of Israel through the Red Sea. (Pa said through the Black Sea, because that one he had seen and "that was wider and deeper than the Red one and who knows about the Red Sea, you just can't believe everything people tell you, not even the Jews.")

Na joh, but he had to wait somewhat longer for his buffalo coat than he had reckoned on. $36.98 was a lot of money at that time and 1936 was exactly the summer when it was so hot and so dry that all cattle, including the neighbours', were too apathetic and too lazy to come over to our fields of green fodder for a sample and an overnight stay. And so Pa was cold for another winter but then things started revving up.

Oh joh, he did buy himself a huge pelt cap that very winter, with thick fur both inside and out. Whenever Pa spoke about that beauty and showed it to people he always said, "Well, we're over the dog and now we just have to cross his tail. Next year!" Or in other words, don't count your chickens before they're hatched.

"What are you talking about, Thiessen? What are you up to this time around?" people asked. But Pa just sneered a bit and said, "Get up horsies!" and took off.

On August 2 in '37, the time had come. That morning there were forty-four black cows and bulls and calves in our fields. They were in a wild grazing and munching competition in our

jeplohnt haud. Toop mett Fraunz, mien Brooda, enn mett Jaunz Oant, enn Kühne Wiense Briss, enn Jehovah Töwse Aunton, enn Liestje Rampels Henritj, saut Voda oppe Pead. Voda haud sich den Kunta Orlik ütjesocht; de groota Donna haud eenen jewaultjen Afterburner, enn wann'a dem aunschitzt, haud'a meea Spied aus een Rehbock.

Joh, aula saute se nü oppe Pead, enn aula weare se soo iewrig aus een Schwadroon Kosoake.

Wiet rundom reede se, eascht langsom em Waste nenn, donn em Siede, enn donn, noch emma langsom, em Ooste nenn. Enn mett ons Mopps, steile Uahre enn mett een extra Tjrinjel enn sienem Zoagel, bie Voda oppem Kunta, wiels daut Grauss enn Jeträajd soo huach wea, daut de Hund nich seehne kunn, waut hee noch too doohne haud.

Enn donn wear'ett soo wiet! Doa stund nü de gaunze Kavalrie, reed toom Aunjriep. Lüd jeräd word nich, bloß de Hund stemmd een fienet Leedje aun, oba hee leet fuats noh, wiels Voda nich mettsinje deed.

Donn worde de Rolle sootoosaje een bät vedeelt, enn sogoa de Pead wißte noch nich waut daut aules sull: Aundasch aus em Woatjeldach, oba nich gaunz Sinndach, so väl wißte uck see.

Voda enn Orlik stunde veropp, enn de Pelzanwärter haud eene dreetinjsche Fortj enne Grauje, enn noh bowe jespetzt, enn hee tald enn hee tald daut Veeh, doa eene Veadel Miel auf, enn bettem Novel enne Säd, sootoosaje. Voda wea soo iewrig aus een Hobo, wann de eenen Zug omme Atj daumpe sach... enn donn... Mett eemol bload Voda: "*Los!*" leet doabie Clotch enn Hund rüt enn rauf, enn donn? Donn bebbad de Ead. See moarachde aulatoop loos, daut Stoff enn Klütasch enn Schiet eenem omme Uahre fluage, jlitj noh Miester Kullah siene Hääd opptoo.

Wiense Briss enn ons Mopps reede enn rande dicht aune Fenz delenjd, doamett de Hääd nich tridj enn noh Hüs kunn. Enn etj stund uck doa aum Tün enn weifeld waut etj kunn, enn bload soo's aule Donna.

oats and alfalfa fields and in our meadows and in the green steps in between. But Pa just let them be and said not a word. I was thinking to myself, "Is he blind, or are we going back to the family estate by the Dnieper tomorrow? Or is he again up to something?"

On August 3 at ten o'clock in the morning, I and the black Angus of "Miester Kullah" realized what Pa was up to. Pa and Franz, my brother, and Preacher Janz's Aaron and Turkey Wiens's Boris and Jehovah Toews's Anton and Liestje Rempel's Hendritj, sat on horses. Pa rode our gelding Orlik and that big devil had powerful hindquarters and more speed than a deer buck. They sat on their mounts, as eager as a squadron of Cossacks.

They took a wide, wide turn, riding slowly to the west and then they all changed direction and rode south and then, still slowly and casually, they headed east with our dogs Mopps, ears erect, an extra ring curled into his tail for the occasion, sitting with Pa on the gelding because the grass and the grain were so tall that he could not see what he was shortly expected to do.

The time had come. The entire cavalry stood ready to mount an attack. There was no loud talk at all. Then the roles were handed out, so to speak, and even the horses did not know what to make of it all. Things were different from the workday but not quite as on Sundays, that much they knew.

Pa and Orlik were at the front and the fur coat candidate had a mighty three-tined fork in his hands, business end up as he counted and re-counted the cattle a good quarter of a mile away up to their belly buttons in standing silage. Pa was as eager as a hobo seeing a train steaming around the corner— and then suddenly Pa yelled, "Now!" while releasing clutch and the dog. The earth trembled and shook as they thundered off together heading straight for Miester Kullah's herd,

De Mejchel wull noch wiese, wea hiea eajentlich Bauß ess, enn hee kleiwd daut'e Soode fluage, enn hee brommd uck bauß, enn leet siene Tung aundathaulw Schooh rütbommle, soo's daut mott, wann'a doll woat. Oba aus hee mett Voda siene Tinje eent aum Hinjarenj tjreajch, soo's een Matador, gauf'ett een Instant Conversion. Oba aunstaut sich oppe Tjnees tooschmiete, dreid hee sich romm, tjwield sich enne Poote, stald sien Zoagel enne Hejcht, enn weifeld doamett aus een Propella, soo's een Rehbock—oba ohne witte Unjabetjse—enn läd loos waut'a kunn, siene Jemeend hinjeraun.

Eascht de jnodefeldsche Lain delenjd, dann soo doll enn schoap enn huppasch rajsch, daut een poah Tjalwa omstelpde enn "MA!" bloade, dann jlitjüt de jrientholsche Lain delenjd, mett väl Jebloah enn emma huppasch. Voda mußt sich noch emma äwa den Boll Mejchel oajre, woona ahm haud vesocht aus Leitenda auftoosate, enn nü bucheld hee sienen Kunta Orlik enne Rebbe, bett he dicht aum Boll wea. Donn resst Voda dem schwoaten Plästa mettem Fortjestäl eent äwrem Bless—noch emma bie dartig Miel de Stund—daut de Boll meddem em hallichten Dach Stearns sach... daut wea ahm lenjdhan aun too seehne, daut he nü opp high beam drebbeld.

Wann doah eena von Metro Golden Meyer jestohne haud, enn sich daut Bild aunjetjitjt, dann wea de gaunze Schwadroon jlitj aum Paunjstaul vebie jeräde, donn derj'chen Chaco, fuats äwre Jrenz, enn donn haulf rajsch noh Hollywood opptoo...

Daut Veeh ständ enn deed, de Schüm enn de Kackenacka fluag... nü weare se oppe Winnipegsche Lain, enn dann noch eene Miel, enn donn weare se mett eemol bie Dirijente Driedjasch em Paunjstaul aunjekohme. "Nü nenn mett jünt Schindasch!" enn donn word de Gate toojemoakt.

Jieda Cowboy tjreajch eenen Dolah, aus'a wull ooda nich, enn se mußte nü wada em Auldach nenn, enn noh Hüs riede. (Enn etj? Etj tjreajch uck een Dollah, oba enn veea Installments äwa veea Joah.)

Bloß Voda reet noch veea Miel wieda noh Miester Kullah, mett Hund enn Fortj, enn väl Wind von hinje.

sending dust and clods and shit flying around the spectators' ears.

Wiens's Boris and our Mopps rode and ran close to the fence so that the herd could not run back home. I stood by the fence yelling and screaming and waving for all I was worth. Michael, the bull, wanted to show who the real boss was in these parts as he clawed huge hunks of sod into orbit and bellowed with a foot and a half of tongue hanging out of his mouth. But when he got four inches of Pa's weapon right into the flank and ass area, he had an instant conversion. But instead of dropping to his knees and doing penance, he placed his tail in high gear and started swirling it like a deer buck but without white shorts, and took off for all he was worth, hard on the heels of his congregation.

First they moved along the Gnadenfeld line so fast and sharply and so much in overdrive that a few calves capsized and then straight along the Grünthal line with much bawling and more gallop. Pa was still mad at the bull for having attempted to unseat him as the lead minister and so he gave Orlik a few hefty digs in the ribs until he was alongside of the bull. Then he hauled out and landed the black bastard one over the forehead—still at thirty miles an hour—so that the bull saw a galaxy of stars in the brightness of day; you could see it all over him that he was now strictly on high beam.

Had there been anyone of those reps from Metro Golden Meyer and had he taken a good look at the entire squadron, he would have had them ride straight past the cattle impounding station, then right through the Chaco, across the border and a half-right straight to Hollywood.

The cattle groaned and moaned with foam and shit flying. Now they were on the Winnipeg line and then after another quick mile, they suddenly arrived at Conductor Driedger's Cattle Impounding Compound. "In with you bastards!" and the gate was closed.

Jenoag, aum Friedach von de Wäatj haud Voda vearefeatig Dohla, enn Miester Kullah haud sien Veeh. Enn aum Mondach vonn'e nächste Wäatj bestald Voda sich derjch'en Eatons Kataloo eenen Biffelpelz, size 46.

Oba doa wea je noch een Dollah äwajebläwe...woa han mett dem? Vleicht emm Kollatjtetala? Weit jefehlt, meine Teuren. Voda läd den Dolah enn een Kowart mett een Zadel nenn, enn säd, etj sull rejchtoo noh Kullasch gohne, enn ahn den Breef jäwe.

Etj kunn donn aul een bät lese, enn unjawäjess—daut wea emmahan meist twee Miel, uck rejchtoo—tjreaj mie de Nieschiea von hinje, enn dann von bowe, enn donn noch von benne too hoole, enn schmeet mie han, enn donn nauhm see mie uck noch den Breef wajch, enn reet den op enn hilt mie den verr'e Uage enn säd: "Lass!" Enn waut stund doa? Doa stund:

"Howyüdo Miester Kullah. Tanks fer de Beffelkoht. Hier ess won Dollar fe die Fertilaiza yür Kattel lief Behaind. If yü vant anoder Diel next yier laik dis yier, jü just say mie, O.K.?"

Yür Christschen Freund enn Naybür Peter-the-Grate."

Every one of the cowboys got a dollar whether he wanted it or not and then they rode into the everyday world of home. (I also got a dollar which I wanted but it was paid to me in four installments over the next four years.) Only Pa rode another four miles to Miester Kullah's place with dog and fork and a stiff breeze behind.

To make a long story short, on the Friday of that week, Pa had forty-four dollars and Miester Kullah had his cattle. And the following Monday, Pa ordered himself from the Eaton's catalogue, a buffalo coat, size 46.

But there was one dollar still left. If you think it was meant for the collection plate you're wrong again. Pa placed that dollar in an envelope together with a note and told me to take a short-cut to McCullough's and give it to the Miester.

I was already able to read a bit and while underway—it was a good two miles, even by short-cut—my curiosity grabbed me and took that envelope away and ripped it open and made me read the note. It read:

"Howyüdo, Miester Kullah. Tanks fer de Beffelkoht. Hier ess won Dollar fe die Fertilaiza yür Kattel lief behaind. If yü vant anoder Diel nex yier laik dis yier, yü just say mie, O.K?

Yür Christschen Freund enn Naybür, Peter-the-Grate."

Nie Wada

Wie worde ons fuats oppe Städ eenijch, daut wie niemols nijch een Wuat äwa disse Schwienarie jemols velude lohte wudde. Tjeena nijch sull irjendwaut weete, waut doa väajefolle wea, wiels wie kunne aul heare, waut dann pesseare wudd, "Ujujujuj, waut woare de Lied sijch bloos dentjche, waut woare de Lied saje?"

Soo wea daut, enn etj jleew, wie weare sogoa een bät stolt doaropp, daut wie een Jeheemnis haude, daut sesst bloos de leewa Gott wisst, enn sesst tjeena. Oba noh fiewentwintijch Joah lohte de Tjäde enn uck de Strenj, woohne daut Jeheemnis fausthoole, een bät noh, enn wann wie Jeheemnishieta ons hanennwada too seehne tjriee, dann brinj wie aul sogoa eenen tjlienen Schmusta äwre Leppe, aunstaut bloos too hiele enn Triebsaul too blose, enn Kloageleeda, aule Stroophe, veea-stemmijch too sinje.

Waut wea? Veea Predjasch enn een Tjrist (enn daut wea natierlijch mol wada etj), haude jeheat, daut'et enne Stäts aul donn enn mol wada doll toojintjch. Toom Biespell, weare Peeta Bruhn, Bruno Wiebe, Johaun Reima enn Jaunzess Willie eenmol tien Doag opp eenmol wajchjefoahre. Enn auls see tridjkaume, koffte sijch Wiebe enn Bruhn fuats jieda noch veea Veadel Laund, während Reima schwind sien Veadel Laund vekofft, enn fe ahn auls Oabeida, Schetjbenjel, enn Pauslocke schaufe musst. Willie, dee Aufkoht, fong zeowents aun auls Bartender too oabeide, wiels sien Jehault auls Aufkoht reatjcht nijch meea too omm seine Famielje too feehde. De eenfache Lied enn uck de Tjoatjevodasch wundade sijch, waut doa woll

72

Nevada—Never Again

We had reached agreement and promised each other that we would absolutely never ever tell this whole messy tale to anyone. Not even to half of one of anyone if it gave such a thing because it was it was nothing but pure mischief and bad in any case and also shameful and if the whole thing ever came out one would hear, non-stop, "Ujujujuj, what will people say? What will people think?"

Yes, we had all promised to commit the matter to utmost secrecy at the time, pledging that we would never breathe a single word of it, but after twenty-five years the chord of resolve tends to loosen a bit and one can already manage a bit of a smirk again—even if not yet a full-blown smile—instead of always breaking into sobs or lamentations.

Well, it is like this. Four preachers and one Christian (and I was that one of course) had heard that already then things in the States were going hard and heavy. For example Peter Braun, Bruno Wiebe, Johan Reimer and Janzen's Willie were gone for ten days in the middle of winter. When they came back Wiebe and Braun immediately bought themselves another section of land while Reimer quickly sold his quarter and started working for them as a hired hand. Willie, the lawyer, started working evenings as a bartender because his wages and salary and income as a lawyer did not reach far enough to feed his own family. The common people as well as the church fathers were wondering what was wrong but when they started into the whole matter they soon returned humming the song, "Must I go and empty-handed?"

pessead wea, enn see vesochte dann je uck Kloarheit enn Lijcht enn daut Gaunze too brinje enn too schmiete, oba see kaume boold tridj, enn sommde daut Leed, "Muß ich geh'n mit leeren Händen?"

"Donnawatta enn Schinda em Schiet!" säd dee oola Schwoat, während Ohm Gerstein, ons judscha Stooahmaun bloos: "Daut jefft een Hupe Zorres!" säd, eea hee aunfong too lache.

Enn soo jinje de Predjasch enn etj nohm Johaun Reima, enn fruage, auls wie dee gaunze nijch berädboare Sach, beräde kunne. Oba Johaun rolld sijch eene Zigarett enn säd bloos: "Nie Wada, oba Nie, Niewada!" enn jintjch tridj aune Oabeit. Enn waut de aundre dree weare? Bruhn, Wiebe enn Willie haude daut soo drock, daut see tjeene Tiet haude, irjenwaut too berede. Na, Willie talld sowesoo nijch, wiels hee nijch too de Tjoatjch jeheat—hee wea nijch bie Jemeend—enn soo kunn wie ahm nijch jeleewat nehme, dem Hallota!

Enn soo bleef ons, de Predjasch enn mie, nuscht nijch aundasch äwrijch, auls ons dee gaunze Sach vom Boddem opp too unjaseatje. Nu ess daut Gaunze, soo auls aul jesajcht, aul fiewentwintijch Joah tridj, oba daut ess aules noch soo enn woah, wertjlijch soo.

Enn soo fuah wie fief nohm Siede, noh de Stäts. Medden em Winta. Wie gauwe onse Frulied enn onse Muttasch Frieheit, Tus too bliewe, enn too besorje, enn Eia uttoonehme, enn uttoomeste, enn noh School toogohne, enn aum Party-line opptooschnacke, enn Hose enne Schlenje too jriepe, enn noh Tjoatj too gohne, enn Spohs too driewe, während wie eene earnste Pflijcht nohjinje. "Noh Kaunsas Frindschauft beseatje," säd wie, daut heet, säd etj, wiels etj goot wisst, woa wie hanfuahre; daut haud Johaun Reima, dee Kanädja mie jesajcht. Jrohds auls wie loosfoahre wulle, fuscheld Reima mie ennet Ooah: "Woarom latst Du de Predjasch nijch auleen foahre? Woaromm wellst Du die de Henj enschwiene? Bitte, bliew hiea!"

"Thunderations and bullshitzky!" said old man Schwartz, while Gerstein, our Jewish store-man, only said, "That will give a stack of Tsorres!" (misery) before laughing.

And so the preachers and I went to Johan Reimer and asked if we could discuss the whole undiscussable matter. But Johan just rolled himself a cigarette and said only, "Nie Wada, but Nie, Nie Wada!" and went back to his work. As for the other three? Braun, Wiebe and Willie were so very busy that they had no time at all to discuss the matter. Well, Willie did not really count anyway because he did not belong to the church and so we couldn't manage to corral him at all; we just couldn't lay the inner hand on him, that rascal.

And so there was nothing to do but for the preachers and I to try and investigate the whole matter from the bottom up. Now everything is already twenty-five years old but it is still all so and true. Joh, joh.

So we five drove south, to the States. In the middle of winter. We permitted our mothers and wives and the little ones to remain at home to do the chores and gather eggs and manure-out and go to school and listen in on party phone line talk a bit and snare rabbits and go to church and have their fun, while we took off in the line of duty. "To Kansas to visit relatives," we said, that is, I said, because I knew very well where we were going; that Johan Reimer, the Kanadier had told me. Just before we started out, Reimer whispered to me, "Why don't you let the preachers go alone? Why do you want to dirty your hands in their business? Stay around, please!"

"No," I said. "Johan, why don't you come along?"

"Mensch, Nie Wada (never again), Nie Wada!" Then he turned on his own axis in his Burrsteewle-boots and went to pitch straw and hay and cow shit. I noticed that he was no longer smoking but had a tooth-pick in his mouth and he worked for his bosses like somebody gone wild.

"Nä," säd etj. "Johaun, woaromm tjemmst Du nijch mett?"

"Mensch, Nie Wada, Niewada!" Enn dann dreid hee sijch enn siene Burrstewle omm, enn jintjch Hei enn Koohschiet stoake. Etj sach, daut hee nijch meea schmeatjcht, sonda een Tähnepoake em Mul haud, enn fe siene Bausse auls een Willa oabeid.

Donn kroop wie enne Koah nenn, enn läde loos. Eascht Schnee enn Ies, dann Ies enn Schnee, oba aum dredden Dach leet de Winta aul enn bät noh, enn auls'ett Owend word, wear'ett aul woama enn scheen, enn wie sage sogoa den easchten Rootbuck; wie haude aul tweedusend Miel tridj-jeljajcht.

Woa wea jie? froag jie. Auls wann jie daut nijch lenjst jeroht habe—wie weare enne Sonn enn Sind City!

"Eea wie de Schwienarie Tus enne Tjoatj opprieme tjenn, mott wie ons daut Gaunze opp Uat enn Städ unjaseatje, enn 'hard evidence' saumle, säd 'Tiny' dee Barjchtholscha Predja C. F. Friese.

"Joh, ons blifft nusch nijch aundasch äwrijch," stemmd ahm Predja Hienrijch Peetasch bie; dee jansja woohna ons Jungess emma vemohnd: "Jungess, jie derwe niemols nijch doll woare, daut ess nijch biblisch!" säd hee.

"Oba See woare je uck weens tweemol den Dach doll!" säd wie.

Donn stald sijch Predja Peetasch von Gortiets han, haud de Been aundathaulf Schooh utenaunda, enn dann pompt hee sijch voll Loft, enn leeht sien Wieseafinja enn siene Uage nohm Himmel nohhejcht wrabble, enn säd opp Huachdietsch, "Mein Zorn ist der Zorn des Gerechten!"

Wie weare aunjokohme, enn fonge onsen schwoaren Deenst uck fuats aun.

Joh, enn Predja Korneeljeus Faust, dee emma säd: "Etj heet Korneel-jesus, enn ut goodem Grund," säd: "Dem Jerajchten ess aules jerajcht, dem Reinen ess aules rein," tjreajch de Wrang

76

Then we piled into the car and were on our way. First snow and ice, then ice and snow but on the third day winter let up a bit and come evening it was beautiful and spring-like in the air and we even saw our first robin, or "Red-paunch" as the Old-Colonier Preacher Nickel said, when we had two thousand miles behind the rear tires.

Where were you? you ask. As if you didn't know—we were in Sun and Sin City!

"Before we can clean up the mess in church back home we have to look around here and gather hard evidence," said "Tiny", the Bergthaler Preacher C. F. Friesen.

"Yes, we have no other choice in the matter," agreed Preacher Heinrich Peters, the one who always admonished us when we were boys, "Boys, you should never not get angry, that's not Bible-like!" he said.

"But even you get angry at least twice a day," we said.

Then Preacher Peters from Chortitz moved his legs apart a foot and a half while pumping his front full of oxygen and then he said with his eyes and his watch-out finger pointing up, "My wrath is the wrath of the righteous!"

Joh, and Preacher Kornieljeus Fast who always said, "I am called Korniel-jesus with good reason," stated, "To the just all things are just, to the clean all things are clean," and grabbed the crank of the gambling machine while throwing in six quarters with his other hand.

Then he pulled the crank down and it started turning in there and turning and spinning and turning some more, then it rolled into low gear, stuttered and choked as four choice watermelon pieces, carved up right through the middle with black seeds against the juicy red and all alike lined up behind the glass.

The red light on top of the machine now blitzt and spun; the machine came alive and howled and screamed and then rang and started growling and busheling quarters. Those quarters

von dee Spälmaschien mett eene Haund too hoole, enn mett de aundre Haund dretjcht hee doa sass Veadels nenn. Dann trock hee dee Wrang rauf, enn dann fong daut doa benne aun too dreie, enn too turne, enn too kullre, enn too diesle, enn dann wada too dreie, enn dann wea daut Gaunze mett eenmol em Low Gear, em läajen Jedriew aulsoo, enn dann stottad daut Jeschnees, donn veschluckt'a sijch, enn veea straume Arbuseschnäde duckte opp; schmocke Schnäde, fein derjchjeschnäde mett schwoate Tjänatjess opp daut roode Arbusefleesch, enn aule stunde se enn eene Reaj.

Daut roode Lijcht opp daut Jeschnees blitzt opp enn dreid, dee Maschien word läwendijch enn juhld, enn schreajch, enn tjlinjad, enn fong aun too bromme, enn donn leet dee too, enn buscheld Veadels. Dee Veadels spretzte, enn ruschelde, see fluage enn see rollde, dee schoowe enn see buchelde, see dreide enn see dreide, enn see tjlätade, enn schnurrde, enn wulle bloos wajch, wajch von dee Maschien, enn kullade bie de Dusende noh ons opptoo. Biem Buschelvoll. Toom Jletjch haud ons stellsta Ohm, Predja Netjel, vonne ooltkolniesche Sort, lange, schwoate Steewle aun. Een Rucks enn dann haud'a dee uck aul enne Grauje, enn leeht dee voll ranne. Toom Jletjch haud uck etj onsen Meddachsätebiedel mett Reatjaworscht, Zipple, Koffe, Kuffels, Reeschetweeback enn jekoakte Eia enne Haund. Etj schmeet daut gaunze Mettbrinjsel opp dee Ambulance-Maschien nopp, enn hilt den Sack unja. Enn noch emma stritzt daut enn stritzt daut; tien Dusend Veadels schnerzte doa rut auls wann daut gaunze Jeschnees een groota Gaunta wea.

Dann word mett eenmol aules wada stell. Twee von onse Predjasch lage oppe Tnees enn lause de Veadels opp, enn schmeete dee bie de Jappsvoll enn mien Sack, enn dann weare aule Stroopfe von dem scheenen Leed too Enj, enn de greiwa Auldach läd sijch wada äwa ons. Etj wull noch een bät Spohs moake, enn fong aun daut Leed "Von der Erde riet mie loos, enn fell ons voll een jiedret Kroos" oba donn tjitjcht Predja

splattered and rang, and rattled and rustled, they flew and they rolled, they pushed and they shoved, they turned and they rolled and they clattered and purred, busily fleeing and escaping that machine by the thousands. By the bushelful. Luckily, our quietest preacher, Nickel, was of the Old Kolonier type and had long, black boots on. These he whipped off in a flash and filled with quarters. And fortunately, I had brought along our lunch sack with smoked farmer's sausage, onions, coffee, stale buns and boiled eggs. I heaved these supplies on the stationary ambulance machine and held the sack under it. It was pouring and pouring; ten thousand quarters squirted out like so much goose shit.

Then everything became still again. Two of our preachers were kneeling in front of that quarter-dispenser, gathering up the last of the quarters and throwing them into my sack and then all the verses of that beautiful song were over and the greyness of everyday silence settled over us. I wanted to have a little bit of fun and started singing the refrain, "From the earth, oh tear me loose, make my sack, fat as a goose!" but Preacher Peters gave me one look with his brush-cut and his look-out finger and said, "Silentium!" and my song became like the muted machine.

Then we departed. We left the hollow-bellied money machine lonely with all the dripping watermelon pieces still inside and made for our car. Leading the way was Preacher Fast with his bulging pockets while behind him tripped Preacher Peters with his pants full and an offering of silver in his cupped hands and then followed Preacher Friesen who bore but meager change since his body engine had its hands full with the holy man's considerable weight. Next came Preacher Nickel barefoot—his foot rags were waving from his pockets—but with his boots in his hands like slop-pails full of quarters. I formed the rear guard with the lunch sack full of money and

Peetasch mie mett sienem Brush-cut enn mett sienem Pauss-Opp-Finja aun, enn säd: "Silentium!" enn dann word mien Leed soo stell auls dee meede Maschien.

Dann jinj wie loos enn wajch. Wie veleehte dee hollbuckje Maschien mett aul de sauftje Arbusestetja doabenne enn begauwe ons noh onse Koah. Veropp jintjch Predja Faust mett siene utjebuhlde Fuppe, enn hinja ahm drebbeld Predja Peetasch mett volle Betjse enn een Opfavoll-Selva enne Japps, enn donn kaum Predja Friese mett weinijch Boajeld; hee haud aule Henj voll sijch selwst too beweaje, wiels hee een seea jestuckta Bibeforscha wea. Hinja ahm jintjch Predja Netjel boaft; siene Footkoddre weifelde ahm ute Fuppe, oba siene Steewle druag hee soo auls Drangamasch volla Veadels. Etj jintjch auls latzta mett dem Meddachsbiedel volla Jeld hinjeraun, während de Worscht enn dee jekoakte Eia und so weiter und so fort enn miene Windbreaka Fuppe mettreisde.

Predja Faust hohld de Koareschlätels ut siene rajchte Betjsefupp, schloot daut Koareklotje op, tjreajch eenen heltanen Eiakauste toohoole enn säd: "Na, enn nu häa mett mien Jeld!"

Sien Jeld? Sien Jeld? Bloos Predja Faust sien Jeld? Aule tiendusend Veadels jeheare Predja Faust? Enn bloos ahm? Wie stunde verrem Hinjarenj vonne Koah mett tjeen Wuat opp onse Leppe, soo auls een Jespaun Osse verrm Aumboaj.

Etj wull jrods mien Sack Mammon enn Predja Faust sien Eiakauste nennschedde, auls Predja Nejtel, dee stella, mett eenmol säd: "Du, Korneeleus, Du wellst aulso nuscht nijch tjristlijch deele?"

"Waut mient ess, ess mient. Waut redst Du hiea von endeele? Enn nu jicha doamett!" kommendead Predja Faust.

Dann säd de ooltkolniescha Predja Nejtel too mie: "Du pauss opp miene Steewle opp, enn loht nijch een Veadel rutjleppe. Wiels waut mient ess, ess mient, enn daut meent uck volle Steewle. Enn nu goh etj mie niee Schooh tjeepe." Enn donn

80

with the sausage and the boiled eggs and so on and so forth in my windbreaker pockets.

Preacher Fast pulled his car keys from his right lower pant pocket, unlocked the trunk of his car, grabbed a wooden egg-crate and said, "Na, now let me have my money!" His money? His money? Only Preacher Fast's money? All ten thousand quarters belong to Preacher Fast? And to him all alone? We stood in front of the back of the car without a word on our lips, like a team of oxen before the steepness of the hill.

I was just about to dump my stack of mammon into Preacher Fast's egg crate, when Preacher Nickel, the quiet one, suddenly announced himself, "You, Kornieljeus, you intend not to divvy anything at all Christian style?" he asked.

"What is mine, is mine. What do you mean, divvy up? Now, on the double!" commanded Preacher Fast.

Then the Old Kolonier Preacher Nickel said to me, "You guard over my boots and don't let a single quarter slip out. Because what is mine, is mine and that means full boots. And now I'm going to buy a pair of new shoes." Then he counted himself eighty quarters into his hand.

Well, then we all felt a little like one fellow's brother-in-law Harry who used to assess new situations by saying, "It's about time we put new belts on the pulley!"

Whatever, we now had to come to some kind of consensus. Preacher Fast resisted and was contrary and had ten Bible verses to support his case, while Preacher Peters had just as many counter verses at the ready, while I sat there on the bumper of the car with the boots and sack full of silver.

Then suddenly Preacher Nickel was back and he announced, "Now it's enough. If things will keep on going like this I will soon say 'Shiet!' aloud! If we cannot immediately come to an acceptable agreement, and I mean an immediate and full agreement, then my boot servant and I will dump the whole

talld hee sijch tachentijch Veadels enne Haund. Na dann kaum wie ons soo väa aul eenem sien Schwoaga Harry, dee bie soohne Sache emma säd: "Na, dann mott wie dochwoll niee Seiden oppe Reemschiew opplajen."

Jenuag, wie musste ons nu dochwoll irjendwoo eenje. Predja Faust stiepad sijch, enn wea jäjenaun, enn hee haud tien Bibelfarzh reed omm sijch too rajchtfoadje, während Predja Peetasch kratjcht soo väl auls Jäjenred reed haud, während etj oppem Bompa mett twee Steewle enn ons Ätesbiedel volla Selwajeld saut.

Boold wea je dann uck Predja Netjel wada tridj enn hee säd seea ruhijch, "Enn nu reatjcht daut too. Wann daut hiea soo wieda jeiht, woa etj boold seea lud 'Schiet!' saje. Wann wie nijch fuats oppe Städ ons opprejchtijch eenje tjenne, dann woat mien Steeweltjnajcht enn etj daut gaunze Jeld doa hinje enn de Rie nenndompe. Brooda Kornusch, wellst du daut doohne, ooda wellst Du daut nijch doohne?"

Predjasch Peetasch enn Friese säde doatoo Amen. Dann fong wie aun entoodeele. Twintijch Minute lohta haud een jiedra tweedusend Veadels, oba tachtentijch weinja fe Predja Nejtel, enn eene Stund lohta haud wie daut Selwajeld fe Papieajeld enjetuscht. Predja Faust behild siene Veadels.

Dann vebeet wie ons een bät, enn dann noch eenmol, enn dann hild wie Meddachschlop noh de mennonietische Oat: enne Koah.

Joh, joh, enn dann fuah wie wada tridj noh Hus, noh Jrienthol enn Kanada. Oba nu goht nijch fuats loos enn vetalt dit aulewäaje wieda, nä? oba dee Eensja, woohna mett ladje Henj Tus aunkaum wea Predja Faust. Dee Veadels haude ahm jedretjcht, enn bedretjcht, enn oppjedretjcht, enn ahm jebaudat, enn ahm jepiesackt, bett hee daut nijch lenja uthoole kunn, enn hee Medden enne Nacht oppstund, dee Koah veleeht, enn auls hee twee Stund lohta von dee Arbuseberstaund tridjkaum, haud Korneeljeus weens tien Pund aufjenohme.

stack of quarters into that back creek. Brother Kornusch, do you want to or do you not want to?"

Preachers Peters and Friesen also said amen to that. Then the dividing started. Twenty minutes later everyone had two thousand five hundred quarters (minus eighty for Preacher Nickel) and one hour later three of us had exchanged the change for paper bills. Preacher Fast hung on to his quarters.

Then we noshed a bit and then some more and then we had a nap Mennonite style, in the car.

Joh, joh, and then we went home again, to Grünthal, to Canada. Now don't go around and tell this story all over the place, understand? But the only one of us who arrived home empty-handed was Preacher Kornieljeus Fast. Those quarters had pressed him and oppressed him and depressed him and bothered him and pestered him until he just couldn't stand it any longer and then he got up in the middle of the night and left the car and us and when he returned some two hours later from the watermelons machines, Kornieljeus was at least ten pounds lighter.

When we returned home, it did not take long for another Mennonite church to be built. People brought sacrifices and hammers and saws and soon the new church was standing bright and ready. This new church was called "Gerechtigkeits-Gemeinde", (Church of Justice) and in this church there were frequent and mighty thunderations against "Gambling and Dance". The bishop of this new church was Preacher Kornieljeus Fast.

When I saw Johan Reimer again he was a bit more lively; he seemed to have enough kopecks again to afford cigarette tobacco. But he still worked for Braun and Wiebe (Wiebe had also become a preacher) and his talk was a little less inhibited.

"I have a new deal," he said, "Another seven years and I am a free man. But do you know what I think they should call Fast's new church? 'Lost Wages, Nie Wada!'" and then he

Auls wie Tus aunkaume, gauf daut boold wada eene niee Tjoatj, enn dee heet dee "Gerechtigkeits Gemeinde" enn doa word väl jäjen Späl enn Daunz jedonnat. Dee Eltesta von disse niee Jemeend wea Korneelius Faust.

Wann Predja Faust mie jefroagt haud, haud etj ahm vääjeschloage, daut dee Jemeend Niewada haut heete sullt. Jie uck?

smiled and rolled himself a cigarette and swivelled around in his old Burrsteewle-boots and set about forking hay.

Een Mickey Finn

Mensche jleewe, see weete waut een Mennist ess, nich? Etj woa Junt vetalle, waut etj jleew Jie jleewe, enn wann etj aul doabie sie, woa etj Junt dietlich moake, enn dee Loag rechtich stalle. Wann Jie jleewe, daut wie mett schwoate Heed enn Bäte, enn een schwoaten Aunzug rommranne auls eene heilje Uniform enn onse Frulied ons hinjeraun schibble, een Schrett ooda dree tridjaun, enn lange Ratj droage, omm äah Foarmaschibbel too vedatje, enn uck den Kopp bedatjt habe enn äwabrestich schmustre, send Jie aulwada faulsch.

Ooda wann Jie jleewe, daut wie meea auls eene Fru habe, ooda jemols jehaut habe, mott etj saje: Weit gefehlt! Nä! Wie habe aule Henj voll mett eene Fru em Hus.

Enn wann Jie jleewe, daut wie Mennoniete, uck Menniste jenannt, twee bie twee rommwanke mett een earnstet Jesejcht verrem Kopp enn Junt eene Haundvoll Pampfleete vetjeepe welle, dee vonne grulje Tiede omme tweede Atj vetalle, vetjeepe welle, mott etj saje, daut wie nuscht nich mett soohne Russeliete enn ähre 144,000 Glommstjapp too doohne habe.

"Na, waut send Jie dann?" froag Jie.

Wie send fe daut Niee Testament, kratjt daut, waut de Jude fe daut Oole Testament send; gaunz eenfach. Wie send meist soo oolt auls de Tiet ess, enn auls wie dem Pohp enn Rom säde, daut hee sich schäre kunn enn sull, stald wie uck de Beijcht enn, wiels wie seea weinich, ooda äwahaupt nuscht nich Grootet too beijchte habe. Wie vestohne ons too benehme, enn wann nich, woare aundre Mennoniete ons aul tridj äwre Sälestrenj nohm gooden Benehme schuwe, ooda uck buchle. Ooda wie ahn. Enn dann vetalle see, ooda wie äwa

"Repant"

So you think you know what a Mennonite is? Well, I'll tell you what I think you think one is and while I'm at it, I'll correct you. If you think we run around in black hats and beards and have a black suit on as a professional holy uniform with our wives walking behind a step or three and all wearing long skirts to hide a barnyard shuffle, with something over their hair and smiling superiorly, you are wrong.

Or if you think that we have more than one wife, or ever had, for that matter, then I can tell you that you are wrong again. We have all hands full with one wife each.

If you think, we Mennonites walk around preaching joy but scowling two by two and wanting to sell you some pamphlets of things happening just around the next corner of time, then I can tell you we have nothing not to do with such modern cults and their 144,000 numerals, either. Nosiree.

"So what are we," you ask?

We are to the New Testament what the Jews are to the Old, plain and simple. We are almost as old as time itself by now and when we told the Pope where to go, we also abolished the doctrine of confession because we have very little, if anything, to reveal. We know how to behave ourselves and if not, other Mennonites will shove us back into our traces of respectability by taking another good look at us, or we at them, and then we will expose them to another round of disapproval by speaking all manner of stuff about each other. That helps.

ahn aulahaund "Pauß opp, oba pauß blooß opp!" enn weifele mett dem Paußoppfinja ahn hinjeraun, ooda see ons. Daut halpt.

Soo's aul jesajcht, wie send soo's de Jude vom Nieen Testament. Wie dentje nich blooß, daut wie rajcht habe, wie weete daut. Enn wann Jie dentje, daut Jie de measche Jude aun ähre Nohmes tjanne, soo's Blumenstein, Herzog, Bernstein enn Weinstock, dann tjenn wie uck kratjt soohne typische Nohmes oppreaje. Wann irjend een Reima, Friese, Wiebe ooda Thiesse Junt vetallt, daut hee tjen Mennist ess, dann well wie ahm nich habe, ooda hee lijcht.

Nich blooß daut. Wann Jie mett mennische Experte räde, woare soohne Junt vetalle, daut jewesse Äjenschaufte sich bie bestemmde Famieljes derjchsatte. Friees, toom Biespell, jefft daut seea väl. De Appe lese jearn Beatja; Wiebe send hinjaridjsch enn stolt opp ähre Demoot; Thiesses striede sich jearn, enn send ditjkoppich (weens soo meene eenje Prädjasch) enn seea intelligent (mien Voda säd mie daut), enn pausse seea oppem Dohla opp. Enn noch eent: aule Menniste send vonne Welt, oba nich een Deel vonne Welt.

Bitte dit nich vejäte, O.K.? O joh, nu fellt mie noch bie: daut jefft Friees, dee etj tjann, dee eene Tugend ute Dommheit moake, enn see wudde leewa noh Belize ooda Madagascar auls opp eene hejchre School gohne.

Enn blooß wiels daut Menniste jefft, dee jleewe, daut see bäta send auls aule aundre, meent oba nich, daut see faulsch lidje.

Wann Jie mol eenen Tjwierinj, ooda Quiring traffe sulle, jleeft nich, daut dee meist soo derjschschnettlich send auls jeweehnliche Tjriste. See send de jratste Fass enn onsem Famielen-Rejista. Enn von eenem Soohnen well etj Junt vondoag eene Jeschijcht vetalle.

Eent von disse Quirings, Cornelius, kaum nohm latzten Tjrijch noh Kanada, enn daut wea eene Lost dissemTjeadel too beoobachte. Daut easchte Joah haud hee mau een Hohma, oba daut tweede Joah wea hee aul een Bumeista, enn buhd enn hohmad toop, enn dann noch meea. "Developing" soo

Just like I said, we are like the Jews of the New Testament. We do not only think we are right about that, we know we are. And if you think you recognize most Jews just by their names like Blumenstein, Herzog, Bernstein and Weinstock, then we can match such nomenclaturing too. If any Reimer, Friesen, Wiebe or Thiessen tells you he is not a Mennonite, then either we won't have him anymore, or he or she is simply a liar.

Not only that, but if you speak to Mennonite experts they can more than likely tell you family characteristics that run through the lineage. Friesens, for instance, are very numerous; Epps are studious; Wiebes are devious and proud of their modesty; Thiessens are argumentative and bull-headed (at least so say some ministers), and high in intelligence (our father told me that), and all are careful with the dollar. The other thing we all are is from the world but not of the world.

Don't forget this one, okay? Oh yes, there is another thing about some Friesens I know and that is that they make a virtue out of ignorance and would rather go to Belize or Madagascar than to higher schools.

And just because there are Mennonites who think they are better than the others doesn't mean they are wrong for thinking like that.

If you ever encounter a Quiring, then you will soon assume that they are almost as average as ordinary Christians. They are the only, but also the biggest, foxes of our familial den. And about such a one, I will tell you a story.

One of these Quirings, Cornelius, came to Canada after the war and he was amazing to watch. The first year he had only a hammer, and the next year he was a supervisor, always building and constructing and fashioning and "developing" as they call it here. Growth and progress are very holy cows in the Mennonite pasture, and we have managed it so that we

nanne se daut hiea, oba seea! Jrata enn meea send seea heilje Tjeaj oppe mennische Weid. Enn soohnt tjenn wie Menniste doohne ohne opp Koste von aundre ooda vonne Natua. Enn wäa soohnt aum basten kaun, ess bie ons Mejchel, dee Darpsboll, äwanacht.

Wann eena dem jenannden Cornelius irjend, mett uck eene gaunz lieseltje Kritik kaum, dann wea hee fuats unjawäjess mett Oabeida toop enn muak hiea enn doa waut enne Tjoatj, emm Tjalla ooda oppem Dack enn Ordnung, enn fuats wisst een jiedra, daut Gott noch een Schoof Heinzelmennchen opp Loaga haud.

Dree Joah nohdem Cornelius Quiring noh Kanada jekohme wea, meend hee Plautdietschräde wea prost. Oba uck aul verhäa, saumeld Cornelius Unjaschrefta, mett dem Ziel tjeene D. P.'s noh Kanada enwaundre too lohte.

Väjen Hoawst muak dis Cornelius Quiring ziemlichen Opprooah enn onse Jemeenschauft enn Jrienthol. Hee säd, daut hee auls Mennonietischa Brooda (dee Mennonietische Breeda send fe de Menniste, daut waut de Jesuite fe den Catholicismus send, enn den Rothschids fe de Jude. Opp dem unjaschten Enj von disse Ladda, hab wie uck sondaboare Utbunts aunDaut Missjoohnprograum wea jrods soo wiet, auls Quiring aules stohne enn lidje leet enn noh Winnipeg trock, wiels de Harr ahm doahan jeroopt haud. Von doa bowe, aulso von Winnipeg ut, drift Quring nu Bujeschafte em Grooten enn meaht sietoobeede, soos's soohne, woohne meene, daut de Welt soo plaut ess auls ääh Jesang, oba de Catholitje habe je uck eene erstaunlijche Reaj Glommstjapp soo's de Solar Templars, ooda de Jude mett Roseanne Barr) reed wea, sich daut Tweedbaste auntooschlute enn sich onse Tjoatj enn Jrienthol bietootrede, "etj enn mie Hus," siene Famielje aulso, meend hee, oba blooß wann wie meea Iewa fe de Missjoohn oppdriewe wudde, wiels de "Harr daut soo wull."

Ritje Mensche vetalle, daut Quiring väl Menniste ut Paraguay fe sich oabeide haft; measchtens plautdietsch-

never do it at the expense of others or of nature. Anyone who can master it is held in high esteem, sometimes overnight.

Whenever anyone ever as much as questions this Cornelius, he immediately sends his men to repair a little this or that in or by the church and then everyone is convinced that God still has his very own emissaries.

Within three years of arriving here, Cornelius Quiring considered it *prost* to speak Low German. Even prior to that, he was campaigning against the admission to Canada of Displaced Persons from Europe, or D. P.'s as they are called around here.

Obviously this Cornelius Quiring was of sterling Mennonite Brethren stock and such are to Mennonitism what the Jesuits are to Catholicism or the Rothschilds to the Jews. At the other end of the scale, Mennonites can dish up some astonishing samples, like the ones who know that the earth is as flat as their singing, but, then, so can the Catholics with their Solar Templers and the Jews with their Roseanne Barrs) One spring morning a year or two after his arrival in Grünthal, Manitoba, Cornelius said, he was prepared to settle for second best and join the local church in Grünthal "—as for me and my house—" he said, but only on the condition it would initiate a more ambitious missionary programme, in keeping with Divine Decree.

This missionary programme was barely in place when Quiring up and left for Winnipeg in response to the Lord's calling. It is from this more central station that Quiring now operates. People say that he imports only able-bodied Low German speaking Mennonites from Paraguay and gives them all the construction jobs and work they need. He pays their way here and remembers them in daily prayer, but they have to promise in writing that they will work for him, and him only, for at least three years.

rädende Tjeadels, den hee de Foaht hiehan betohlt, mett dee Bedingung, daut see Dreejoahlang blooß fe ahm den Hohma noagle lohte. Butadem vespruak Cornelius Quiring fe siene Oabeida aula too bäde, oba seea!

Enn soo word Cornelius eascht ritj, enn dann "wohlhabend" enn druag Schooh mett emma spetzere Tees veropp. Boold wea Cornelius dann uck foakna enn foakna enn Toronto. Bieaun meahd hee sien Roop, enn boold wea hee, soo's hee mie mol vetald, meist oppe Stoop von een Eltesten enn Rußlaund.

Eascht wea Cornelius eenmol em Moonat enn Toronto, enn dann boold jieda tweede Wäatj, en soo wieda enn soo fort. Siene Fru Mathilda strohld äwa daut gaunze Jesejcht, daut see daut soo goot haud, enn ahr freid daut uck een tjlienet Tjniepsel, daut aule aundre Jemeendeschwestre sogoa een bät neidisch weare, daut see soohn grooten Säjen aun Ritjdoom von bowe jeneete durf. Oba donn wisst see oba uck fuats bäta, enn kaum too Ensejcht, enn dankt dem Harrn fe sien Säjen, nich Ritjdoom.

Quiring gauf de Tjoatj, siene Breeda, väl Jeld, daut wisst een jiedra; uck woss sien Raddungsenn soo's dem Hohn sien Kaum.

Soo's aul aundre, sogoa enne Bibel, kaum Cornelius Quiring opp domme Jedanke—-progressive—-nanne se soohnt, enn soo's vom Apostel Paulus uck aul jesajcht word: "seine große Kunst machte ihn rasend." Eascht de Molosch, dann Jrienthol, dann Winnipeg, dann Toronto, enn nu wea Las Vegas aune Reaj.

Mett Cornelius Quiring haud etj äwareen, daut wie twee bett dreemol enne Wäatj enne Banj em Health Club em YMCA saute, enn wie doa toop schweete, enn ons vom Daump beoabeide leehte. Etj rand too dee Tiet eascht twee bett dree Miel, schwomp eene lange Striep, enn Jedanke von Elloag bett Zaporozhje, enn dann speeld etj mie toop mett dem Noakschieta Bruder Cornelius auf.

So Cornelius became first rich and then wealthy and wore sharper-toed shoes all the time. Then Cornelius was soon often in Toronto. His reputation rose quickly to that of an Ältesta or bishop back home in Russia. First he was in Toronto on big business once a month and then every two weeks and so on. His wife Mathilda was beaming with pride that she had it so good and that all the other sisters in church slightly envied her husband and her riches. But then they quickly knew better and helped Mathilde praise and thank the Lord for blessings, not riches.

Everyone knew that Quiring sometimes gives a lot of money to the church. Such givings work here and everyone says, "Cornelius Quiring has Rettersinn" which means he has been blessed with a sense for salvation. People know that the Lord giveth to Cornelius so mission work can grow and multiply.

As with some others dating back to biblical times, Cornelius Quiring had arrived at some silly notions—progressive they call them here—and had gradually incubated them, and as once said of the Apostle Paul "Every man's work shall be made manifest: for the day shall declare it." For a good while now, Cornelius Quiring had not only gone to Toronto on business but bigger business, still, even took him to Las Vegas. But these roundabouts are known only to him and to me; he tells me these things like a brag-confession, when we work out at the Yealth Club at the Y. and have a good Schwitz together in the nude. Exposing yourself when in the nude comes easily. Cornelius then fully reveals himself, thinking that I would never say a thing to anyone. Even if I did "no one would ever believe you," so said Quiring, because "your headquarters are not really in The House of the Lord, I heard say." There and then he had me and we both you knew it. My credibility was not blue chip.

On his fourth visit to Vegas, Cornelius met a woman. Again, maybe. To maintain a good appearance, Cornelius entered

Noaktje Mensche habe daut leijchta too vetalle, see habe nuscht nich too vesteaje. Soo jintj ons daut uck.

Enn soo vetald hee mie aulahaund, enn meend doabie, "Du kaunst wieda vetalle, waut Du west, wiels Du tjen rejchtja Brooda best, jleewt Die sowesoo tjeena waut!" Aha!

Etj wea, säd hee, nich blue chip! "Diene Office, head etj saje, ess nich im Hause Gottes!"

Aulwada Aha!

Oppe veade Reis noh Las Vegas, haud Cornelius eene Fru jetroffe. Aulwada, wäa weet.

Omm eenen gooden, opprejchtjen Endruck too moake, haud hee ahr auls siene Fru em Hotelrejista aunjejäwt. Soohn Moot, soohne Opprejchtijchtjeit mildad siene Schuld aul weens oppe Halft. Enn wäa weet...wann Cornelius disse vebiestade Fru mett de Bibel mol jrindlich enne Nachtlang beoabeide wudd, wudd see, eea de Hohn dreemol tjreie wudd, vleijcht toom Harrn kohme?

Dee Daum, Cornelius siene haulwe Fru, fe de eensaume Nacht enn Las Vegas haud dem "Cornie dear" biem Cocktail-drintje een Mickey Finn enn sien Sturrack nennjleppe lohte.

Auls Cornelius den näjchsten Morje een bät lohta auls jeplohnt wacka word, word hee dree Dinja fuats oppe Städ enn: ahm ruzht de Kopp soo's aule Donna, siene noch emma onbetjeade Fru wea enne Wille Hundat veschwunge, enn see haud dee Gardiene, enn uck aules, waut enn de Hotelstow too stehle jintj, utjeriemt.

Tridj enn Winnipeg... Mathilda wacht jrods bute ver ährem Milljoondohlahus enn Pritchard Farms mett dree Garazhe opp den Diakoon, Jasch Block, dee ahr mett too Tjoatj nehme sull.

Eea see enstiehe kunn, kaum de Polizei mett eene riepe roode Tjoasch oppem Dach vonne aundre Sied aunjeruzht.

Emm Grande Mirage Hotel enn Las Vegas haud eene Misses Cornelius Quiring seea jestohle, "Weete See, waut daut too bediede haft?"

her name as his wife in the hotel registry. That stroke of courage immediately reduced his sin by one half, for, after all, had he not had the courage to claim this woman as his wife? And who is to say that she would not even be saved by him, the Lord willing, before the cock would crow three times?

This half-wife slipped something into Cornelius's drink that cocktailing night and it knocked him out. A Mickey Finn they call it in such circles.

When he awoke at 5:30 the next morning, Cornelius noticed three things: that he had a wild headache, that the woman-wife was no longer around and that his billfold was empty. Then he fled, without noticing that she had also stripped the entire room, and, who knows, possibly half of the Grande Mirage of everything stripable. Security, "damn them" Cornelius told someone when he came home, had not failed to notice.

Back in Winnipeg, Mathilda was waiting outside by the porch close to the three-car garage of their million dollar villa in Pritchard Farms for a ride to church, that fair Sunday morning, by the deacon, Jasch Block, when a car, with a revolving fully ripe cherry on top beat Jasch to pick Mathilda up. They came to question Mrs Mathilde Quiring for theft in the hotel "Grande Mirage" in Las Vegas.

Na Goondach Obraum!

De Obraum Pankrautz Familie ess em basten Ella enn läwe em Woolstaund, tweschen Cuauhtemoc enn Quinta Lupita enn eene stohtsche Villa em Staut Chihuahua, Mexico. Kratjt soo auls enn Rußlaund sienatiet auls Menniste mett Jeld, woohnt noh aul dee Missionsdriewarie äwrijchjebläwe wea, enn measchtens enne Koloniee biem Nippa enn Ommjäjend lage, noh Peetaborjch fuahre omm enntootjeepe, enn de hiesje Generation von Sardis ooda Yarrow, B. C. noh Vancouver fuahre omm sich aulahaund auntootjitje, enn dann sogoa Dit enn Jant koffte, deede daut uck de mennische Ladies von Vineland oppe Niagara Haulfensel enn ähre ditje Buicks ooda noch jratre Koahre omm noh Toronto too foahre, während de Mennofrulied ut Jienthol, mien Heimatdarp, noh Winnipeg fuahre omm de Lauftjes ladijch too tjeepe. Enn enn Mexico deede de ritje Menniste, mett dem selwjen DNA enne Odre... daut schetjt ahn von Cuauhtemoc noh de Chihuahua Staut, wann nich sogoa wieda auf, noch väl wieda auf, enn noch dolla noh de latzte Mood.

Väaje Wäatj fuah de Obraum Pankrautsche voll Daump noh Väahre nohm jratzten Shopping Centre enn Chihuahua, woa se sogoa een Lauftje mett Hustiere, aulso een "Pet Store" haude. Fuats rajsch biem Engang von dit groote Stooah stund een buntet Klohtje, enn doabenne saut een Popka, een Popajei aulso, enn dissa wea too vetjeepe, sogoa seea billijch, "Blooß $50.00, aulso feftijch Dohla" enn amerikaunsche ooda kanadische Dohlasch. "Bett nutoo $500.00, oba schmock utjeleaht, enn kaun väle Spoake vestohne enn uck räde."

Howdy, Abe!

The Abraham Pankratz family is in the prime of life and prosperity. They reside between Cuauhtemoc and Quinta Lupita in a stately villa and all in the State of Chihuahua, Mexico.

Just as in Russia, when Mennonite women with money, left over after numerous missionary endeavors, and mainly residing in their colonies located by the Dnieper River and farther afield, went to Saint Petersburg for shopping sprees, their later counterparts from Sardis and Yarrow B. C. went to Vancouver to inspect wares on sales, while the Mennonite ladies from Vineland in the Niagara Peninsula took their Buicks or bigger to Toronto, and the Menno Womenfolk from Grünthal, my home town, ventured to Winnipeg. Obviously and similarly the DNA of prosperous Mennonitism asserted itself in Mexico as well, and sent the ladies from Cuauhtemoc to Chihuahua City or even further, more stylish.

Last week Mrs Abraham Pankratz was shopping full speed ahead in Chihuahua at the largest shopping complex which even features a "Pet Store". To the immediate right of the entrance to this establishment in a brightly coloured cage sat a Popka, aka parrot, and he was for sale, much reduced for "only fifty dollars" in American or Canadian currency. "Previously $500.00, fully trained, multi-lingual."

"Why so cheap?" This Popka had spent three impressionable years in a House of Pleasure, or as the explanatory note, more elegantly and less tainted stated,

"Woaromm soo billijch?" Diss Popka haud sich dree Joahlang enn eenem Freudenhaus, aulso em

Maison de Plaisir oppjehoole; diss Goaschthaumel mett bunte Flijchte wea daut Kohme enn Gohne vom internationalen Publikum jewant, enn kunn sogoa een bätje mennischet Plautdietsch. Enn doawäjen wea hee soo billijch. Aunstaut fief hundat Dohla wea diss, een bät vekohmna Fada-Scherniesel, oba kluag, utjelohte, enn läwendijch, nu fe feftijch Dohla too habe, toop mett Klohtje.

De Pankrautzsche docht kratjt soo's Mennoniete dentje: "Too billijch, omm nich too tjeepe, enn wann'et senne mott woa etj siene Sproak een bät beschliepe," betold daut Jeld, enn nauhm ahm mett noh Hus.

Tus aunjekohme, weare uck jrods de Pankrautz Mejalles, tridj vonne Menno Privaut School aunjekohme, enn worde von dem Popka emm sinndoagschen Sponsch bejreest. Feftien Minute lohta kaum de Nohbaschfru, de Jeat Reimasche vebie, wiels see nieschierijch wea, den nieen Gaust too seehne. Enn uck aul wada bejreest dee Popka ahr enn siene feinste Sproak, "Buenos dias, señora" enn siene Coloraturastemm.

Pintjlijch omm Klock Sass kaum dee Bauß vonne Famielje, Señor Obraum Pankrautz, een wietjereisda Koopmaun enn Industriella noh Hus, enn säd, hee wea reed toom Äte. Dee Popka, nu aul Peeta mett Nohme, tjitjt sich Bauß Pankrautz seea ooltnäsijch aun, läd sien Kopp oppe Schulla, bedocht sich kort enn bejreest ahm enn sien bastet Plautdietsch: "Na oba, Goondach Obraum!"

Maison de Plaisir, and so this bawdy winged rascal was used to international comings and goings of those in need, including even a bit of Mennonite Plautdietsch. And that was the reason he was so cheap: instead of five hundred dollars, this somewhat tainted in manners and speech rover, but known for his brisk intelligence, was on sale for fifty dollars, cage included.

Mrs Pankratz's thinking assumed practiced routine, "Too cheap not to buy, and if need be, I will convert his tawdry language," paid for him, and was off.

Back home, the Pankratz girls, just back from the Menno Private School, were greeted by the new guest of the house Popka in refined Spanish. Some fifteen minutes later the neighbours' woman, Frau Gerhard Reimer passed by since she had seen and heard the spangled bird carried into his new home. And again the Popka uttered a pleasantry in Spanish, Sunday style, elegantly chirping "Buenos dias, señora" in Lily Pons coloratura!

Punctually at six, the head of the family, Señor Abraham Pankratz, a widely travelled industrialist, announced himself with a brisk flourish, ready for dinner. The Popka, already Peter by name, gave him a snoopy once-over, laid his well-cocked head slightly to a contemplative angle and called in his best Popka-Plautdietsch, "Howdy Abe!"

Dee Mieagrope

Wää een gooda Mennoniet senne, ooda woare well, mott tjenne:

a) mette Henj eene Kooh maltje
b) Plautdietsch vestohne, räde enn schriewe
c) Arbuse tjnippse
d) Tjinja aufhoole
e) Missjoonsenn habe
f) Tratjchtmoakasch oppseatje, ooda selwst tjnibble
g) weete, waut een Mieagrope ess, enn den uck bedeehne!

Daut ess dee mennischa Katetjismus, kort en dietlich; soo steiht daut jeschräwe!

Kratjt soo's aule Läsasch, dreedusend, wann nich sogoa meea, docht etj emma, daut dee Mieagrope von dem vondoag hiea dee Räd ess, blooß eene mennische Enrejchtung ess, enn uck aul emma jewese wea. Etj sie een Errtum unjaläje, enn mott mien Fehla toostohne enn berejchtje.

Oba well wie doch mol gaunz vom Aunfong aunfange. Soo's ditt: Bie auldem docht etj oba natierlich besondasch stoatj aun mien Onkel mett dem etj disse Reis noh Indonesien unjanauhm, wiels wie ons doch mol toop betjitje wulle, woa hee enn sien Voda, Pappa Doc ut Elloag, dee MIssjoonoa Johaun Obraum Thiessen Senior, ver boold hundat Joah (wie schreewe nu daut Joah 1975), jegohne enn jehaundelt, enn jeheelt enn betjead haude. Den Oolen, heiljen Voda, noh dem etj jenohmt worde wea, haud wie, aulso sien Sähn, Dr John

100

The Rendering Cauldron

If you intend to be, or become a Mennonite in good standing, you have to:

Be able to milk a cow by hand
Understand Low German, also speak and write it
Thump watermelons to determine quality and ripeness
Learn to hold a baby to relieve itself by way of toilet training
Have a sense of mission
Visit chiropractors regularly or practice the art
Know what a rendering cauldron is and how to operate it

This is the Mennonite catechism, concise and in writing!

Just like the majority of my readers, three thousand plus and counting, I believed that the rendering cauldron, a.k.a. *Mieagrope*, the topic of today's discussion was exclusively a Mennonite institution, and had always been such. I have to confess the error of my ways and correct this faulty assumption in writing, as follows:

But let us start this endeavour at the very beginning. While reflecting on this matter, my thinking was concentrated on my uncle with whom I undertook this venture to Indonesia, and with common intent of taking a reflective look there, where he and his father, Pappa Doc from Kitschkass, Ukraine, the missionary-medic, Johann Abraham Thiessen Senior, had almost one hundred years ago (the year of our venture was 1975), travelled and served and healed and converted the lost, the afflicted and the fallen. The old, holy father whose name

101

Thiessen, Junior, enn etj dee Tiet äwa emm Dentj, wann uck mett korte Unjabrätjunge auls hiea enne Vetall aul aunjediet.

Wie weare nu, endlich doa, enn, wiels de Nieschiea eenem nich blooß Tus porrd, sonda uck wann eena sich opp Reise bejefft; dee foaht kratjt soo foaken enn jearn mett auls Frulied. Enn soo kaum daut, daut oppe Ensel Bali aunjekohme, von de Margaret Mead, dee ooltnäsje oba jegrommde Struckhatjs, Ähratiet behaupte deed, daut dee Ensel daut rajchtschuldje Paradies wea (kaun senne, oba wann de Amerikauna doa eascht aunfange rommtoomulwere enn too dreimoazhe, blifft daut nich lang een Paradies, vleijcht een Nohmeddach), etj fuats omme Atj von mien Loaga, dijcht bie Denpasar, mie mol daut Paradies soo meea aum Raund betjitje wull. Etj wea noch tjeene Minut unjawäjess auls etj uck aul enn eenem Darptje aunkaum, woa de Mensche soo vejneajcht auls freschbetjeade Breedamejalles aum Nippa ooda uck Tus dicht bie Jrienthol weare.

Oba doamett wea dann uck aul de Vejlitj too Enj, wiels dee Frulied zwoa aula schmocke Batik Ratj druage, oba vom Nowel noh bowe bett oppe Hoahspetz gaunz enn goa noaktijch weare. "Hiea ess noch väl Missjoon too driewe," docht etj soo bie mie, oba saje deed etj nuscht, wiels miene Uage daut too drock haude. Dee Frulied enne Uage too tjitje foll mie schwoa, wiels daut Meddelstetj tweschnem noaktjen Nowel enn Bless lentjt soo seea auf. Enn etj kaum daut opp vereascht mett dem Odme meist nich noh.

Aulso jintj etj mett'e Henj soo ziemlich deep enne Fuppe romm, enn betjitjt mie disse niee Missjoonsbestaun. Oba aunstautt mie soo rejchtijch too konzentreare, woo etj Tus enn Jrienthol von dee groote Sinde vetalle wudd, enn woo eena de Betjeararie vonne utjewossne Noakschietasch aum basten aunstalle kaun enn sull, folle mie soohne lestje Nebensejchlijchtjeite enn, enn uck bie, wiels een Professa enn Marburg, selwst een jewesna Missjoonoa, mie mol gaunz

became mine, with agenda attached, was much in our minds, meaning in his son, Dr John Thiessen Jr., and mine, when we retraced steps and purpose in that far country beyond many horizons.

And now we were finally there, and because curiosity bordering on snoopiness, is part of the human baggage which spurs man ever on, even on a trip, and with such curiosum being as commonplace and assertive to come along as is womenfolk, there was a threesome in on this venture, namely, my uncle, Snoop and me.

So it happened that we arrived in Bali, of which that nosy, but educated battle axe Margaret Mead claimed that this Island was the true and original Paradise (that may well be, but once the Americans commence ransacking anywhere such Paradise lasts a day at most) I set out from my quarters close to Denpesar, to check things out. I had not walked ten minutes before I arrived in a hamlet where the inhabitants were as happy and carefree as recent converts to the Mennonite Brethren faith by the Dnieper or back home in Grünthal, Manitoba, Canada.

But shortly all comparisons failed because these Balinese women, wore flowery skirts of Batik; however beyond and above, starting at the navel and right up to the apex of their hairdo, they wore next to nothing; meaning, for worse or better, depending on your squint or mine, they were stark naked. "There is much mission work called for right here and now," I made mental note to myself, but I said nothing because my eyes had all hands full with their own mission of taking it all in. To look such womenfolk in the eyes proved difficult since the curved middle portion between navel and brow was a distraction of rare order. So much so, that I had trouble catching up with all the extra huffing, now called for.

When consternation strikes, it is time to take a stroll with deeply pocketed hands and I did just that as I inspected the

earnst vetald haud, daut äwa tachentig Prozent vonne Missjoonoare, sich too dee Relijoon betjeat haude, dee see betjeare sulle.

Soo deep wea etj enne easchte fief Minute aul jefolle, auls etj dee Frulied ohne een schlajchtet Jewesse ährasiets, biem soo meea noaktijch Rommranne sach! Mie schweet. Enn nu word daut aulatoop noch oaja. Een Mädtjstje von eenjefäah drettien bett achtien Joah oolt, enn gaunz ohne Tjleedie, tjreaj vonne Frulied, biem Kokusnätschalle Orda mie Roosewota too reatje. Enn auls etj daut drunk, enn daut Mejaltje bieaun fruag auls etj vleijcht een vebiestada Hollenda wea, säd etj blooß noch: "Etj weet uck nich meea gaunz, wäa etj sie," enn auls mie biem Roosewota drintje aunfonge dee Leppe too weppre, enn de Henj too tetjre, enn see mie dann lieseltjess enn leeftolich doatoo noch de schweetje Stearn mett een bloomesträmeljet Strieptje Zeijch wescht, weare miene Tjnees blooß noch Kolodets, enn etj musst mie han enn dohlsatte. Mien gaunza oppjespoada Missjoons enn Radasenn haud enn fief Minute opp vereascht vespält, gaunz vespält.

Enn bie auldem mald sich mol wada mien mennischet Jewesse, oba uck mien Senn fe dee Rätjnunge em Läwe; gaunz kloa enn dietlich jesajcht: woo onjerajcht daut Läwe doch measchtens senne kaun. Tjeene twintijch Joah tridj haud etj em Moulin Rouge enn Paris goode veatijch Euros, wann nich meea, utjejäwt omm mien easchten Striptease too seehne: een Frumensch stund doa oppe Biehne enn hohld twee, aul een bät vewaltjte Easdschocke ut ährem Brostbiedel, enn hiea weare de straumste Eevasch ver mie mett jestuckte, riepe, spetze Kruckebeete, enn aules gaunz omsonst. Enn auls etj dee frindelje, oba leijcht sindje Frulied dann noch biem Kokusnät toopsaumle schmock noh dee mennische, tjristlijche Oat holp, schlentjat dee eene noaktje Lady mie gaunz nattjes enn lieseltjes, soo meea toofallijch eent aum Rissel (etj

missionary patch of potential. However, instead of paying supreme attention as to how I would report back home in Grünthal about the heavy duty sins far afield, and how to properly set about saving such grownup heathens in the nude, all manner of errant notions came to mind, including the one of a professor in Marburg, himself a former missionary, who once commented with due seriousness, that more than eighty percent of missionaries he knew had converted to the religion they were meant to convert.

That is how deeply I had fallen in my steadfastness of purpose within five minutes when I experienced the women around me, who without a trace of a sullied conscience, walked and pranced and sang as they went about their chores, stark nude, save for the skirting issue. Things got worse. A young girl about thirteen to eighteen, and without a trace of garment received instructions from her superiors, busily occupied in shelling coconuts, to hand me a drink of cool rosewater. And, while gently imbibing this refreshing potion, this lithe beauty casually inquired whether I, perchance, was a lost Dutchman, to which I feebly responded, "I don't quite know myself as to who I am" and while I was still lost in drink, with lips twittering and hands trembling, she gently wiped my sweaty brow with a flowered strip of cotton material, my knees turned to jelly and I had to sit me down. My vast amount of missionary reserves compiled over many decades now failed me, utterly failed me.

On top of all the confusion, my Mennonite conscience as well as my practiced mercantile comparisons announced themselves, reminding me just how unfair life generally is. Barely twenty years ago I had paid at least forty dollars in hard earned cash at the doors of the Moulin Rouge in Paris to see my first strip tease…there, under the lights, stood a lady not acting her age on the stage, as she produced two somewhat wilted potatoes out of her bust basket while here, right before

meen de Näs) mett äah Raubeltje, daut etj toop mett mien
gaunzen Missjoonsenn eenfach lang hantjeiweld.

Toom grooten Jletj kaume dann uck langsom dee darpsche
Maunsmensche vonne Oabeit noh Hus, enn daut gauf
Auflentjung. Etj hab hiea erwähnt, daut dee Maunslied vonne
Oabiet, soo dochte etj mie weens, tridj noh Hus kaume. Uck
wada een Errtum.

Wiels, wann doa Oabeit wea, soo deede de Frulied dee enn
dissem Paradies, soo meea auls manke Menniste enn
Rußlaund biem Tjeajmaltje. Daut wea Fruesoabeit. Enn
doamett soo goot.

Enn waut wea hiea uck väl too doohne? Oft, Jetjätjs, tjliene
haulfwille Schwientjes, mett een ditjen Buck auls een
aufjedeehnda Prädja enn Rußlaund, Heehna oppem Hoff,
Schaute, reinet Wota, enn aules enn Hülle enn Fülle, woo
sulle dee sich daut drock moake?

Dee Maunsmensche doa spälde measchtens den Dachäwa
mett dolle, kurrje Hohns, enn oajade dee enn, doamett dee
sich toodoak jinje, enn biete enn hassre leahde, wiels aum
Sinndach gauf'et emma Hohnstjriej enn Denpasar. Enn wiels
daut jesatzlich strenj vebode wea, kaume omm soo meea
Mensche, enn tjitjte too, bie de Dusende. Een jieda tohld twee
Dohla, enn boold wea uck aul de Arena voll, enn dann jintj
daut mett dee Hohnsprietzarie loos, daut Schnodda, Bloot
enn Fadre fluage. Soo kaum daut Pack, measchtens
onbetjeade Schnerniesels enn ähre Fruees enn Tjinja, too Jeld.
De measchte Mensche emm Publikum weare Butendarpa,
aulso Utlenda ut Amerikau ooda ut Dietschlaund, enn wiels
etj uck doa meddemang saut, word etj dann uck boold enn,
daut väle von de Tootjitjasch sogoa Hilfsarbeiter enn
Missjoonoare ut Amerikau weare, enn uck een tjlienet
Schwittje Doopsgezinde, wiels de Hollanderie sich enn
Indonesien soo derjchjesatt haud, daut een jiedra wisst, wäa
waut wea, uck noch dartijch Joah nohm Tjrijch. Natierlich

me, the most bountiful of Eves, garden fresh, romped around me and all armed with firm, ripe and luscious gourds and all for free for the eyes to feast upon! And then, meaning now, when I set about to assist these obviously errant women in gathering coconuts in my finest Mennonite manner of being ever ready to aid and abet, one particularly luscious model, very gently but distinctly and hopefully accidentally swiped me a gentle one on the schnozzle with her high beam, and my lights went out, sending my entire sense of mission and all I stood for, for a sprawling tumble.

As fortune had it, the men folk of that bewildering village slowly came home from work and diversion came to my assistance. I claimed these men came home from work. Mistake, yet again.

Since, if there was work to do, the women did it in this Paradise, similar to the Mennonites in Russia when it came to milking cows. This was women's work. End of discussion.

Furthermore, what work was here to be done? Fruit, vegetables, little piglets, half wild with pot bellies similar to a retired Mennonite minister, aged fifty two in Ukraine, chickens on the yard, shade everywhere, clean water, and everything in profuse abundance, why be busy and to what end?

The men of this region and mentality spent most of their time with angry and aggressive cocks and trained them to be as mad as hell and taught them to bite, slash and kick because, come Sunday, cock fighting was as regular and as common in Denpesar, the little capital city, as church going was back home. Since cock fighting was strictly forbidden by law, all the more people flocked to watch fighting action; people by the thousands assembled to watch the Sunday forenoon fun. Entrance fee was two dollars and soon all arenas were filled to capacity to see snot, blood and feathers fly; obviously this half converted rubble of humanity, including women and children

beschwiemde biem Hohnstjampf atelje Frulied, wiels daut bie dee Sort soo Mood ess, wann dee mol daut Läwe enne reiwe Natua betrachte. Enn aules noh daut Thema: Wann aul Dootschlohne, dann sull eena daut doch mett dee Mensche doohne, enn nich missaja Hohns dee Tjapp aufriete! Wiels etj dochwoll een eenjamohte bruckboare Mensch sie, haud daut haulfwille Pack, em Darp nu aulwada, Noakschietasch, Vetrue too mie jewonne, enn soo jintj daut mett'e Vetall boold loos.

Dee ellre Maunsmensche woohne too de Burzhojschijcht jeheade, kunne noch eenjemohte Hollendisch, enn donn biem Rum mett Kokusnätmaltj drintje, jintj daut aulnoch jlei mette Vetall loos. See weese mie aules, waut mie intressead, wulle mie uck de schmockste Mejalles vekupple, enn aula schmeatjde see, tjwelsdade rundommendomm, speaje ut, enn schobbde sich de Luj bett aune Fuj!

Aum dredden Dach, biem Schemmawoare, kaum eena vom Nohbadarp enn nauhm den Darpsstarschie enn mie opp sien motoriseaden Rickshaw mett, enn wie fuahre mett sass Miel de Stund enne Wille Hundat nenn; see wulle mie waut wiese. Enne Tweschentiet haud mien Onkel, aulso dee Pappa Doc Junior, daut mett siene eajne Sach aundawäjess aule Henj voll; daut gauf väl Trajchttoohalpe, wiels de leewa Gott kunn je uck nich emma enn aules auleen beschetje.

Wie kaume noh feftien Minute aun Uat enn Städ aun. Doa aum Raund von een dijchten Bosch stund eene oole Serai, nich bewohnt. Uck stunde doa Descha enn oola Steehle romm, enn uck noch een bät Teetijch enn Jescherr wea doa too seehne.

Doa weare uck noch een poah nieschieje Mensche ute Nohbaschauft toojekohme, enn een poah Frulied, noch emma soo meea auls Eva emm Paradiesgoade aunjetrocke, sade ons Papayas, Mangoes, Arbuse enn Benana enn aundre Fruchtsorte bie de Kommvoll väa. Uck haud dee Starschie Schwiensfleesch enn eenen haulwen Hohn fein jebrot, mettjebrocht,

came to money quite handily. Most of the assembled were foreigners, Americans and German tourists, including foreign aid workers and missionaries from all over. Since I was right in the middle of it all, I even noticed some Ana-baptists, because the Dutchmen of all stripes had formerly contributed so much to the local colour in Indonesia that everyone knew everybody else even thirty years after the last war was over. During the cockfights more than a few women regularly fainted as is generally the case with this gender when life takes on basic form and action. Obviously the prevailing sentiment applied here as well: if there is killing to be done, then it should involve mankind. Why waste the excitement of death on useless cockerels?

Since I probably am a fairly trustworthy Mensch at base, back in the village again, the assembly of nudists trusted me and we engaged in animated exchange.

The older generation of men who belonged to the burger class still spoke Dutch, and when rum and coconut milk started to flow in abundance much conversation ensued. They showed me all I was interested in, and even attempted to barter a few of their choice beauties, while the men folk were constantly spitting and scratching themselves wherever and whenever an itch announced itself, generally much below the beltline.

On the third day at gloaming, a fellow from a neighbouring village took the village elder and me on his motorized rickshaw, and we set out puttering at six miles per hour to a site of common intent, which they wanted to show me. In the meanwhile my uncle, Pappa Doc Junior was up to overdue holy business all over the original Thousand Islands because you simply could not leave all the essentials for God to do on His own.

We arrived at the intended destination after some fifteen minutes. There at the edge of an verdant jungle stood a shack,

enn wie aute, drunke hollendschet Beea, schmeatjde, daut'et
reatjad, enn reete Resse.

Langsom rolld dee oola Tjeadel dee Vegangenheit auf, enn
vetald, waut see too eenatiet hiea en dissem aufjeläjnen
Wintjel Frähjoah jedohne haude. "Doa," wees dee oola Donna
mett sien krommen Dume, "stund ons Mieagrope mett
Kokusnäteelj jefellt enn aunjehett bett daut Schmäah
doabenne ruzhd enn bruddeld, enn enn dem onse Vää-
vodasch dee Mensche, wann uck measchtens butendarpsche
Bätaweetasch, woohne ahn nich pausste, de Zube aufnauhme,
ahn de Rinj enn de Omegas aufstreepte, ahn de Schooh enn
Betjze uttrocke, enn ahn mett een Bouquet Garni, aulso
Schisnick, Päpakrut, Päpatjäna, Dell enn Luabäabläda
schmock goa brohde."

Etj wea bie aul de Vetall soo schmock auls Tus een Jrienthol
enne Sinndachschool, wiels, wää weet, waut disse Jungess
mett mie väahaude. Vleijcht ritjt etj ahn aupetietlich.

Weit gefehlt; disse Tjeadels weare modern enn haulfbetjeat
jeworde, enn ahn schmatjte Hohnsschintjess enn Schwiens-
fillet, fein jereatjad bäta auls homo sapiens, aulso Onsaeena.
Vleijcht uck, wiels etj mett hollandschet Beea, Heineken,
spendobel wea. Vleijcht uck, wiels see wisste, daut etj mie doch
seea jestiepad haud, eea see mie enn den Miagrope noh dee
oole Wies nennjeschmäte haude.

Mie intressead dann oba doch dee oola Mieagrope, enn
irjendwaut kaum mie aun dee straume oole Enrejchtung
emm Schemma gaunz wietleftijch bekaunt vää. Etj betjitjt mie
den, enn see holpe biem Betjitje. Dee Mieagrope haud bowe
een Messingraund, enn doa stund doch tatsejchlich, eene oole
Enschreft: (Dit wiedre ess eene Äwasatung utem
Hollendischen).

"Fe miene Breeda enn Bali, oba blooß von nu aun toom
Schwien fe Jreewe enn Rebspäa utbrohde, hab wie auls
Breedajemeend ut Elloag aum Nippa enn Rußlaund junt den

somewhat dilapidated, not inhabited. Some tables and worn chairs also stood around as well as some chinaware and cutlery.

A few curious onlookers from the neighbourhood had also assembled, and some women, dressed in their Eve in the Garden costumes served us papayas, mangoes, watermelons and bananas in copious abundance. Also, the village elder had brought along pork and half a chicken, well cooked and we ate, drank Dutch beer, smoked and talked widely and well.

Slowly the old fellow unfurled the past and what they had all done in this remote patch of their world. "There," the old bard said, pointing with his gnarled thumb, "stood our rendering cauldron filled with coconut oil and heated up until the oil starting frothing and bubbling and into which our forebears deposited people who displeased them, but mostly such removed from our immediate clan, and know-it-alls in any case, and after stripping them of their clothes, and ridding them of their rings and Omegas, then shoes and pants, and together with a bouquet garni, consisting of garlic, summer savory, pepper corns, dill and laurel leaves, they dumped them into the seething broth until they were nicely cooked."

During this conversation I was as nice and pious as back home in Grünthal in Sunday School, because, who knows, what these wily old boys had in mind with me. Maybe they considered me a choice morsel?

I was proven wrong again; these fellows were modern and semi-converted and preferred chicken legs and fillet of pork, well smoked, to homo sapiens, meaning me. Also, it came to me that they were extending gentle cordialities because I treated all assembled liberally to Heineken. Then again, it might have occurred to them that I would have put up whatever resistance it took before I would have allowed myself to be deposited in a cauldron of seething furore. And, said resistance, then as now, is considerable.

Mieagrope jestefft! Pappa Johaun Thiessen, Dokta enn Missioonoa, nu enn Bandung, Java."

Latzte Maldung ooda Breaking News soo's CNN daut jiede dree Minute aunsajcht:

Daut kaum manke Kaunibaule dann doch boold too eene Spoolinj enn ähre Jemeend, gaunz noh de mennische Oat, soo's daut mott.

Dee Aufjefollne stead, daut dee jejräpne Kaundidaute nich verhäa dee Tjapp reseat worde, wiels see muchte tjeene Hoah enn ährem Eintopf, uck Stew jenannt.

Bie de niee Jemeend, dee sich eenfach de K. J.'s (Kay Jays) nanne, daut heet Kannibaule Jemeend, woare de Opp-Too-Ätende verhäa aulso dee Tjapp ennjeseept, dann jeschropt enn dann kohme see schmock kohlkoppich enne Breaj.

Guten Appetit! Bon appétit, ooda, soo's de Hollenda sajcht: *Smackelich eten!*

While taking all this in, past and present, the cauldron held a remote attraction, something vaguely remembered. I casually inspected it and the older fellows joined in the scrutiny. The top of the rendering cauldron was faintly but discernibly surrounded by a bronze ring, and it held the answer to my fascination: it contained an inscription, old but prevailing, to the curious eye. It read, now translated from the Dutch:

"For my Brethren in Bali, but as of now only for the rendering of pork cracklings and spare ribs, we, the Mennonite Brethren Congregation from Elloag by the Dnieper River, dedicate this *Mieagrope* to you. Pappa Johann Thiessen, doctor and missionary, now resident in Bandung, Java."

Latest Update or Breaking News as CNN has it every three minutes:

Among the cannibals a congregational split occurred, similar to accustomed Mennonite schism example.

Those belonging to the new direction had taken offence that the captured cauldron candidates had not been properly divested of crown hair since they objected to hair in their stew.

In the new congregation, which simply called themselves the C. C.'s, the Cannibal Congregation, all those soon to be ingested will have their heads shampooed, then shorn before they are properly deposited bald and blank in the brew for stew.

Guten Appetit! Bon appétit, or, as the Dutch have it: *Smakelik eten!*

Schnuftje, woa best Du?

Aum tweeden Novamba aune 1944 jintjch Jasch Blocke
Hein, dee sijch kratjcht donn aunfong Harry too nanne,
enne School seea stiewbeensch romm. Sien lintjchet Been deed
ahm em tweeden Stock weeh, enn hee wea mett eenmol soo
schmock auls een Laum; äwahaupt wea diss sesst utjelohtna
Wribbelwrips schmock, ontlijch, ducknäsijch, enn soo's de
Molotschna enn onse Jäjend säde "artig". Daut foll nijch blooß
mie opp.

Jeweehnlijch moake sijch de Mensch Jedanke, wann mol
eena ute Jleis rutscht, enn goastrijch, ooda jäjenaun, opp-
stoarnoasch ess, enn eegol äwre Sälenstrenj klunje well. Oba
Hein-Harry wea vondoag mack auls eene Sommapogg enn
seea iewrijch emm Schmocksenne. Etj muak mie sorje. Soo's
auls jesajcht, jintjch Harry mau seea scheiwelhassijch, enn
biem Sette oppe Schoolbeintjch haud eena tweschen sien
Hinjarenj oppe lintjche Sied ruhijch een Twee-bie-Veea
tweschne Moazhback enn Beintjch schuwe kunnt, wiels hee
enn dee Jäjend soo empfindlijch wea, enn sien Been soo enne
hejcht trock auls ons Hund, Mister, wann hee eene Reif aun
eene framde Koah sitt.

Auls hee mie dann noch fruag auls etj mol mett ahm, bitte,
enne Meddachspause toop noh de Setjreet kohme wudd,
docht etj mie: "Na! Na!"

Enne Setjreet aunjekohme, schloot wie de Däah von benne
mett de Kraump too, enn etj musst aun Harry nu een bät
doktre. Harry haud aum Hinjarenj, aune lintje Back twee
Entzündunge, dee ahm morschijch weeh deede. Wann daut

Snuffy, where are you?

On November 2nd, 1944 Jake Block's Henry, who had just started calling himself Harry at the time, walked around very stiff of leg. His left leg hurt him a lot in the second storey, and his behaviour, most uncharacteristically, was that of a lamb and in general this livewire had been reduced to a meek, well-behaved, docile pilgrim, or as those of higher Low German like to term it "exemplary in thought and action." I was not the only one to notice a former naughty rover now bordering on "born-again" status.

Generally people display concern if someone slips out of the ruts of propriety and is naughty, or contrary, fractious, and constantly given to stepping over the traces. However, Harry's case was more concerning: he was as docile as a frog in high summer and eager to be a good boy. As observed, Harry today walked with a discernible list and while sitting on the school bench of hard wood, you could easily have slipped a two by four between his left ass-cheek and the seat since Harry lifted that part of his sensitive anatomy up and away similar to my dog Mister when he encounters a strange car and applies his expertise to the rubber.

When Harry then asked me if I would, please, accompany him to the outdoor biffy come noon recess, I thought to myself, "Na!, Na!"

We arrived at the biffy and locked the door with a crooked cramp and I was now meant to doctor a bit. On his left posterior, Harry displayed two badly infected sores, which hurt him a lot, a great lot. Had Harry suffered similar affliction between nose and gills, he would have not been able to

Schlemms bie ahm auna Back, bowe, aulso tweschne Näs enn
Tjeewe jewast wea, haud hee woll nijch kunnt, soo auls
jeweehnlijch, schmocke Frautze riete. Enn auls etj dee von
ahm mettjebrochte Wautepuzheltjess bruckt omm ahm den
Metäje ut siene Schlemmsa ruttoodretjche, dann stund Harry
soo seea oppe Tees, daut hee meist säwen Schooh lang wea.
Dann hohld Harry een Doostje Korboolsaulw vonne
Watkins-Sort väa, enn donn schmäad etj ahm enn bett hee
opphead soo winjsch auls auls een Joahlintjch, daut den
Diestel enn de Oatschät mett de Hinjabeen enn grenautstje
Bieta hassat, too senne.

Von dee Schoolsetjreet tweemol soo wiet auls Schmett
Friees Tjnals een Steen schmiete kunn auf, wohnd Betschla
Hauns Weltj, woohnen de Mensche Schnuftje nannde. Dies
Hauns Weltjch wea een sondaboara Kauz, wizhrijch enn
tjoanijch, iewrijch enn rootnäsijch, oba goot too liede. Verr'm
Tjrijch wea hee de Väasettenda vonne jrientholsche Nazi-
partie, too dee uck mien Voda, Arbuse-Klosse, Tobias Jaunz,
Stooah Jinta, enn noch een haulwe Dutz aundre jeheade.

Enn während dem Tjrijch oba uck nohäa, wea Schnuftje
bieaun uck de Darpsbootlegger, enn doamett haft hee meea
Säjen enn Jletjch auls maunjch een Prädja utjedeelt.

Enn too aul dem wea Schnuftje uck noch een Looslada, dee
flaumend doll woare kunn, oba dann uck measchtens seea
leewtolijch word, enn jeweehnlijch wea. Soo's jesajcht, goot
too liede, wear'a.

Oba wiels hee wea, waut'a wea, enn jiedet Darp enne Welt
soohn Tschudack bruckt auls Mohtstock, sootoosaje, mett
dem de aundre sijch vejlitjche tjenne, word Ohmtje Hauns
Weltjch han enn wada jenertjt. De Darpsjungess oajade ahm
enn, enn foddada ahm rut. Measchtens word Schnuftje nijch
mol doll, hee wea daut meist jewant, soo een bät de
Proowsteen too senne.

cut an amusing display of grimaces and faces of rare order as per usual. Then when I applied two cotton pompons which Harry had brought along for the medical procedure to squeeze copious amounts of pus out of his abscessed ass, Harry stood on his toes, then his tippy toes and only stopped mounting until he was a good seven feet tall. Harry then produced a tin of carbolic salve of the Watkins variety which I smeared into his sores until he stopped acting like a frisky colt bent on kicking the single tree of any transporting vehicle into smithereens.

From the school biffy to where Bachelor Hans Woelke lived, the distance was twice as far as Smithy Friesen's Corny could throw a stone.

This Hans Woelke was a peculiar pilgrim; he was fidgety but tough, eager and red-nosed but likeable enough.

Before the last big war, he was the self-appointed chairman of the Nazis in town to which belonged my father, Watermelon Klassen, Toby Janz, Store Gunther, and half a dozen others. All had in mind to join Hitler and occupy Ukraine and retrieve their former homes, rightfully theirs.

During the war and then again afterwards, Snuffy was a part-time bootlegger as well and in this trade he managed to dispense more blessings and joy than most ministers of the word, and at a lower price.

In addition to all named Christian attributes, Snuffy was also a fire-brand who, on occasion, could get mad as hell, but then quickly resumed a steady pace of reserved wherewithal as becomes a model Anabaptist.

In short, he was a likeable enough presence.

Since Hans Woelke was what he was and every village is entitled to a fiery jester as a measuring gauge of human behaviour, Snuffy was occasionally teased. The boys of the village challenged and provoked him. Mostly he was used to such minor irritations and he let it go since "boys will be boys." He didn't even get all that mad, he was used to it, since he represented his own standard.

Soo auls jie junt aul dentjche tjenne, word Schnuftje dann uck aum Hallowe'en Owend Opfa vonne Dommheite. Enn uck wada aune '44. Jintasch Eddie, Julius (Schrooda) Klosses Obraum, een jnerrja Schledonz, enn uck Blocke Harry troffe sijch soo's jiedet Joah biem Schnuftje ver siene tjliene Koht, enn eewde Schowanack. See stelpde sien Hiestje omm, see läde een Sack mett Heehnafadre bie ahm oppen Schorsteen, enn see stette ahm mett dem Soagbock de Husdäah too. Enn auls see daut verrejcht haude, roopte see aule dree: "Schnuftje, woa best Du? Wie welle die mol Goondach saje!"

Daut jintjch doa verre Däah een bät lud too, oba Schnuftje kaum nijch rut. Donn docht Blocke Harry, hee wudd doch mol opp den faustjetjlamden Soagbock noppsprinje enn een bät extra schelauje. Enn daut deed'a dann uck. Schnuftje, oba, kaum nijch rut. Hee bleef benne, soo dochte de Jungess. Waut see nich weete kunne, ess daut Hauns Weltjch sich de Tiet äwa hinja een Pappelboom, dusend Joah oolt enn sass Zoll ditj vestuak; een sasszollja Boom reatjt ahm too. Auls ahm daut aulatoop dann doch too lud enn too groff word, nauhm Schnuftje een haundeljet Bratt mett twee Näjel soo meea aum Enj rutsteatje, kaum omme Atj jeschlitjt, enn heiwd dem Harry eent äwrem Hinjarenj, daut dissa meist oppem Dack schoot.

Dee Näjel aum Schnuftje sien Priejelstock weare root fe Rosta, enn doawäjen musst etj Harry enne Setjreet twee Doag lohta aune hinjaschte Back doktre. Enn etj jleew uck noch vondoag, daut etj vleijcht haud Dokta woare sullt, oba dann haud etj nijch äwa mien Beroop Jeschijchte vetalle durft, enn doawäjen socht etj mie dann doch waut mie scheen jeiht ut; enn toom Deel uck wiels Mensche, dee säwen Schooh lang woare, wann eena ahn de Hinjaback beoabeit, mie dann doch een bät engrule.

As can readily be imagined, Halloween became Hans Woelke's annual scapegoat occasion. And so, in 1944 Gunther's Eddie, Julius (Grain Crusher) Klassen's Abraham, a sneering scoundrel, and Block's Harry met at Snuffy's little hut to dispense naughtiness in the form of pranks. They knocked over his biffy, deposited a bag of chicken feathers on his chimney, and then wedged a saw horse into his door, preventing let and entry.

Having accomplished their round of pranks, all three of them called, "Snuffy, where are you; we intend to wish you a pleasant Good Evening!"

When Snuffy did not answer, their calls they turned up the action and increased the volume of summoning. Harry then took matters a step further by mounting the saw horse, thereby playing the cock of the roost the better.

He called and he crowed but Snuffy failed to respond.

Small wonder, Snuffy was hiding behind a poplar tree, just behind his hut, a poplar tree a thousand years old and six inches thick gave him adequate cover. When Harry's coloratura warble of calling Hans Woelke became too much, the latter's coxcomb swelled, he grabbed a prepared plank with two nails ripe with rust at the end and swatted Harry a mighty one straight on his *dupa* which damn near sent Block Junior airborne.

Rusty nails in the podex of most anatomies quickly do their bidding and so I graduated into medical proficiency for two days on end, doctoring Harry's sorry ass. I believe to this day I would have made a fair enough practitioner of Hippocratic calling but then the wider world of story-telling would have been off-limits to me and you, the reader, would have been the loser. The other reason I chose to postpone response to the call of caring for the physical man is that I simply am too much in awe of patients who stand seven feet tall when their private parts plead for the helping hand.

Revolwamissjoon

Etj haud mie väajenohme, ditmol Israel nijch too velohte bett etj dee twee äwajebläwne Templasch doa jefunge haud. Oba daut's leijcht jesajcht. Woa fangt eena aun? Etj wisst bloß, daut eent een Niefeld wea enn de aundra een Enns, enn daut wea oba uck aules.

Daut see doa dijcht bie Nazareth woll sette wudde, kunn etj mie goot väastalle, wiels doa wohnde een Schoof dietsche Jude en een Darp, dee fe de Ashkenasie uck nijch väl waut äwrijch haude.

Oba finj dee mol…

Etj fruag. "Na, woo sitt'et dee?" word jefroagt.

"Soo een bät vebiestat," säd etj.

Von soohne Sort jeft daut hiea dree Milljoone, daut halpt weinijch," säd mien Frind Sascha Waldner, een Moskau Jud, enn dee tjand sijch enne Welt ut; hee wisst sogoa woa Winnipeg wea.

"Etj woa die waut saje," meend Sascha, een jewesna Admiraul, nu een Schlorrekapitän. "Vondoag haft de kaunodscha Bootschaft een Empfang, enn doa woat uck Freelein Bronfmaun senne, enn wiels see Jeld haft, haft see uck Vebindunge enn Palanka soowesoo. Froag ahr."

Etj drunk opp dem Empfang Chivas Regal wiels etj wisst je, daut dee Schnaupsfebritj enne Bronfmaun Henj wea, enn etj leet ahr daut seehne, daut etj mett dissem Produkt ommtoogohne vestund.

"Freelein Bronfmaun," säd etj, "etj brinj jearn Opfa enn drintj disse Buddel ut, wann See mie eenen Jefaule doohne

120

Revolver Mission

I was firmly resolved not to leave Israel this time until I had found the two remaining Templers. However, such is easier said than done. Where do you start? All I knew is that one was called Neufeld and the other one Enns, and that was all.

I could well imagine that they lived close to Nazareth because a good number of Jews lived in a village in those parts and these chose not to have all that much to do with the Ashkenazi either.

But how to find them?

I asked around. "What do they look like?" was the counter question.

"A bit lost, I imagine," I said.

"There are at least three million of the lot which fit the description, that's not much help," said my friend Sascha Waldner, a Moscow Jew who knew the world; he even knew where Winnipeg was.

"I'll tell you something, though," said Sascha, a former admiral, now a pilot of the fireplace, in cosy slippers, fleece-lined. "There is a reception at the Canadian Embassy tonight and Miss Bronfman will be in attendance and since she has real money, she also has connections and clout. Ask her."

At the reception I asked for Chivas Regal as the beverage of choice because I knew that the Bronfman Family were the distillers of favoured libations, and I casually, but persuasively, had her notice that I knew how to handle a good Scotch, or two.

woare. Etj seatj twee Templa-Menniste Niefeld enn Enns, dee sijch doa dijcht bie Nazareth opphoole selle."

"Morje biem Freehstitj em Desert Hotel hiea enn Beer Sheeba woa etj Ahn daut saje." Enn wiels etj wisst, daut de Israelischa Jeheemdeenst soo eene schoape Näs haud aus een ooltkolniescha Eltesta fe Gummreife, jleewd etj ahr daut.

Biem Freehstitj—wie aute Herinj, jekoakte Eia enn Howajrett—säd Freelein Bronfmaun, "enn dem enn dem Darp jefft daut eenen Niefeld enn een Enns. Enn wann See welle, foah etj Ahn doahan."

"Ess daut oppem Gummesel too wiet?" stald etj mie bescheide, soo aus sijch daut fe een Mennist jeziemt.

"Joh."

Aulso leit etj mie doahan kutscheare.

Daut wea nohm Meddachschlop auls wie doahan kaume. Etj stald mie dee twee em Jeist soo väa aus twee eensaume, vebiestade Schop, soo enn bät auls mennische Professasch, dee aum Okanagan sette, enn daut scheene Wada doa lowe, enn den biljen Pries fe Appel preise, oba ennalijch sijch jieden Dach noh Wienepetj enn Schneediehne bange. See wudde woll irjendwoa oppe Väaleew sette, enn eena wudd Frind-schauft nohfädme, enn de aundra enne Offenbarung romm-blädre, enn beid vebiestad senne, soo auls daut mott, wann eene hiea ooda uck doa auls Mennist em Jaumadohl rommd-wault, soo docht etj mie.

Oba, weit jefehlt, soo aus Prädja Happna emma säd.

Doa weare se! See saute doa mett een poah Berliena Jude, spälde Schach, enn weare seea iewrijch enne Vetall, aus wann se morje haulf Rußlaund ennehme wulle, enn äwamorje soo bieaun Kanada besatte. Daut see sijch hiea tusijch feehlde, word eena enn, wiels see aulatoop dietschet Beea drunke. Vom Faut.

Etj jintj noh de Weatsche, enn bestald fief Jläsa Beea, nohdem etj mie be Freelein Bronfmaun soo seea bedankt

"Miss Bronfman," I said, "I am happily prepared to make sacrifices and polish off this bottle myself if you would do me a favour. I am looking for two Templers Mennonites, one Neufeld and one Enns, who supposedly reside in the region of Nazareth."

"Tomorrow at breakfast in the Desert Hotel right here in Beer Sheba I will inform you where they are." And since I knew that the Israeli Secret Service has a nose sharper than an Old Colony bishop sniffing out rubber tractor tires, I believed her.

At breakfast—we ate herring, boiled eggs and oatmeal porridge—Miss Bronfman said, "There is a village just west of Nazareth which one Neufeld and Enns do indeed call home. And if you want me to, I'll take you there tomorrow with my car."

"Is it too far for me and my bicycle?" I asked in false modesty, the kind that behooves a Mennonite.

"Too far," she replied.

And so I let her chauffeur me to my site.

We arrived at the village shortly after the noon nap, called siesta in hotter climates. In my imagination I saw two lonely and lost sheep, much like Mennonite professors, who are spending their twilight years in the Okanagan Valley of B. C. and praising the gentler climate and the cheap price of apples, but daily yearn for Winnipeg and its snow banks and related company, including me. They would most likely be sitting in the shade on a porch, with one tracing relatives while the other one would be busily leafing around in the Book of Revelations, and both lost and lonely as it becomes a Mennonite pilgrimming in the Vale of Sorrows, both here and there, so my thinking went.

Fact of the matter: "Far, far off the mark," as Preacher Heppner said most every Sunday back home.

haud, aus sijch daut fe eenen Maun von Welt jeziemt. See schmustad bloß enn säd: "Anytime, gellaunta Oohmtje," enn fuah auf.

Daut Beea fresch aunjetaupt, stund oppem Desch, enn etj späld den spendowlen ritjchen Onkel ut Amerikau. "Thiesse, ess de Nohme," säd etj, "enn dit ess dochwoll Oohmtje Niefeld?" "Joh, daut sie etj, Kolja Niefeld, enn dis aundra Missa ess Doft Enns. Riet ahm mol den Oarm ut biem Haundreahre, joh? Wiels hee tjemmt sijch emma noch uck em Ella seea stoatj vea. Enn wann Du een ajchta Thiesse best, sull die daut nijch schwoa faule."

Na joh, daut eena sijch mett disse Tjeadels vetalle kunn, daut wea etj aul enjeworde. Oba eascht word etj mett dee Berliena Jude bekaunt jemoakt. Daut weare seea oppjeriemde Tjeadels, enn see haude woll uck meea mett dem Fiddelboage auls mett eene Mestfortj too doohne jehaut.

Etj saj toom Niefeld: "Etj tjann Tus eenen Reima enn daut ess een haulwa Tjäla, kunn daut opplatzt noch Frindschauft senne?"

"Ess daut een Bejchterieta? Wann joh, dann ess daut mien tjlienaVada vonne Muttaschkaunt, joh."

"Joh."

Donn meend Enns, soo bieaun; "Oba daut näjchste Beea bestall wie, enn Kolja waut daut betohle. Wie send noch emma deemootijch, oba nijch oam."

Na, soo jintj daut han enn tridj, enn etj wea hiea, etj meen doa, boold gaunz tusijch. Nohm dredden Beea hold etj de Buddel Chivas Regal, Jeschentj von Freelein Bronfmaun, äwadähl, enn dann kaum wie noch dolla enne Vetal nenn.

"Saul etj dem Thiesse vetalle, woo daut mett ons aules pessead, ooda wesst Du, Doft?" fruag Kolja Niefeld.

"Na, wiels Du emma äwadrifst, woa ejt leewa vetalle," säd Kolja.

There they were! They sat with a couple of Berlin Jews, were playing chess, in animated discussion as if planning to occupy all of Russia tomorrow and also Canada the day after for good measure. They felt quite at home here as I could tell by the fact that they were all drinking German beer from the tap.

I walked up to the manager of the pub, a lively lady, and ordered five glasses of beer after I had thanked Miss Bronfman, courteously, for the ride as it becomes a cosmopolite. She, Sadie Bronfman, as she asked me to address her now, smiled and said, "Anytime, my gallant gent," and departed.

The round of beer, nicely tapped, stood ready before us, compliments of the rich uncle from America. "Thiessen is the name," I said, "and this, I assume, is Mr Neufeld?" "Joh, that's me, Kolja Neufeld, and this runt is David Enns. Tear off his arm when you shake hands, will you? He still thinks he is awfully powerful in spite of his advanced years. And if you're really a Thiessen of the old stock, you should manage to tear off his member with ease and put him in his place, long overdue."

Well, the fact that you could strike up a conversation with this variety of Templers was obvious. First off, though, I was introduced to their friends, Jewish fellows from Berlin. They were obviously accomplished enough company who had more experience handling fiddle bows than manure forks.

After taking the social scene in a bit, I remarked, "I know a fellow by the name of Reimer at home and his mother is from the Kehler clan, could he be related?"

"Is he a raconteur? If so, then he is a small cousin from my mother's side, indeed."

"That's him, alright!"

Then Enns rather casually said, "But we will order the next round of beer and Kolja will pay for it. We are still humble but not poor."

"Daut send nu aul boold dartijch Joah tridj auls wie eemol enne Turkei weare," sad Kolja loos. "Wie haude ons eene Koah jekofft, enn fuahre em Laund vonne Moohre omhäa. Dann saj etj toom Doft, 'Du, Doft, well'we doch mol eefach nohm Ooste foahre, eenfach mol noh Syrien, enn seehne, auls de Mensche daut doa soo plätrijch jeit, aus emma jesajcht woat, joh?' Enn Doft netjkoppt, enn wie fuahre äwre Jrenz. Mett een Tank voll Gauss enn eene Fust voll Backsheesh tjemmt je eena enn soohne Lenda doch ernoa romm,' saj etj.

"Na joh, daut jintj aulnoch jlei, wann uck jieda twintijch Verscht irjend een Ooltnäs enne Uniform ons opphild enn mett de Loop rommpoakad. Daut see doa nijch lese kunne, wisst etj fuats. Etj reatjcht ahm emma onsen Paus äwakopp, enn hee laus den derjch enn head eascht opp auls etj ahm eenen Rubel gauf, enn donn leet hee ons wieda foahre."

"Aum tweeden Dach auls wie derjche Wieste fuahre, enn daut soo eensaum word, daut sijch doa nijch mol Kameele han vebiestade, saut mett eemol eene oole, misaje Mumtje aum Wajch. Haulf doot, wea se, enn weifeld soo lieseltjess, daut eenem daut jaumad. Heet wear'ett soo auls aule Donna, enn dreeveadel vedarscht wea see sowesoo."

"Oba Doft, dis vebruckta Missjoonoa, dee gauf nijch eea Fräd bett etj stellhild, enn äwaroasch fuah, enn ahr mett-nauhm.

"Wie holpe ahr hinje enne Koah nenn, enn wie freide ons, daut wie noch mol wada mennische Samerieta späle kunne, kratjcht soo auls se ons daut Tus jeleaht haude. Enn eea Doft wada doatweschen räde woat, woa etj Die saje, daut wie, Doft enn etj, doa uck boold een Scheetiesa enne Fupp haude. Daut mott vleijcht nijch, oba eena schlapt bäta, wann eena soohne Stritz de Nacht bie sijch haft. Enn woo wie too dee kaume, woat de Jeschijcht Die vetalle, nijch etj.

"Na, joh, oba wie send je noch emma unjawäjess. Wie weare noch tjeene haulwe Stund jefoahre auls de Fru doa hinje

126

There quickly was a good deal of back and forth and all in our mama-loshn as the Jews call the mother tongue, and we all felt rather homey as happens when the tongue speaks the language of heart and soul. After the third glass of beer, I produced a bottle of Chivas Regal, compliments of Miss Bronfman and our conversation assumed desired perspective.

"Shall I tell Thiessen what all has happened to us on our life's journey, or do you want to David?" asked Kolja Neufeld.

"No, since you always exaggerate everything I would rather do so myself," said Kolja.

"It's almost thirty years ago now that we once were in Turkey," Kolja started off. "We had bought a car and travelled through the land of the Moors. And then I said to David, 'David, listen, why don't we simply travel due east and travel to Syria and find out for ourselves whether people live as modestly over there as is commonly said, okay? And David nodded and we crossed the border. With a tank full of gas and dukes full of baksheesh, one can get on quite well,' I suggested.

"Well, things ran quite smoothly even if every twenty versts or so some ragged joker in a uniform stopped us and poked around with a rusty barrel of a gun. The fact that nobody in that region could read I knew almost from the start. I always handed the guards our passports upside down and then they read our passports on and on until I handed the ruffian a ruble and then he immediately waved us on."

"The second day as we travelled through the desert for a thousand miles and more and things were so desolate that not even a camel got lost in those parts, there, suddenly, sat an old wretched woman by the roadside. She was obviously half dead as she waved feebly and you couldn't help but feel sorry for this dying creature. It was hotter than hell and we were about three-quarters dead of thirst ourselves.

"But David, this semi-retired missionary, left me no peace until I stopped, backed up, and took this hag along. We

platzlijch seea oppläwd. See hild Doft enn mie mett eemol
jiedem een Revolwa em Jenetj enn wull Jeld, Backsheesh enn
onse Passa enn weet de Donna waut noch aules habe. Waut
bleef mie äwrijch? Etj klunjd oppe Brams nopp, enn hild stell.
Dis frulijcha Maunsmensch word seea groff, enn auls wie
rutkroope, tjreaj wie beid eent äwrem Heeft mett ähre, siene,
meen etj, Stritz, daut eenem de Tähne em Kopp klaupade.

"Na, etj nijch ful enn nijch domm gauf ahm too vestohne,
daut wie ons Jeld hinje enne Rumpelkohma enne Koah
haude, enn etj muak dee ohp. Toom Jletj wea hee kratjcht soo
rachulijch aus etj jehopt haud, enn dann schluag etj too. Enn
Doft Enns uck vonne aundre Sied, oba dis Wiestensähn wea
nijch ut Kardond, enn soo gauf daut een schratjcheljet
Schermetzel. Doft fuchteld mett sien Tjnippsmassa romm,
enn etj leet miene Fuste seea lud prädje. Oba dis Mooah wea
grulijch jäjenaun. Na, jenuag, noh feftien Minute haud wie
ahm mack, oba mett ons Bloot enn uck sient wea daut
Schetjsaul nijch spoasom ommjegohne, enn ons sach daut aus
bie eene Schwienstjast.

"Na joh, enn waut nu? Wie entschloohte ons dissen endlijch
macken Donna hinje enne Rumpelkohma nenntooschuwe,
enn wieda too foahre. Enn daut deed wie dann uck.

"Tjeene haulwe Stund lohta word wie wada oppjehoole, enn
diss Scherniesel, weet de Donna, sajcht wie selle mol hinje
daut Datjzel opmoake.

"Enn doa lach nu de elendja Mohdesack, meea doot aus
läwendijch. 'Wäa haft dit jedohne?' well hee weete. "Dochwoll
Gospodjien Davied Daviedoff," saj etj, enn wies ahm Doft sien
Massa. Oba Doft sajcht: "Etj? Etj mol wada? Kolja Abramvot-
isch, dee schluag ahm mett de Fust too gooda latzt de Näs
twei, enn vebuhld ahm den Kopp, hiea tjitjch."

"Na jenuag, see nauhme ons den Schlätel vonne Koah emm
neajchsten Darp wajch, enn stoppte ons enn. Noh eene haulwe

128

assisted her into the back seat of our car and were happy that
we still had it in us to be good Mennonite Samaritans, just as
they had taught us back home. And before David again has a
chance to interrupt my tale, I should tell you, that we two had
acquired a shooting iron ourselves, simply because you tend
to sleep better with a metal squirt gun in your pocket when
the shades are drawn, even if our conscience announced itself
on account of our faith. But as to how we acquired the
revolver the story will reveal it, not I.

"Well, but we were still en route. We had not travelled for
more than half an hour when our woman passenger on the
rear seat suddenly sprang to life. She held a revolver to David's
neck and to mine and demanded baksheesh, our passports,
and God only knows what else. What was I to do? I braked as
sharply as I could and stopped. The feminine man became
very rough and when we got out of the car both David and I
got a hefty smack right over our heads with her, I mean with
his weapon, so that the teeth in our heads started clacking.

"Well, I knew of similar tactics from way back home on the
Dnieper and so I told him as best I could that we had
everything he wanted in the trunk of our vehicle and I started
opening it up. Fortunately, he was just as feverishly greedy as
I had hope for and so I landed him a good one with the full
force of divine righteousness. And David, for once, also
jumped into action, and we started a sudden but thorough
working over of this nefarious thief, only to discover that this
miserable runt was not of cardboard manufacture and soon a
bloody donnybrook of the Machno variety was in full bloom.
David busied himself with his pocket knife while I held forth
with a sermon in which my dukes did the preaching.
However, this Moor was most resistant. Well, after some
fifteen minutes off non-stop action we managed to subdue
this lousy Sukensien aka s.o.b. To say that our lot, or fate, or
call it what you will, had tapped blood from all sides sparingly

Stund, kohme dree Soldohte aun, enn een Maunsmensch enn Zivil, enn kaume ons enne Chelodne beseatje.

"Wäa haft den Mooah dootjeschloage?" "Tjeena, soo wiet auls wie weete," gauw wie too Auntwuat.

"Schohd," säde se, "wiels diss Doodja wea aul twalw Joahlang de jefährlijchsta Deef enn Merda, enn Terrorist enne arabische Jeschijcht, enn sien Rejchta tjrijcht oppe Städ fiefhundat Dusend amerikaunsche Dohla."

"Donn entschloote Doft enn etj ons, daut wie ahm vleijcht beid een bät biem stoawe biejestohne haude. Enn see tohlde ons daut Jeld boa ut."

"Nu drintj wie noch een Beea, wiels de Jerajchtijchtjeit strenjt noch emma soo aun, daut eenem meist aunfangt too darschte."

would be a falsehood; fact is the scene reminded of a hog butchering back home.

"But what now? we seriously pondered. So we decided to stuff the subdued party, finally, into our trunk and resume our trip. And that's what we did.

"Not half an hour later, we were again stopped and this shady scoundrel in uniform told us to open the trunk of our car.

"And there before us all now lay this miserable maggot bag, more dead than alive. 'Who did this?' was his question. "Probably Gospodjien Davied Daviedoff," I answered, and showed the guard David's knife. But David said, "I? I yet again, as always? Kolja Abramovitsch, he broke his nose with his fist at the end of the debacle and put a dent or two on his head, here look!"

"Whatever, in the next village they took the keys of our car away and threw us into the local prison. After half an hour, three soldiers arrived, as well as an official in civilian attire; all four came to look us up in the chelodne."

"Who killed the moor?" "No one, as far as we know," was our answer.

"Too bad," they said, "because this maggot bag was the most dangerous thief, murderer and terrorist in the wider vicinity and in Arab history for that matter, and his judge will receive five hundred thousand in cold cash in American dollars."

"Then David and I decided that we together probably stood by him during his last minutes on earth. And then they paid us out in cash and on the spot."

"And now it is time for a final round of beers. While recapitulating that final hour of justice enacted, one tends to sweat a bit, even years after the fact."

Een Joonafesch em Nippa

Auls ruhm twee Joah tridj Kauspasch Hein mie vetald, daut siene Grootellre ähren Tjastdach omm een gaunzen Dach enn Chortietz veschowe haude, wiels kratjcht omm dee Tiet de groote Feschasch ut Elloag enn Roosendohl eenen joonaoatjen Wels jefonge haude, wea dann uck de Dach auls disse Jeschijcht eene Weaj jelajcht word.

Dee Grund ess eenfach. Kauspa jeheat too de gaunz weinje Mensche, enn Jrienthola noch doatoo, dem etj waut jleewe kaun enn dooh, enn doamett sie uck etj enjeschlohte. Wiels auls Resserieta doaf enn saul eena de Sälestrenj vonne Woahrheit strapazeare, uck sogoa soo seea utratjche auls 'ett jeiht. Enn daut well etj vondoag mol oppe Proow stalle. Vleijcht jletjcht mie daut, ohne den Sälestrang tweitooriete ooda äwatooklunje.

Enn soo's jesajcht: Kauspa ess doch een bätje opprejchtja, sesst wea hee nijch een bekaunda Bankier enn Steinbach jeworde. Wiels bloos ut Jrienthol too kohme, reatjcht nijch too omm enn Steinbach de Easchta Offiziea enne Credit Union too woare. Den eensjen Pries woohna Kauspa fe siene groote Konst tohle musst, ess daut ahm de Hoah utjinje. Enn mie uck, oba etj nauhm daut nijch mol haulf soo jeneiw mett de Woahrheit, weens bett nutoo nijch.

Joh, oba wie wulle vondoag doch fesche gohne, aunstautt bie de Resserietasch romm too dwaule. Aulso: Kauspa vetald mie, daut siene Grootellere enn Chortietz enne Ooltkolonie, doa nijch wiet vom Nippa auf, soo's aul jesajcht, ähren Tjastdach väavelajcht haude, wiels de Mensche eenen Fesch

The Jonah Fish in the Dnieper

When about two years ago Henry Kasper told me that his grandparents' wedding had been moved up by a full day in Chortietz because exactly at that time fishermen in Elloag and Roosendohl had caught a Jonah-fish like monster out of the deep, it was also the day this story was laid in the cradle.

The reason for this is simple enough. Kasper is one of the few people around, including fellow Grünthalers, whom I can believe anything at all, and that includes me. As a raconteur you are meant to stretch and test the traces of truth to their limits. This being so, I intend to do so today, long overdue. Maybe if I'm lucky I'll manage to do so without ripping the traces or unduly stepping over the boundaries of truth.

As said, Kasper is a bit more honest, for otherwise he would not have risen to prominence as a banker, and that in Steinbach, were folks know something about the big buck. The only, but considerable price Kasper paid for his considerable talent, was that he lost his hair early on. So did I, but I did not take matters of really, really true as seriously as he did, at least not up to date.

Joh, but today we intend to go fishing instead of sitting around and dishing out tall tales or listening to them. Now then: Kasper told me that his grandparents in Chortietz in the Old Colony, close to the Dnieper River, as mentioned, had moved up their wedding celebration by a full day because the fishermen yet to be named had at the very time caught this fish, so large, that a fully fledged wedding party could eat its fill and invite half of the neighbouring village of Elloag and all

aune 1927 emm Somma jejräpe haude, enn dis Fesch wea soo groot, daut sijch een Gaustjebott doaraun saut äte kunn, enn dann noch haulf Elloag doatoo, enn gaunz Roosendohl sijch de Doarm uck noch vollheiwe kunne. Oba, soo's daut aul emma wea: wann een Fesch jejräpe woat, dann mott eena den oppe Städ oppäte, sesst woat de oolt enn stintjcht.

Daut easchte Mol auls soohn Maleea aul mol meist pessead wea, wea auls Jesus aum See Genezareth een poah Dusend Mensche ver sijch haud, enn den hungad, enn Hee enn siene Jinjajemeend kratjcht donn mehrere Fesch vonne Joonasort jejräpe haude, enn Hee dee oppdesche leet. O joh, enn wiels daut doa gaunz dijchtbie eene Batjarie jefft, woa dee Ua-Uagroottjinja von Goliath enn Simson Bultje noh de Resserieta Oat backe doohne, enn von soohne Bultjess reatjche fief bett sass too, enn dann ess uck aul eene Dutz voll (von dit wudd etj goanijch woage too räde, wann etj mie doa aum Heiljen See nijch selwst een poahmol de Kaldune mett een Simsonbultje volljeprommelt haud), enn doabie word mie aulahaund opp Uat enn Städ dietlijch, uck daut de Feschasch aul emma een bät meea Spälruhm mett'e Woahrheit haude auls de Golfasch ooda de Professasch, enn uck de Jrienthola.

Enn daut saul heete: Wann Jesus mie von dem jewaultjen Gausjebott vetald haud, wudd etj ahm aules jleewe, oba wiels mol wada aulahaund Tiet enn Mensche tweschen Fesch enn Oppschriewsel doatweschen kaume, saj etj: "Wäwaeet!?"

Na joh, oba wie send je meist biem Gaustjebott, enn de Joonawels ess noch deep em Wota. Oba soo's jesajcht: Kauspa vetald von dissem Fesch, oba uck mien liefhauftja Voda vetald soo meea kratjcht dautselwje, enn wiels hee doabie, daut heet biem jriepe doabie wea, well etj uck ahm ditmol jleewe, enn ahm too Wuat kohme lohte. Enn dann wea je uck noch een aundra een bät doabie, enn daut wea der Besten Einer, aulso Ohmtje Arthur Kroeger, eena von de Tjräjaschklocke

134

of Roosendohl to line their innards as well. However, as has always been the case, when a fish is caught, then the eating of it better commence with dispatch since it deteriorates by the minute and the stinking by the hour.

The very first time a similar malheur occurred is when Jesus, on the Sea of Galilee, had a few thousand hungry people around him and He and his congregation of disciples had just caught a few fish of similar size which He promptly served up.

And as it happened, that there was a bakery conveniently close by where the great, great grandchildren of Samson and Goliath baked loaves of bread of story-telling size, meaning five to six to a dozen. (I would be reluctant to introduce this tale if I had not had my personal fill of such Samsonite loaves by the Holy Sea); it was there, and on the spot, that all manner of Scripture became very clear to me, as well as the fact that when you deal with fishermen, you ought to measure truth by varying degrees of standards, the same being true of golf players, professors and fellow Grünthalers.

All I mean to say is this: If Jesus would have told me about a mass feeding, I would have believed every word He said, but because considerable time elapsed between the catching of the fish and the documentation thereof, I would add, "Who knows?"

Na joh, but we are edging closer to the wedding feast and the Jonah fish is still in deep water. But, as already stated, Kasper made lively mention of this fish and so did my father and since their stories amounted to the same, for once, and since my father had personal involvement in the catch, I choose to believe him this one time and so I will let him have his word in the matter. There was another person involved in it all and he was no ordinary witness; he was none other than Arthur Kröger, member of the Kröger Clock making family, and even if he was no personal witness to the episode, he came upon the scene scant minutes later after the wagon,

Famielje, enn wann dissa uck tjeen diretjchta Zeij wea von dem gaunzen Unjanehme, wea hee oba doch dee Maun, dee een poah Minute noh dem dee Entjelwoage mett dem Rekord, aka Joonafesch, doabowe vom Nippa von twee tweedusend- pundje Kuntasch jetrocke, noh Elloag jefeaht word, doa vebie kaum, enn sach, waut doa pesseat wea. Enn diss Arthur K. haft mie disse Jeschijcht aul dreemol vetalt (eenmol verre Tjoatjch, woa noch tjeen Mensch buta de Piano-House Leewe jeloage haft) enn jiedesmol ess dee Jeschijcht deeselwje, enn jiedesmol tjemmt Ohm Arthur doabie de Schweet oppe Stearn, enn daut Tetjre enne Stemm.

Joh, enn soo vetalt ons Zeij Arthur Tjräja, een gottesferjchta Mensch enn soo opprejchtijch auls dee jenannda Bankier Kauspa, kaum daut, daut auls see aun de seea schoape Atj oppem Wajch bie Roosendohl kaume, enn dee Joonafesch weens dree Meeta hinje äwrem Woagebax rutstuak, dann haud mien Voda dee Kuntasch extra eent äwajeresst, doamett see mett de jewaultje Lohd omme Atj kaume. Uck haud Voda dee tjliene Jungess, dee dutzendwies hinja dem Feschwoage rannde, jesajcht, daut wann see nijch schuwe wudde, waut Zeijch enn Lada hoohle kunne, hee ahn woomäjlijch uck eent äwaresse wudd, wiels de Fesch mott nu stauntepee, aulso huppasch, noh Ungasch em Spitja oppe Wijschschol toom wääje.

Joh, enn auls de Feschzoagel donn soo wiet hinje rutstuak, krautzd enn murjcheld dee eene Hollinj aune roosendohlsche Atj een Meeta deep, enn dree Meeta lang emm Haulfkulla, enn disse Rät ooda Holinj ess bett vondoag too seehne. Miene Uage laje hieamett Zeijchniss auf!

Na joh, daut ess aules scheen enn goot, oba eea de Joona- fesch krautze enn murjchle kunn, enn eea dee bie Ungasch oppe Wischschol nopp, ooda bie de junge Freese biem Gaustjebott too de Tjast oppen Desch kaun, mott dee jejräpe

bearing the record breaking Jonah fish pulled from the Dnieper by a team of two thousand pound geldings all the way to Elloag, and what all transpired en route. And this Arthur K. has told me this same tale three times (once in front of the church where no person has ever told a lie except Piano House Löwen), and each telling was identical in detail and at every telling of the tale, Arthur K. breaks out in a sweat and a quiver befalls his voice and his hands to this day.

Joh, and this witness Arthur K., a God fearing man and as honest as the named Kasper, reports, that when they negotiated the sharp curve on the outskirts of Roosendohl, with the Jonah fish protruding a good three meters out of the wagon box, my father had to let those mighty geldings have an extra measure of the whip so that the wagon, fish and the driver managed the turn. Also, my father had commanded the dozen and more kids who were chasing after the adventure, to push for all they were worth, for otherwise they, too, might get the lash since the fish had to be moved with due haste to the Unger mill for an urgent scaling.

And so, since Jonah's tale protruded so far out, it scratched and scraped and gouged a semi-circular dent a meter deep and three meters long in the Roosendohl corner and this excavation is visible to this day. My own eyes bore witness to that event and now you have it in writing! But, as already stated, that is all fine and good but before that Jonah fish could manage all its scraping and gouging, and before it could be landed on Unger's scale, or served to the waiting Froese wedding day masses, it had yet to be caught and it was at this event that my father, for the first and probably last time in his life became the man of the hour, and a real hero.

I asked my father at home, meaning behind Gnadenfeld, whether his swimming was really as good as he frequently boasted. "Well," he said, "I do not really know and I do not intend to exaggerate or boast but there is one thing I do know

woare, enn hiea word mien Voda toom easchten enn woll uck toom latzten Mol toom Held.

Etj fruag Voda Tus, aulso doa hinja Jnodefeld, auls hee emm Nippa wertjlijch soo goot haud schwamme kunnt auls hee emma säd. "Na," sajcht'a, "daut weet etj nijch, enn etj well je uck nich äwadriewe ooda puche, oba eent weet etj, enn daut ess, de Lied, oba besondasch de Jungess aum Nippa säde enn vetalde foaken, daut auls Obraum Thiesses Peeta aunfong jieden Dach em Nippa bie Elloag aun too schwamme, dann haude sogoa de Fesch Leah aunjenohme, enn dee schwomme von donn aun bäta, stoatja enn strauma. "Daut haud etj ahn biejebrocht," vetald Voda. "Enn daut wea auljemeen bekaunt," säd'a noch, enn dann wisst wie.

Auls etj Voda dann noch fruag, auls hee wertjlijch doabie jewast wea, auls de groote Joonawels jejräpe word, speajch hee ut, schmeet siene Metz enne Auschkuhl nenn, enn säd: "Toom Donna han, woo foaken mott eena de Woahrheit vetalle eea dee em Jedajchtnis backe blifft? Nijch bloos wea etj doabie, oba ohne mie wea de Fesch noch bett vondoag em Wota, wiels een Wels von äwa dusend Pund too jriepe, ess eene Sach, dem oba utem Wota rut too tose, enn noch een extra Kapitel fe sijch!"

Donn speajch sijch Voda noch eenmol enne Grauje, enn vetald wieda: "Joh, wann etj nijch de stoatjsta Scherwaunda tweschen Peetaborjch enn Odass jewasst wea enn den Fesch rutjetrocke haud, haud daut de roosendohlsche Hollinj mever nijch jejäwt, enn Freese haude uck nijch veeahundat Jast bie de Tjast soo schmock saut too äte jäwe kunnt."

"Na joh," meend Voda dann doch, "daut Mahla Ungasch ähre twee Kuntasch Orlik enn Starschie mie een bät holpe schod je uck nuscht, oba daut measchte bleef mol wada opp miene Schulre lidje, enn etj musst schuwe, schweete, tratjche enn retauje, daut de Schnodda Fiea foot."

and that is: people, but particularly the young boys by the Dnieper often said then when Abraham Thiessen's Peter started swimming everyday in the Dnieper then even the fish caught on and since then their swimming was noticeably improved, stronger and more elegant. "It was I who taught them that," father said. "And that was a fact generally known in the area and beyond," he said, and then we knew.

When I then asked my father whether he had been in attendance when the big Jonah fish was caught, he spat in a wide arc, threw his cap into the ash pit and thundered, "How often do I have to tell you the truth before it dents your memory? Not only was I present but without me that fish would be in the water to this very day, because catching a fish in excess of a thousand pounds is one thing, to drag it out of the river is a chapter unto itself."

Then my father spat in his hands once more and continued, "Joh, if I had not been the strongest of the heavyweights between Petersburg and Odessa the Roosendohl excavation would never not have happened and Froeses would not have managed to feed four hundred people and more so well at their mighty wedding feast."

"Na joh," father then added, "the fact that Miller Unger had two geldings, Orlik and Starschie who helped me a bit in the effort did not exactly harm the endeavour, but most of the heavy pulling was left to me, and I had to push, sweat, pull and strain until my very snot caught on fire."

"That whole episode transpired as follows," said my father. "We set out from Elloag very early in the morning towards the Dnieper with the single wagon pulled by Unger's two geldings and before long we had a dozen or more small boys sitting on the wagon because they all wanted to come along for the ride. They knew that I had already seen a fish in the Dnieper as large as a deep sea ferry, if not bigger. And this Jonah fish (this is what Jasch Wiebe, later the bishop the

"Daut kaum aulatoop soo," säd Voda: "Wie fuahre aul tiedijch zemorjess von Elloag nohm Nippa mett dem Entjelwoage mett Ungasch ähre twee Kuntasch aunjespaunt, enn wie haude uck aul boold eene gaunze Reaj tjliene Jungess oppem Woage sette, wiels de wulle aula mett. Wiels? Joh wiels, etj haud aul tweemol eenen Wels em Nippa jeseehne, dee mie soo groot auls een Huagseeprohm väakaum, wann nijch jrata. Enn dissen Joonafesch (soo nannd Jasch Wiebe, woohna nohäa enne Scheenwäsa-Tjoatjch Eltesta word), dee vestuak sijch, wiels hee dochwoll ohnd waut ahm jebrode wea.

Na joh, oba wie haude doch daut rejchtje mettjebrocht, omm den riesjen Wels de Nieaschiea opp den Hoake bietoobrinje. Etj nauhm von Tus eenen grooten Heihoake, eenen Strang, dumeditjch, enn uck een Stetjch Ohs mett, (dit wea een groota Herinj, dee noch ut Praisse staumd, word vetalt, enn etj jleew daut, wiels dee stentjad noch emma de haulwe Ooltkolonie voll), enn donn fuah etj mett de Lomm langsom, gaunz langsom, emma värewajch, emma lieseltjes värewajch, enn leet den Hoake mett daut Stetjch Ohs soo omme sass bett acht Schooh deep derjch daut Wota schlape. Enn soo jintjch daut schmock enn sejcha emma wieda, bett dem Joonawels dann doch dee Nieschiea too groot word, enn hee sijch entschloot den Hoake mett Ohs, wann nijch sogoa miene gaunze Lomm ennem Schlucka mett een Haups nenntooprommle, enn dann gauf daut eene groote Wall, eene seea groote Wall, auls de Joonawels full spied erreatjcht haud, enn mett dem Ohshoake oppriemd, enn doabie een poah vonne tjliene Jungess enne Lomm em huagen Boage rutschoote, wiels de Wels mett eene Krauft, dee eene vleijcht bie de Entretjung erläwe kaun aunsad, oba sesst nijch!

Toom Jletjch gauf daut dann noch nijch den Dneprestroj, den grooten Daum, aulso haud wie meea Spälruhm den Wels sijch uttoobe too lohte. Enn daut deed diss jewaultje Fesch

140

Schönwieser Church, called this monster of the deep) kept hiding, probably knowing of his fate on the skillet.

Na joh, but we had brought along the essentials to arouse the curiosity of the giant fish for the hook. I took from home a heavy duty hay hook, and a sturdy length of hope, thick as my thumb and a good sized piece of carrion (this was a big herring, brought along from Prussia of a former day, I was told, and I believed it since half of her Old Colony reacted by pinching their nostrils shut as I passed by) and then I paddled my boat slowly, very slowly and always straight ahead, and softly straight ahead and dragged that choice piece of carrion at a depth of six to eight feet through the water. And so I proceeded nicely and surely ever on until, obviously curiosity got the better of the fish and so he decided to go for it and he opened up his magnum sized funnel to swallow the bait but likely also the entire boat and in the ensuing chase a huge wave formed, a really huge wave when the Jonah fish attained full speed ahead, and cleaned up the carrion hook and in so doing a few of the boys I had on board flew out of the boat in a high arc, since the monster exhibited the kind of force and power which one would normally expect at the Rapture but hardly otherwise.

Fortunately the Dnieperstroj, the huge hydro-electric dam had not yet been built, and so we could allow Mr Jonah some play room to rummage a bit. And this is exactly what this mighty denizen of the deep did. He had taken the bit between his teeth and he took off until the waves covered half of Elloag so that all the eager swimmers took off, straight for the safety of the shore.

Na joh, since children will be children, including teenagers, my cousin Peter's little Peterkin managed to climb aboard Jonah's back while it was executing an elegant curve and to enjoy a free ride at twenty kilometers an hour, if not even a bit more.

dann uck. Hee haud daut Jebett tweschne Tähne, enn läd loos, daut de Walle hinja ahm boold haulf Elloag unja Wota sade, enn de Schwamasch bloos rut enn wajch stusde.

Na joh, wiels Tjinja enn uck groote Tjinja enne Welt soo sent auls se send, jletjcht mien Fada Peeta sien Peetatje daut, bie eenem grooten Boage, woohna de Wels muak, opp den Fesch biem schwamme oppen Ridje nopp too krupe, enn omsonst mett too foahre, soo bie de twintijch Kilomeeta de Stund, wann nijch sogoa meea.

Oba daut wea dem Joona dochwoll onmacklijch, enn soo pitscht dee eenmol mett dem Zoagel, daut Peetatje onjeheia huag enn wiet derjch'e Loft schoot. Aum näjchsten Dach auls de Wels dann endlijch sien Läwenszwatjch jedohne haud, enn bie de haulwe Ooltkolonie too de latzte ennere Ruh jekohme wea, vetald dis Peetatje mie, daut hee soo huag jefloage wea, daut hee de Lorelei haud seehne kunnt. Oba auls etj ahm dann fruag, auls daut uck wertjlijch soo wea, veläd hee de Lorelei enne Vetal noh Kiev, enn daut nauhm etj ahm dann uck eea auf.

Aulso wisst dis Jung von nu aun, daut eena bie de Woahrheit bliewe mott, uck wann eena Thiesse mett Famieljenohme heet, noh dem Motto: "Äwadriewe? Joh, oba leaje? Bloos, wannet senne mott."

Joh, oba wie wulle je dem Fesch doch noch weaje, wiels sesst jleewt je tjeena eenem daut; daut ess doamett uck nuscht nijch aundasch auls mett de U.F.O's. Aulwada een Probleem: Ungasch ähre Wijchschol tjlintjt bie sasshundat Pund ut, enn soo nauhm Ungasch Obraum enn etj eene Tjriezsoag enn schneede dem Joonah enne Medd derjch, enn fief Minute lohta wisst de haulwe mennische Welt dann uck, daut tweemol sasshundat Pund emmahan twalwhundat Pund jefft, enn woomäjlijch een Rekord wea.

Jenuag: daut jintjch dann uck fuats seea doll enn meea auls hundat Desche enne Nohbaschauft knoade enn stände, enn

However, after the fun of it wore off, Jonah had had enough of the freeloader and he whipped his tail with gusto sending Peterkin flying off through the air. When, the next day the fish had finally fulfilled his calling and had found his final resting place in the belly pits of half of the Old Colony, Little Peter told me that he had flown so high that he spied the Lorelei on the Rhine from his lofty flight. But then when I asked him if this were really so, he re-located the Lorelei to Kiew, slightly less distant, and I accepted his reduced fare.

And so this boy learned a valuable lesson, meaning that the truth must prevail even if your name is Thiessen, according to the time honoured maxim: "Exaggerate? Sure, but lie? Only if need be."

Joh, but we have every intention of weighing the fish, for otherwise no one will believe this grand, true story; no different from the thousands of UFO sightings, but where's the evidence? A problem, yet again. The Unger scale had a limit of six hundred pounds and so Unger's Abraham and I took a cross saw and cut Jonah into two sections and five minutes later half of the Mennonitism of the world knew that two times six hundred pound amounts to twelve hundred pounds and represented a record.

And so, things got very busy since a hundred tables and more had to be set up in the immediate vicinity and shortly these stood neatly arranged and all moaning and creaking with crooked legs on account of all the giant dishes of Jonah catfish and their collective weight on festive wedding tables.

By way of conclusion, it should be mentioned that the grandchild of the bridal couple happens to be the Kasper guy here mentioned and since he is a man who combines a brilliant career in banking with honesty bordering on boring, probably another first in the Mennonite fold, it is time he were honoured by having a commensurately huge fish mounted to the immediate right of the main entrance to the

tjreaje kromme Been von aul de Komme enn Schiewe voll Joonawels.

Enn noch waut aundret too Schluss: De Grootsähn von dee Brutlied, aulso de Hermaun Freese, dee je kratjcht dann Tjast haude, ess dee jenannda Kauspasch Hein, woohna Jrienthol, enn uck mie een bät too de Woahrheit verholp, enn enne Credit Union de Easchta Offiziea word. Enn wann etj een bät meea vonne Fundraisers hild, wudd etj bedde, daut soo boold auls mäjlijch enne steinbachsche Credit Union een Dentjmol fe Henry Kasper mett dem Fesch oppstalle sulle. Wiels ohne de Joonawels enn sien wundaboaret Fleesch wea diss Molodetjs Henritj, dee Freese Grootsähn aulso, enn mien Frind nijch soohn vetraffelja Tjeadel jeworde!

N. B. Wiels wie enn disse Jeschijcht ons soo meea gaunz aune Woahrheit jehoole habe, sull etj noch erwähne, daut de Nippa goot dree Zoll flacha word auls de Joonawels endlijch von mien Voda enn dee twee Kuntasch rutjetrocke word. Daut saul sijch oba mett'e Tiet wada utjejlitjcht habe, head etj saje.

Steinbach Credit Union. If I had not long since sworn off all involvements in Fundraisers, I would assume personal initiative in the matter. It's obvious enough that he got the proper start for any venture as a grandson of the wedding couple of that memorable day.

N. B. Since it is fully obvious that the truth not be spared in the telling of the tale, it should be mentioned that the water level of the Dnieper fell by a full three inches after the Jonah catfish was finally dragged out by my father and the two geldings. I heard say that nature over the years has corrected this shortfall.

Tiendusend Dohla
($10,000.00)

Auls etj vondoag eenen anonymen Breef mett een Scheck äwa tiendusend Dohla tjreajch, mott etj dochwoll een bät domm jetjitjt habe, wiels Mister, ons dietscha Schäfahund, betracht mie dree Sekundelang, enn fung dann opp Dietsch aun too juhle. Tjeen Wunda. Woo foaken tjrijcht Onsaeena tiendusend Dohla enn eenem Klompe ver Weihnacht soo meea boa oppe Haund? Bie mie ess daut selden, enn etj freid mie.

Enn wiels Wiehnachte doatoo ess, daut eena sijch freit, enn soohne Freid uck deehle saul, well etj dit uck fuats berejchte, enn junt dann lenjere Tiet en Ruh lohte.

Daut kaum soo…Wann eena sijch aum Hoat opereare lat, dann mott eena een gaunzen Wesch Papiere unjaschriewe. Etj hab dee nijch jetalt, oba daut kunne weens twalw Stetjch jewast ooda uck jewese senne. Waut etj aules unjaschräwe hab, weet etj nijch, oba daut wea dochwoll meea auls etj docht. Wiels? Joh, wiels, soo auls jesajcht, etj hab eenen haulwwäjes grooten Scheck vondoag jetjräje, die bie auldem rutkaum, enn dee haft mett miene Hoatoperatsjoon too doohne.

Daut heat sijch eenfach nijch aultoo schmock, oba etj hab vesproake bie de Woahrheit too bliewe, enn daut Woahr- heitspeat lentjcht mie toop mett aule dusende nieschieje Lesasch enn disse Rejchtung: Daut haud sijch dochwoll soo

Ten Thousand Dollars
($10,000.00)

When I received an anonymous letter today with a check enclosed in the amount of ten thousand dollars, I must have broken out into a stupid grin because Mister, my German Shepherd, looked me over and then started to howl in our native tongue. Small wonder. How often does such a one as I receive such a pile of money just before Christmas? Rarely, and I was delighted.

And since Christmas is meant to be a festival of joy, and one is meant to share happy tidings, I intend to do just that and then mind my happy business for days on end, grinning secretly to myself.

How did this all come about, you'd obviously like to know? If you are to undergo surgery, explicitly a series of heart by-passes, one is required to sign a whole ream of documents. I did not count them all, but they may well have amounted to twelve in number. As to what I all signed, I do not know, but probably a few more than I remember. The bottom line is that I today received a sizeable check and that check has everything to do with my heart operation.

None of what I have to report sounds all that good, or even modest, but I have no choice in the matter, since I am a man of few words and such words invariably approximate fidelity. The horse which I intend to mount and ride today, is the steed of honesty and it takes me straight to the thousands of readers

langsom rommjerät, daut etj uck goode Siede aun mie, enn enn mie, hab enn dit haft aulatoop doatoo jefeaht, daut Mensche sijch nu doch fe mien plautdietschen-tjristlijchen Bennamensch intresseare, enn eenfach aun mien DNA biekrupe wulle. Enn wiels etj normalawies doch väl too deemootijch sie, omm soowaut tootoolohte, haude sijch doch een poah opp Schlitjwäj aun mienen Dokta, dee mien Hoat verr twee Joah enn fief Moonat opereare wull enn sull enn uck deed, raunjemoakt, enn ahm jefroagt, auls hee nijch een bät von mien Hoat, wann hee daut aul soo straum bie de Operatsjoon enne Henj hilt enn gootmootijch haujre wudd, nijch vleijcht een bätje von dee Sied oode uck vonne schmockste Städ von miene Valentienmaschien enn een Glaustje lieseltjess nennstritjche kunn, enn ahn dann opp disse Oat mien DNA vemeddle?

Enn bie aul de Oppräjness bie de Operatsjoon, enn miene sesstje groote Leewtolijchtjeit, hab etj dochwoll eenen Vertrag unjaschräwe, enn irjendeene Lady ooda uck twee wulle mien Hoat sijch too Hoate nehme, enn see deele nu opp ähre Oat mien Hoat fe sijch enn ähre Tjinja, enn wäaweet, waut see noch aules mett mien Bennaschtet väahabe omm een bätje Oafgoot sijch enntoofuppre?

Enn soo kaum daut aulatoop. Auls etj mie dann doch dee unjaschräwne Papiere vondoag zeowentz derjchlaus, sach etj uck, wäa sijch, sootoosaje, aun miene Bennakaunt vejräpe haud, biejekrope wea, sootoosaje, enn etj phoond ahr, enn deed seea mennisch enn säd, daut haud etj doch uck soo seea jearn omsonst jedohne; eena mott je auls Mennist doch reed senne "Opfa too brinje" enn etj wull uck noch wiedret vetalle, woohnt je eenem soo ver Weihnachte uck leijcht fellt, oba see schneet mie auf enn säd: "Nä, nä! leewa Frind, etj sie uck mennisch, enn wann etj eenen Bargain seeh, dann foht etj too. Dankscheen! Enn nu woa etj noch joahrelang, hopentlijch

I have gained over many years, with the majority of these settling for nothing less than home-made truth. Somehow word must have gotten around that I have well hidden streaks of virtue in me, good sides to my rounded features, and this had obviously attracted a secret admirer or two, at most, and who have taken an interest in me and in my Low German Christian inner man and were intent on snooping around in my DNA, if not downright prepared to acquire a sample of it. Since I am normally much too humble to permit such audacities, mild-mannered and well intentioned as they may be, those ever on the lurk for forbidden fruits in their many forms, had obviously found some sneaky way of establishing contact with the operating doctor two years and five months ago. Since my doctor, a former student, has a stellar reputation, world-wide, and is known for his brilliance, but also his benevolence, he had obviously succumbed to their urgent pleas and agreed to stroking tiny amounts of my DNA into their sterilized vials, brought along for the occasion, while gently fondling my Valentine machine in his skillful hands during the "surgical procedure."

On account of all the excitement during the operation, and my proverbial loving kindness shot through with copious amounts of compassion to boot, I must have signed a document enabling some lady or other, or both, to take my heart to heart and so, obviously, she had intentions of pocketing my noble essence as she perceived it, for her and her future progeny, and who knows what else she might have in mind when going for my genetic propensities?

And that is how it all came about. When I tonight finally took a closer look at all the papers I had signed, I noticed name and address of the party who had managed to gain access to my secret chambers, and so I phoned her and gave her the Mennonite treatment, claiming, as I did, that I would dearly have loved to accommodate her every request free of

mien Hoat mett Die deehle, enn daut fe Die enn Diene Sach puttre lohte. Freist Du Die nijch?"

"Joh."

"Dann Froohe Wiehnacht, enn daut gaunz von Nieem Hoate!"

"Enn Die uck!" säd etj, enn sung bieaun mett Betoonung "Ein reines Herz, Herr schaff in mir!"

charge, and to that end I would obviously have been prepared to make all manner of sacrifices, and whatever else comes to mind during the festive season, but she cut me off in mid air, saying, "No, no, my dear and good friend, I, too, am a Mennonite and so, when I see a bargain, I go for it! Thank you from the bottom of my heart! And as of now I am about to share my heart with you for years on end and let it putter for you and your ways. Does that not make your day a happy one?"

"You betcha!"

"Merry Christmas to you and I mean that from the cockles of my new heart."

"And the same to you!" I responded, while she softly, but with as much feeling as she could muster, hummed, "Yours is my heart alone!" and added "Dein ist mein ganzes Herz!" in German, which is at the heart of the Christmas season.

Entretjt

Auls etj noh Dietschlaund kaum, wea etj noch meist soohne mennlijche Jungfrau auls de measchte mennische Tjriste daut send, enn uck aul emma measchtens weare. Mie latjt de Tugend vonne Näs, enn etj wea soohn jehuarsomma Jinja mett toojeschneadne Betjze, enn reine Unjabetjze volla "Du mottst een goodet Biespell senne" met reinem, feinem Siedtwärem utjeneit.

"Die Zeit ist kurz, o Mensch sei weise...

Laß eine gute Spur zurück..." sung eene Melodie rundommeklock enn jiedet Oah.

Oba daut sull nijch doabie bliewe, enn wann etj nijch ver Sonneunjagang vondoag doavon berejchte woa, fangt miene Tugendnäs wada aun too latje.

Wie saute emm enjlischen Seminar enn Marburg, enn doa, wiels etj goot Enjlisch kunn, kunn etj mien Lijcht scheen dache lohte, enn Peihohn met bunten Zoagel späle. Enn bie aule Demoot, jintj mie daut aulnoch scheen een bätje too stolzeare. Vondoag wea von James "The Turn of the Screw" aune Reaj, enn uck "For whom the Bell Tolls" von Hemingway oppem Jeleadenzaddel.

Aule groote Literatua haft daut aun sijch, kratjt soo auls een Iesboajch, daut mau een bät bowe rutstatjt, daut measchte blifft unjrem Wotaspeajel, ooda uck enne Betjze, unjrem Pojas, sootoosaje, vestoake.

Mie jäjenäwa aun eenem vonne groote Desche saut jeweehnlijch een Freilein Nohmens Liesa Butefisch. See wea ella, oba schmock, enn see schmeatjt selwstjedreide Paparossie, soo

152

Enraptured, or A Fall in the Spring

When I first arrived in Germany, I was a virgin Mennonite Christian youth like most others are, and have always been. Virtue leaked from my nose, and I was an obedient disciple with tight fitting pants and spotless shorts, full of "setting a good example" embroidered with silk yarn on my drawers.

"Time is short, oh man be wise…

And leave behind a worthy track…" was the melody ringing around the clock in my every ear.

However, I was heading for a conversion of inversion, and if I do not report on my Waterloo, my virtuous nose will shortly break out again in a bothersome leak.

We were studiously engaged in an English seminar in Marburg, and since I knew English well, I was able to keep my light shining and play the peacock with a gaudy rudder. In spite of all my humility, I rather enjoyed strutting my stuff, particularly if an audience was handy. Henry James "Turning of the Screw" was due tonight, as was "For whom the Bell Tolls" by Hemingway on the scholarly agenda.

Great literature has in common with an iceberg that only a bit breaks the surface, most of it remains hidden below the water line, or pants for that matter, where essentials are contained by a belt.

Opposite to me at a great table sat one Miss Liesa Butefisch; she was older than average but very well kept and she smoked hand rolled cigarettes as was in vogue at the time. Moreover, she took a shine to my presence, and even a shy country

auls daut too dee Tiet noch mood wea. Butadem muak see
mie Uage, daut word sogoa soo een fromma Butendarpa auls
etj enn. Etj schmeatjt nijch, oba mie kaum trotzdem aulnoch
ernoa Ruak ut miene Näs; mien Heiligenschien, uck Halo
jenannt, wea soo heilijch, daut dee reatjad.

Etj räd donn kratjt soo auls de Dietsche daut jearn enn väl
doohne, groote Ooltnäsijchtjeite, enn kaum mie doabie, kratjt
soo's daut mott wann eena enn Dietschlaund studeat,
wijchtijch enn jegrommt väa. Omm soo meea wundad mie
daut Liesa mett eenmol lieseltjes ver sijch han säd:

"Grau ist alle Theorie,
Doch grün der Lebensbaum."

Enn auls see daut säd, plintjad see mie polluksch too, enn
schmustad, enn nijch blooß daut…auls wie ons em Seminar
aunfonge too jachte, woo eena the screw turns, aulso dee
Schruw dreiht, aum basten äwasatte sull, dann stritjt Liesa
mie unjrem Desch mett een jeheemet Beentje ooda Footje
äwa mien Schänebeen, enn puttad bie mie aun mien rajchten
Ballyschooh aun.

Na, soo waut wea mie nijch mol enne MCI enn Gretna
pesseat, enn etj veschluckt mie, enn kaum daut mett dem
Odme meist nijch noh. Wäa haud daut jedocht? docht etj
mie…

Oba daut sull aun dem Fahrjoaschowend noch dolla kohme,
wiels Liesa haud Fiea jefoht, enn wull mie aunstetje, enn
miene Onschuld begnaubere, enn doamett unje aunfange,
weens soo kaum mie daut väa. Daut Thema wea bie
Hemingway enn sien wackelnda Tjlinja aunjekohme, enn
langsom fong uck dee nu aun too bimmle, wiels Liesa haud
mien rajchten Schooh mett ähre boafte Feetjess utjetrocke,
enn schoof mie den unjrem Desch tridj, enn mie ohnd waut,
joh, mie jintj een Lijcht opp. Enn daut Lijcht word egol dacha,
enn dacha! Etj trock den Schooh stickum nohda, enn sach,
daut Liesa een Schneppelduaktje doanenn jelajt haud. Mie

bumpkin, like my pious self, from a remote village, noticed her eye on me. I did not smoke and yet, quite a bit of smoke issued forth from my nostrils; my *Heiligenschein* aka halo was so hot and holy that it smoked.

At the time I had already learned to behave like a German university student, and I spouted a lot of state of the art, cutting edge pomposities, and felt both important and erudite while so doing. Suddenly my attention took a spell of a surprise as Liesa quoted Goethe's Faust into space:
"Grey and dull, all theory
But green abounds life's budding tree."
And, shortly after softly sharing her little memorized commentary with some of us in the know, she directed a secretive glance at me across the table while coyly smiling... and not only that...when we started arguing how best to translate the screw turns, or how, and if the turning screw could be managed, Liesa stroked my shin with an invisible foot and knocked softly at the sole of my Bally shoe.

Well, this had not even happened to me at the Mennonite Collegiate Institute in Gretna and I now I choked a bit and had difficulty maintaining the rhythm of my breathing. "Who would ever have thought of life's surprises, such as these," I thought to myself.

And yet, things were to get much worse on that fair spring evening, since Liesa had caught fire and wanted to spread it in my direction and nibble at my virginity, and to that end she started at the bottom of things, or so it would appear. The topic of discourse had arrived at Hemingway's Bell which shortly began tolling in my direction since Liesa had slipped off my right shoe with her barefoot toes, and when she pushed it gently back to me under the table, I sensed real trouble; I saw a light of sorts. And that light became bright, then brighter! I rather surreptitiously pulled back my shoe and took a look, and could not believe what Liesa had been up to,

schweet mett eenomol soo auls aule Donna, enn Liesa haud mie, sootoosaje, Help toojeschowe. Etj wescht mie den Schweet, enn Liesa tjijchad, oba mau soo's eene Turtelduw.

Etj trock mie mien Schooh wada aun, enn docht aune schwoare Laust vonne Tugend, väle, väle Joahre oppjespoat, enn vespruak trotz groote Vesuchung fromm, oba blooß fromm too senne, enn too bliewe. Wann eena fromm senne well, kohme mie emma seea huagdietsche Weda, soo's jehorsaum em Dentj.

Daut Seminar muak Pause, enn wiels etj Onnwada wittad, docht etj, etj sull vleijcht blooß bosijch noch mien Quateea schibble, enn vonne mäjlijche Sind, soo auls Joseph em Oolen Testament uttjniepe. Blooß daut Barfüssertor delenjd, enn mie verre aunkohmende Sind enn Versuchunge (aulwada Huagdietsch, wiels daut aulatoop soo earnst word) hinjre Däah bie mie enn miene tugendhaufte Stow vestätje. Etj ohnd Trubbel en mien Moralbereich, enn mie schweet noch emma, kratjt soo's Tus wietauf enn Kanada frähjoah biem utmeste. Ooda noch dolla. Uck word mien Odem knaup, wann etj aun Liesa enn äah Schneppelduak docht, enn woo sie mie daut enn mien Schooh tooschoof. Em Schnellepduak em Schooh? Wäa kunn opp soohne Jedanke kohme, woo ess daut blooß aulatoop mäjlijch?

Daut Seminar fung wada aun, enn nu saut etj wada kratjt oppe selwje Städ, enn docht, "Waut nu?" Haud Hemingway daut uck mol soo schwoa jehaut auls etj? Woo woat dis Dach endje?

Oba etj wea je een tjoanja, stoatja Maun, volla Tugend, enn een Väabild fe aule, enn stiew volla Onschuld, oba etj haud noch nijch literarischet ooda moralischet Betjannis auf-jelajcht, auls Liesa mie aulwada omme Atj leewtolijch tooplintjad, enn mie mien rajchten Ballyschooh verre Däah unjrem Desch, sootoosaje, tooschoof, enn mie ditmol sogoa mien Tjnee stritjt. Daut Schneppelduak musst aulwada

down there; she had placed a handkerchief in my Bally. I broke out in a real sweat with Liesa providing a bit of solace for the occasion of the hour. I wiped my brow, while Liesa giggled, a chortle, more like a turtle dove.

I casually returned my shoe to its proper place and sought refuge in the reservoir of virtue, filled up over many, many years, and now promised to be good, really good, even in the face of temptation. Anytime I make pious resolves of chastity, I invariably seek refuge in the language of prayer and church, High German, where I manage to locate the term obedient humility more readily.

The seminar took a break, and since I sensed heavy weather ahead, I entertained returning to the safety of my living quarters and flee, like Joseph in the Old Testament, in the direction of virtue and virginity. Just sprint down the Barfüssertor (Barefoot Alley) and hide behind the door of my trusted quarters from impending sin and temptations (back to High German vocabulary).

I smelled trouble in the realm of morality, and I was sweating heavily, just as in my better days while mucking out the stable. Only that my sweating was more profuse.

And also my breathing became laboured and heavy laden when I thought of Liesa and her handkerchief. A hankie in my shoe, really? Who would ever arrive at such a notion?

The seminar resumed and I was sitting on the same spot, thinking to myself, "What now? Had Hemingway ever had such a hard time of it? How is this day meant to end?"

But I was a sturdy, stalwart man in my best years, full of home-grown resolve and an example to many and stiffly chocked full of innocence, but I had not yet borne literary or moral testimony as I intended to do, when Liesa again gave me a sly wink, while sliding my right Bally shoe to the door of my feet and, stroking my knee under the table. The handkerchief again had to resume its mission as I bent to

jehearijch deehne, auls etj mie nu betjcht, omm mie wada miene latzte Liebeslohd too betjitje. Enn wess woah! Ditmol haud Liesa ähre schmocke lilableiwe Unjabetjstjess doanenna jelajcht, enn nu bimmeld mie dee Hemingway-Tjlinja gaunz donnasche enne Uahre, enn etj kunn mie nijch meea rade.

Tjeene twintijch Pead haude mie rade kunnt, auls etj nohm Seminarschluß Liesa opp aule Been hinjeraun wackeld.

Weidenhäuserstraße 47 oppem Tweeden Stock wohnd see, enn doa schorrd aun dem Owend miene Onschuld, miene Tugend, enn aul miene, mett säwentwintijch Joah een bestje morsch jewordne Heilijchtjeit toop.

Etj wisst noch nijch waut mie pessead wea, auls Liesa mie daut Wuat fohte, woohnt wie Tus "rautze" nannde, enn aule Sproake mett eenmol biebrocht. See läd mie ähre schmocke Beentjess omm mien Hauls, enn foot mie mett dee soo iewrijch oba uck leeftolijch omm, auls wann sijch Frindschauft aul dartijch Joahlang ut Rußlaund, ooda sogoa Sibierjen kohmend, nijch jeseehne haud.

Nohm dredden Mol bielohte, kaum etj wada een tjlien bät too mie, enn docht, etj wea entretjt. Enn wann nijch etj, dann aul de Äwaje. Etj fuah flucks enne Betjze nenn, enn schibbeld fuats nohm Baptistenheim, woa aule Huagbetjeade wohnde, enn biem Doahanranne, wad etj, daut dee aula veschwunge senne wudde.

Oba nuscht nijch wea. Dee lage sijch doa romm, haude von The Screw Turns tjeene Ohninj, enn von Whom the Bell Tolls noch weinja, enn wulle, soo's auls äah groota Chef, dee Baptisten Prädja Hans Hattenhauer opp Englisch säd "do a little Bible with you, brother."

Oba etj wea enjeworde, daut dee breeda Wajch dijcht biem schmaulen Tugendwajch vondoag mett eenmol väl mackelja too piljre jintj. Omme tweede Atj stund miene Mutta wada soo's jeweehnlijch, oba stautt mie too vemohne, tjitjt see mie vestendnisvoll aun, enn weifeld mie leewtolijch mett ährem

inspect my recent load of love under the table. And sure enough: This time around Liesa had deposited her pretty little violet blue panties into my Bally while the Hemingway Bell was now thundering in my every ear. I was beyond all salvation.

No twenty horses would have been able to contain me as I loped with a list after Liesa once the seminar ended. Weidenhäuser Street Number 47, second storey was her address, and it was there that my virginity and my virtue, and all my holiness accumulated over a span of twenty seven years—granted a trifle frayed at the edges—surrendered unconditionally, simply capitulated, in the face of such well stocked erotic arsenal.

I had not yet come to my senses when Liesa gave me a tutorial in wrestling, which we called grappling back home. She placed her shapely legs around my neck and administered a home-made embrace with much eager vigor like relatives do when they meet again after thirty years separation from Russia, or Siberia for that matter.

After the third coming, I regained a semblance of my senses and knew I had been enraptured. And if not, surely all the others had been taken home. I punched my legs back into my pants with a vengeance (they had made me do it) and briskly took off, straight for the Baptist Home, where all the really saved resided, and as I shuffled along, I was concluding bets with myself that they would all be gone, gone, disappeared!

But nothing of the sort had happened. The converted lounged around, had no idea about the Turning of the Screw, and even less about For whom the Bell Tolls, and wanted to, as their head honcho, the Baptist minister, Hans Hattenhauer, said, in English, "do a little Bible with you, brother."

However, I had that spring evening discovered that the broad way alongside the narrow path of virtue provided much more commodious pilgrimming. Around the second

Schalduak too. Enn dann wea etj uck aul wada bie Liesa unjre Datjch aunjekohme, omm bie ahr miene näjchste schwoare Load auftoolaje.

corner of my frantic journey my mother stood, as usual, but instead of lowering the boom of the Riot Act, she looked at me with compassionate understanding, and gently waved at me with her good-natured apron. Within minutes, I had again arrived undercover at Liesa's love nest where I laid off my final load of heaviness for the day.

Wann Jie daut bue

"Wann Jie daut bue
Woat daut Woatj:
Etj moak den Räjen
Enn Jie dee Oatj."

Auls Gott soo red, wea Hee jrods doabie pienich Enjlisch
enn Plautdietsch too leahre, enn daut wea uck kratjt dee
Tiet auls Hee dee Oatj, woohne Hee uck Ark nannd, ennet
Wota schoof.

Eena haft hopentlich doafäa Vestendnis, woaromm etj
eascht nu, too gooda latzt, mien grootet Weete enn disse Sach
toom Utdruck brinj. Dee Auntwuat ess eenfach: Jeat Ens, dee
latzta Bauß vonne MCI storf latst, enn nu ess de Tiet jekohme,
siene Jeheemnisse uttookrohme. Enn von dee jefft daut eenje
Doose voll.

Aulso schnalt Junt schmock aun, enn dann well wie foahre!

Jeat Ens, ooda noch rejchtja, Gerhard Ens wea een
Jeschichtla von Gottes Jnod; hee vestund sien Metier. Daut
hee seea oolt word stund ahm too Good; hee kunn sich aun
meist aules dentje, woavon hee red and leahd. Sien Jedächtnis
fong bie Bismarck aun, enn leet nich noh. Enn daut ess uck
toom Deel woarom etj ernoa väl weet: hee wea mien Leahra.
Butadem wea Gerhard Ens aulnoch opprejchtich, eene
Tugend, dee nich opp aule Prädjasch too traft.

Daut ess uck wijchtich too erwähne, daut Ens obzwoa
Leahra enn Prädja, uck een eenjemohta jescheida Mensch
wea, wann hee uck mau von Reinlaud kaum. Hee wea

If you will build it

"If you will build it
They'll come to park,
I'll let it rain
You build the Ark."

When God thus spoke, He was busily studying English and Low German, and that, coincidentally, was also exactly the time when He had the Ark, which he called His schooner, committed to water.

Obviously and understandably, you wonder why I only now intend to reveal my considerable knowledge of these things, the answer to which is simple: George Ens, the last great head honcho of the MCI recently died, and the time has come to exhibit his secrets, many in number.

So, fasten your seatbelts and hang on!

George Ens, or, more accurately Gerhard Ens was an historian of God's grace; he knew his métier. The fact that he lived a very long life was a professional asset; he could remember most everything of which he spoke and taught. His memory started in the Bismarck era and never let up. And such, in part, is why I am fairly knowledgeable myself; he was my teacher. Moreover, Gerhard Ens was also known for his honesty, a virtue not attributable to all men of the Word.

It is important to note that although a minister and teacher he was also a relatively decent enough human being, with more integrity than even most of the Reinlander. This is a contagious property. I mention this only because as a

opprejchtich. Soohnt stetjt aun. Etj erwähn dit blooß, wiels etj auls Benjel twee ooda dreemol biem Jeschichtevetalle vesocht too äwadriewe, oba daut word nuscht, enn boold säde de Mensche etj wea jlitjwajch enn sogoa eendoontijch. Aulso hab etj miene deemootje Opprejchtichtjeit toom Deel von Jeat Ens, dem Prädja.

Daut Äwaje aun miene Opprejchtichtjeit tjemmt von Ruth Wiebe, dee mie aul von dee Tiet aun tjannt, auls etj Betjze mett lange Lempe aunfong too droage. Ruth tjannt mie aul lang enn goot, enn helt opp mie. Enn soo pessead daut, daut aune Dazumal, ruhm hundat Joah ver Frähjoah, see mie twee Tickets gauf omm oppe Jungernfoaht vonne benannde Oatj too reise.

Dit stemmt oba doch nich gaunz, enn miene Natua mald sich, bie de Woahrheit too bliewe. Ruth gauf mie, gratis, twee Bed and Breakfast Billets ooda Tickets fe de Oatjfoaht. Enn, soo's jesajcht, omsonst, ween's soo meea. Auls Dankboatjeit velangd see, daut etj Noah loht zeowends biem Auffoodre halpe sull, besondasch waut Pead enn Tjeaj aunbelangt. Etj naum dee Tickets dankboa, enn mett mien Hoot enne Haund, aun.

Nu fellt mie oba doch bie: Ruth stalld noch eene wiedre Bedinjung: Etj sull tjen Wuat von disse Erfoahrunge vetalle ooda schriewe, bett Leahra Gerhard Ens von Reinlaund nohm hejchren Bähn utjewaundat wea. Enn wiels Ens nu wajch ess, opp emma utjewaundat, ess de Tiet jekohme, daut Gaunze too vetalle, wiels miene Vetalblos mie schudahauftijch dretjt, enn mie Orda jefft, etj saul noch vondoag dee wertjelje Jeschijcht von Noah ann siene Oatj vetalle.

Jieda, dee enne Sinndachschool eenjamohte oppjepausst haft, enn sogoa enne MCI Weetenschauft utem Schleef jedrunke haft, tjannt dee Jeschijcht von Noah enn siene Oatj jeneiw.

youngster I may once or twice have exaggerated the telling of a tale, but otherwise I was so honest that I came across as monotonous and even boring. And so, obviously, I have come by my honesty and even truthfulness in part from Gerhard Ens and I even admit to it, even though he was a preacher.

The rest of my honest framework comes directly from Ruth Wiebe, who has known me from the day I wore my first long-limbed pants. Ruth does not only know me long and well, she even takes kindly to me. And so it happened that three days before yesteryear commenced, she gave me two free passes, also termed billets by people of my learned stature, for the maiden voyage of the Ark.

This is not altogether accurate as is my nature and so I intend to correct this slight deviance from virgin truth. Ruth gave me two bed and breakfast tickets for the Ark. And free of charge, gratis, if you will, at least damn near: By way of recompense I had to assist Noah with the late night chores pertaining explicitly to the horses and cows. I accepted the tickets with due gratitude.

And, yes, Ruth posted another stipulation: I was not to reveal a word about my experiences until Teacher Gerhard Ens from Reinland had migrated to the offices of The Higher Ministry. And since he has done just that or, he has just done that, the time has come for me to tell the tale, since my raconteurial bladder urges for release as to how the story of Noah and his Ark transpired.

Anyone who has paid some degree of attention at Sunday School and also at the MCI, has a pretty accurate under-standing of the workings of Noah and the Ark.

Such not in the know will today receive a tutorial in these matters. Most importantly, there are two matters related to this story which are not generally known. Number One: God also permitted two people of every kind to board the Ark, but, since the Mennonites could not agree on who qualified, God

Soohne, dee mol wada nich oppjepausst habe, woare vondoag enn soohne Sache derjch mie beleaht. Wijchtijch ess too behoole, daut daut twee Sache toom Thema jefft, dee nich bekaunt send. Numma Eent: Gott gauf Erlaubnis daut twee Mensche von jieda Sort uck oppe Oatj Schulinj seatje durwe, oba wiels de Mennoniete sich nich eenje kunne, gauf Gott ahn, aulso ons, de Frieheit, sass Menniste doanenna krupe too lohte: twee Ooltkoloniea, twee Molotschna enn twee vonne Breedajemeend. Ahm bleef eajentlich nuscht nich aundret äwrijch, wiels dee Stund enntoostiehe wea jekohme, enn donn gauf daut soohn Pu-Hu, enn soo väl Jejacht, enn Jezank, daut de leewa Gott de Henj ve luta Vetwievelung enne Hejcht schmeet, enn lud word, auls Hee roopt: "O.K., O.K., heat blooß opp. Stop! Stoj! Jie tjenne sass von june Sort oppe Oatj schetje, oba dit Jejacht enn june Jemeend mott oppheare, fuats oppe Städ!"

De tweede Sach ess kratjt soo eenfach. Weens bett vondoag: Etj woa, eea de vondoagsche Sonn unjajeiht, Junt kratjt vetalle, woa dee Oatj schließlich enn endlich daut Anka em Wota schmeet, enn woa Gott enn Noah ähre groote Lomm too finje ess.

Na, enn nu weet Jie soo meist aules enn weete uck, woaromm Gerhard Ens noch soohn weetenden Schmusta em Soatj druag. Hee wisst waut, waut wie nich wisste, oba hee wisst uck, daut dee Dach kohme wudd aun dem etj daut aules utkrohme wudd. Doawäjen sien Schmusta!

Oba nu schwind tridj noh dee Oatj, sesst lajcht Noah noch ohne ons auf!

Kratjt soo's bie de CNN enn aul de Breaking News, jieda rettlang, jintj daut oppe Oatj too. Auls de Foaht endlich loos jintj, wea jieda schmock, enn fein, enn fromm, enn dankboa, enn deemootijch, enn een jiedra jintj aun siene Oabeit; oba auls donn de Räjen kaum, enn dann uck fuats Ammawies poascht, enn dann daut uck noch Wind enn Storm gauf, enn

permitted six of the faith to board: two Old Koloniers, two Molotschnaers, and two Brethren. He really had no choice in the matter because that hour of decision caused such an uproar, so much arguing and quarrelling and so much dissension, that He simply threw up His hands in despair and cried, "Okay, okay, ust stop. Stop! You are allowed to send six of your kind to the Ark, but I will not tolerate any further arguments and trouble in your congregational ranks!"

And matter number two is very simple, even if a great, indeed secret mystery. At least up till today: I will, before the setting of today's sun, tell you exactly where the Ark finally dropped anchor and where it can be located.

Well, and now you know most everything and also know why Gerhard Ens wore a smile when knowingly reposing in the coffin. He knew something we didn't know, and he also knew that one day I would tell his story. His farewell smile revealed the pleasure of knowing.

But back to the Ark for otherwise Noah might just take off without me.

Similarly, to the news on earth, breaking news, transpired on the Ark. At the outset everyone was well behaved, and pious and grateful and humble and everyone going about assigned duties, but when the showers came, and then the rain, and then pouring rain and then torrential downpour, and howling of storms, formerly good behaviour and many promises slackened and the inhabitants of the Ark, including Mennonites started, as Luther observes of the Children of Israel, to "murmur".

The first hour or so when the Ark gradually took to water and animals and humankind swam after the Ark in frantic supplication, like the finest of "Nippaenja", meaning those semi-godless roughnecks from Elloag, people both here and there had little to say; their gratitude was simply too overwhelming. But then when the exceptional became

daut de Tietäwa, Dach enn Nacht soo's utem Faut Wota von bowe strulld, leeht daut goode Benehme noh, enn väle Vesprätjunge worde schlaup, enn dee Oatj-Ennwohna, uck de Mennoniete, funge aun, soo's Luther von dem Volk Israel schrift, "too murre." See gromsaujde, schindeade, wattade, enn weare oppstoonoasch, enn heiwtänsch biem Räde.

De easchte Stund, auls de Oatj sich oppem Wota macklich muak, schwomme Tiere enn Veeh enn Mensche bie de Dusende ons hinjeraun, enn jaumade enn prachade enn hielde, wiels see mettfoahre wulle. Enn wie oppe Oatj weare dankboa enn vejnäjt, enn weare ons aulatoop goot. Oba, soo's daut dann soo ess, wann daut Butajeweehnelje toom Auldach woat, leeht daut goode, dankboare Benehme boold noh, enn de goastaje Oat buhd sich em menschlijchen Hoat wada Nasta.

Dit troff uck fe de Mennoniete oppe Oatj too.

Den easchten Owend sung wie jemeenschauftlich "Ströme des Segens" enn "Wirf ihm das Seil zu" enn uck "Bruder, laß den Mut nicht sinken" enn wie bäde schmock enn räde sinn-doagschet Plautdietsch. Oba aum tweeden Dach, bestunde de Molotschna aul opp meea Rasiene emm Bobbat, enn see wulle wittet Bultje stautt Groffbroot, enn uck ditjen Schmaund too de Howajrett aunstautt Schliesamaltj, enn Tweeback mett Konfitüre, aulso dobbelt jeschmät, während de Ooltkoloniea sich noch bescheide mett Derjchnettskost toofräd gauwe.

Daut aundre oppe Doagesrejista wea daut ua-oolet mennische Probleem von de Doop, enn woo wie daut begohne sulle. Aul daut Jeräd von "rain checks" wea nu vebie, uck vonne dreaje Dartjajoahre word nich meea jeschwietat. Wann daut Probleeme gauf, vetald Noah daut dem leewen Gott, dee jieden Owend biem Schemmawoare oppudckt. Hee saut dann hinje oppem Afterdeck, schmeatjt Piep, enn besorjt siene Arbusebestaund. "Joh!" säd de Oola, "daut Obraumtje

routine, good behaviour let up and naughtiness asserted itself in the human condition.

This was true of us Mennonites as well: The first evening we sang in common accord "Streams of Blessing", "Throw out the lifeline", and "Brother, you're drifting too far from shore!"and we prayed nicely, and all spoke Sunday-like Plautdietsch, but come the second day, the Molotschnaer already demanded raisin bread with two scoops of raisins, instead of dark rye bread, and coffee with heavy cream and oat meal porridge, with an extra dash of cream instead of skim milk, and buns with marmalade instead of no spread at all, even though the Altkolonier and the Old Order were still quite humbly satisfied with average fare.

And next on the agenda was the age-old problem of the God anointed form of baptism and how now to go about it. It was obvious to all that the rain check stunt had now become all too literal. This problem resolved itself with dispatch because Noah reported the squabble to the dear Lord, who arrived every evening without fail, and sat afterdecks, smoking his pipe and tending his watermelon patch. And sure enough, the Old Fellow, as he was widely called, said that He intended to grow watermelons, His favourite fruit, since a goodly slice of choice watermelon, center cut, was just as important to Him as a good pipe of tobacco, after dinner with a glass of German pilsner beer served with a hefty roast of pork. Obviously we Mennonites aboard God's schooner were no match for the Jews and since they had gained the upper hand with their Grand Chief casting the deciding vote, the topic of baptism had been wiped clean off the slate.

I have to confess to a bit of backsliding myself. Initially I wrote Ruth everyday in grateful praise but as the work with horses and cows mounted, my gratitude diminished in direct proportion. There was much more work than to be done than I had expected on the cruise. Feed the cattle, milk the cows,

von eene Arbus schmatjt mie kratjt soo goot auls miene Piep, ooda een goodet Glaus dietschet Beea toom Schwiensbrode."

Wiels de leewa Gott toop mett siene judsche Jeschwista sich fe aules interessead, enn dee aulatoop den lenjeren Oarm haude, word mett dem Thema vonne mennische Doop boold eent fe aulemol oppjeriemt.

Etj mott toojäwe, daut uck boold etj een Backslider word. Aunfenjlijch schreef etj Ruth jieden Dach enn miene groote Dankboatjeit, oba auls de Oabeit mette Pead enn Tjeaj toonauhm, leeht miene Schriewarie noh, enn miene Dankboatjeit word blauß. Daut gauf opp dem Cruise bediedend meea Oabeit auls etj jerätjend haud. Daut Veeh foodre, Botta scholtjre, dee Bottamaltj tjeele, dee Schliesamaltj de Oame, dee daut aulewäje jefft, sogoa oppe Oatj, jäwe, Glommskuake brode, enn dann wea uck aul de Dach too Enj.

Wann etj uck aum leewsten enn soohne Sache diskreet bliewe well, weare de Tjeaj dann uck boold bollsch, de Kobble hinjsch, de Hunj enn Hose ransch, enn de Säje bursch.

Daut jratste Probleem oba wea de Noahsche; see wea eene Hoohjohnsplum, Struckhatjs enn Heiwtähn aules enn eene Persoon, enn schlemma auls eene grommsaujende ooltkolniesche Fru, dee em langen Winta enn Minot, North Dakota mol von Mexiko head, enn woo billijch enn riew doa de Huwe weare. Dee Noahsche kollbätjad den gaunzen Dach äwa, enn wea soo kurrijch auls eene Kluck, enn uck noch bausijch doatoo, enn niedatrajchtijch sowesoo. Daut jriesd mett dee Oole ut, enn eena kaum meist nich too Ruh. Nu word mie uck aulahaund schwind dietlijch, kratjt soo's de Bibel sajcht, enn woaromm Noah soo grulijch oolt wea, een woahra Antique, soo's de Enjlenda saje. Waut Joahre aunbelangt, wea dee vebruckta, missaja Deffat nich ella auls fief ooda ruhm sassenzastijch, oba ahm sach'et meea noh achthundat. De Noahsche wea dee easchte bewesene Hypochonderin oppe Welt. Ahr deed meea weeh auls em

centrifuge the milk, skim the cream, churn butter, cool the buttermilk, hand out the skim milk for the poor ever among us, even onboard, fry cottage cheese patties, and then the day was as good as done.

Even though I prefer to remain discreet on the topic, the cows soon were in heat, the mares stallion inclined, then pregnant, and the colts skittish.

The biggest problem, though, was Mrs Noah; she was a battle axe of rare order and worse than a nagging Old Colony Mennonite woman who once caught a brief skin flick of the shack fevered women in Minot, North Dakota. She was a chronic complainer and bossy, bordering on bullying, to the point where proper rest was a rarity. Soon things became clear to me, just as the Bible says, why Noah was so extremely aged, a genuine antique. In terms of years, this emaciated, paltry cock pigeon was no more than sixty five or sixty six but he looked like eight hundred, more give than take. Mrs Noah was the first documented hypochondriac, she suffered from more afflictions than were listed in any medical textbook; something always hurt or ailed her without surcease, either a headache, or the crop, or varicose veins, or rheumatism in its many forms, including sciatica, or her spleen was acting up. "My goodness, me," I felt like saying. She lamented and complained mostly in vulgar Yiddish known to the Ashkenazi, and enough to give anyone the splits in the head and that before the days of common aspirin.

And yet there were many moving experiences on board as when the Old Fellow arrived and we Mennonites gathered for an impromptu Song Fest and we sang to raise the roof, had there been one. When we sang "Let us gather at the River", He was genuinely touched and He smiled with His face and his heart as he served us wine and beer aplenty, while partaking of an ample barbecue or an *asado* on the Promenade Deck.

Doktabuak steiht; irjendwaut deed ahr emma weeh, ohne Unterlaß, entweda ahr reet de Kopp, ooda de Kropp, ooda de Kraumpodre, ooda de Rietinj von jieda Sort, enn Flät sowesoo, ooda ahr deed de Milz baudre. "Oba, meine liebe Zeit," wull etj boold saje. See laumentead, enn kloagd measchtens opp prostet Jiddisch, auls Ashkenasi bekaunt, enn jenuag doavon omm mie Kopprietinj enntoojoage, enn aul daut eea daut opp jieda Atj Aspirin too tjeepe gauf.

Enn doch haud wea scheene, sogoa erjriepende Erfoahrunge oppe Oatj, soo's wann dee Oola oppduckt enn wie Menniste toop mett ahm een impromptu Senjafast hilde. Wie sunge bett sich daut Dack hoof, wann daut een Dack jejäwt haud. Wie sunge, "Sammeln wir am Strom uns alle" enn Hee freid sich mett Hoat, Seel enn Uage enn spendead goot Wien enn Beea toom Barbeque ooda Assado oppem Promenaden Deck.

Waut mie oba aum scheensten jintj, enn, etj jleew, dem Oolen uck, ess wann Hee sich doa aum Desch em Schulinj breet muak, enn Hee noh de mennische Oat Sonnebloomesoht knackt, sich de Spiekomm bedeend omm de Schluwe uttoospiee, enn doabie vetald. "De Amerikauna woare nochmol unja Franklin Delano Roosevelt fe een Hohn enn jieda Topp sorje, enn daut woa etj uck, oba wiels etj Sozialist sie, woa etj uck jiede Famielje oppe Ead een Swimming Pool opp een Joah enrejchte enn vollranne lohte, enn dit Vesprätje hab etj jehoole!"

Enn soo jintj daut emma wieda. Wann ijendeena jleewt, daut dee Texana Dit enn Jant vonne Bewoterung vestohne, dann sull Jie mol seehne, waut dee Oola aules kaun, wann hee den Rainmaker spält.

Wie haud ons noch ich gaunz saut jewundat, auls eene wiedre Äwarauschung fellijch wea. Dee Räjen haud aul eene Wäatj nohjelote, de Sonn jintj jieden Morje tiedja opp, daut wea woam, dann heet, enn mett eenmol wea uck aul Laund

The most memorable of those days was when the Old Fellow relaxed on His easy chair on the deck and told stories. "The day will come, " He said, "when Franklin Delano Roosevelt will promise to put a chicken in every pot of America. I will do better than did in my capacity as a Socialist: I will not only provide a swimming pool for every family on this globe but keep it brimful for an entire year."

And so things went on and on. If anyone thinks that the Texans know a thing or two about irrigation, then you should have seen what the Old Fellow can do when He takes over as the Rainmaker!

We had barely had our fill of wonder and attendant miracles, when we were in for another surprise. The rain had abated for a full week, the sun got up earlier each day in all its blazing glory, and then there was land to be seen. Since the Blacks on the Ark and the Americans were busy beavers as per usual, they had constructed a huge hatch at the rear of God's schooner, where they and we let out the water buffaloes for a daily swim. We did the same thing at the prow of the vessel where the horses were let out to swim and frolic. Both sets, fore and aft, were now harnessed to do their mission. In the bow the horses pulled, swimmingly, while at the afterdeck the buffalos snorted, paddled and pushed, and in short order we docked at the Molotsch; it was here that the Old Fellow and Admiral and Head Honcho, the authoritative Trinity, assumed control. At the Molotsch two passengers, one Reimer and his wife were asked to bid us all God speed, and to get on with settling the Molotschna Colony.

We had not yet had our adequate fill of astonishment and concluded with a few choice hymns of farewell, when the Ark meandered back into the Black Sea, heading for the Dnieper River to Chortietz. There the Peters disembarked and laid out the Old Colony.

enne Sejcht. Wiels dee Schwoatasch enn de Amerikauna oppe Oatj soo pienijch auls Biebabatj weare, haude see hinje aune Oatj eene groote Luck jebut, woa see dee Wotabeffel jieden Dach rutleete, omm too schwamme. Wie deede donn dautselwje Väare aune Spetz vonne Oatj, enn leehte de Pead rut omm too schwamme enn sich too vejnäje. Beide Sorte worde nu aunjespaunt, enn durwe ähre Konst bewiese. Väare trocke de Pead, daut'et plenschad enn ruzhd, enn hinje schnoowe enn bruddelde enn paddelde de Beffel, enn boold wea wie uck aul enne Molotsch. Hiea äwanauhm dee Starschie, dee Eppaschta, dee Admiral, dee Dree-Eenijchtjeit de Kontroll. Een Reima enn siene Fru tjreaje Orda hiea uttoostiehe, enn boold de Tjleenjemeend too jrinde.

Wie haude ons noch nich saut jewundat, auls daut aulwada värewajch enn veropp jintj, enn nohdem wie noch een poah Aufscheedsleeda jesunge haude, wea wie aulwada oppem Schwoaten Mäa, unjawäjess noh dem Nippa noh Chortietz opptoo.

Doa steaje de Peetasch auf, enn jrinde de Ooltkolonie.

Aum näjchsten Morje reisd wie een Stetj wieda enn leehte den Anka bie Elloag rauf, woa de latzte enn baste Menniste aufsteaje. Ditt weare de Resserietasch, dee Jeschijchtevetallasch, dee Rudy Wiebe noh, dee menschliche Aristokrate send. See vetalle daut Bennaschte noh bute han.

Enn nu weet Jie uck woaromm Gerhard Ens soohn weetenden Schmusta druag, dee lenja wiere woat auls sien Soatj, enn dee ahm jlitj nohm Nippa opp Jantsied nauhm.

Next morning we headed north for a piece and dropped anchor at Elloag, where the last and the best of Mennonites left the schooner; these were the raconteurs, the tellers of the tale, so says Rudy Wiebe, who calls them the aristocrats of humanity. They tell the real story of the story.

And now you know why Gerhard Ens had a knowing smirk which outlasted the coffin and took him straight for the Nippa in the beyond.

Bielohte

Auls etj aune vearentachtentijch enn Paraguay plautdietsche Jeschijchte väalaus, wisst etj toom easchten, enn woll uck toom latzten Mol, opp waut verr'e Jedanke een Reiseprädja ooda uck een Evangelist foaken tjemmt. Soo väl Lied kaume mie tooheare, enn mie tooklautsche, daut, haud etj staut Literatua de Bootschauft jestreit, etj too Jeld enn Ruhm jekohme wea, enn dann daut bett vondoag rund omme Klock, vleijcht sogoa rund ommen Kelenda drock jehaut haud. "Diss Thiesse ess opp sien Stetj soo goot auls de Evangelist Reima," säde de Mensche. Audre veea hundat meende: "Joh, joh, bäta auls Reima, bloos oppjrejchtja, eajentlijch schod!"

Kaun senne. Etj tjann Evangelist Reima nijch, weet bloos daut etj siene Spoare han enn wada too ritje tjrie, enn daut hee daut soo drock haft, auls aule Mensche, woohne foaken flunkre.

Waut etj noch weet ess dit: auls etj vondoag de Enjlenda jäjen Paraguay enne Weltmeistaschauft Footbaul späle sach, foll mie bie, daut etj aul eenmol de Jugendmaunschauft von Paraguay jeseehne hab. Daut wea uck aune 1984 auls etj, soo's aul jesajcht, meist beriehmt enn ritj jeworde wea, oba nijch word, wiels etj staut de Bibel Plautdietsch emm Chaco streie deed. Wann eena opprejchtijch bliewe well, mott eena Opfa brinje, nijch? Oba etj haud je uck aul lang tridtj bäta weete sullt, wiels daut Janz Team mie aul dit enn Dietschlaund enn miene Jugendjoahre enne lohte Feftjajoahre dietlijch jemoakt haud.

Na joh, oba tridj nohm Footbaul. Wann eena hiea enn Kanada derjch Sport toom Ruhm enn Jeld kohme well, mott

Futbol

When I was on a reading tour of Paraguay in 1984 I knew for the first and probably the last time what it must be feel like; what manner of thinking is native to itinerant ministers, or evangelists for that matter. So many people came to hear me hold forth and to give me standing ovations, that, had I spread the Word instead of true stories, I would certainly have harvested both fame and currency and would be frightfully busy to this day with a pocket note book calendar in every pocket to remind me of a very busy schedule, Mennonite style. "In his way, this Thiessen is as good as the Evangelist Reimer," people said. "Yes, yes, he is better than Reimer and more honest in any case; too bad, how sad, what potential gone to waste, if only he could fib more slyly!"

That may well be. I do not know Evangelist Reimer but I know that I managed to sniff out his tracks here and there, and knew that he was just as busy as most people are who fib just for the fun of it.

What I do know is this: When I today saw the English National Soccer Team playing against the Paraguayans on TV, I remembered personally seeing the Paraguayan Youth Team in action at that time. This also transpired in 1984 when I, as mentioned, almost came to riches, in addition to fame, but did not manage to do so because I spread Low German stories among the masses instead of doing Bible. If you want to remain honest, you have to be prepared to make sacrifices.

However, I should have known better for a long time since I witnessed the Janz Team Evangelists in action in Germany in the fullness of my youth in the late Fifties.

eena eascht weens fiefdusend Dohla utblädere, wiels toom
Eishockey mott eena von bowe bett unje sijch Panzasache
auntratje sonst schleiht eena sijch enn feftien Minute entweda
schwoat enn bleiw, ooda buhlijch, ooda doot. Golfspäle ess
nijch billja. O joh, enn verrem Spell mott eena noch iewrijch
bäde, daut saul biem Jewenne halpe.

Enn doawäjen ess Footbaul hiea tjeen populäre Sport: dee
tjemmt too billijch.

Toom Footbaul, soo word etj enn Paraguay enn, bruckt
eena goode Lunge, hoade Feet, Tees, dee noh Väare welle, enn
mau een Baul fe twee-entwintijch Spälasch. Enn dann jeiht
daut loos. Oba seea!

Een Brun ut Nielaund enn Paraguay hild een Uag opp mie,
doamett etj daut doa too seehne tjreajch, woohnt fe miene
blausse Onschuldsuage enn miene utejeplatjchte Jesennung
goot wea. Hee fruag mie, woovält Prozent vonne kanaudsche
Indiauna betjeat weare, enn auls etj säd: "Daut weet etj nijch,"
säd hee seea bestemmt: "Von dee Sort weare 98% von
mennischa Haund hiea enn Paraguay emm tjristlijchen
Hock." Amen.

Oba aum Sinnowendnohmeddach jintjch etj aunstaut
Meddachschlop too hoole noh de Jugendmaunschauft äah
Footbaulspell. Aulso ohne Brun, enn siene tjristlijche Fuchtel.
Woa see spälde wea leijcht uttoofinje: doa woa soo's aule
Donna jebloat word, enn woa dee Mensche soo oppjereajcht
weare soo auls eene haulwe Minut noh de Entretjung, doa
wull etj han.

Etj wea aunjekohme. Dee twee Maunschaufte haude uck
ohne mie aunjefonge, enn stände, enn warjde enn puste,
enn—joh—uck daut, fleatjchte, daut Tjwiel enn Schnodda
mau soo fluag.

Daut daut soo iewrijch toojintjch wea mie fuats dietlijch,
wiels de Indiauna jäjne Menniste spälde, enn wiels see sijch
sesst soo seea goot senne musste, enn uck soo tjristlijch weare,

But back to the soccer pitch. If you intend to attain fame and wealth via sports in Canada you better be prepared to fork over $5,000.00 even before you start, since playing ice hockey requires you to wear a suit of armour from head to toes; otherwise it won't take fifteen minutes before you are black and blue or dented, or more commonly, even killed a bit. Playing golf is no less expensive. Further, if you intend to make a good impression on the masses, you should kneel for Divine Guidance prior to the whistle being blown for action; that is a partial and effective way to ensure victory.

This is the reason why soccer is not a popular sport closer to home; you can play it on the cheap.

Playing soccer, as I came to know in Paraguay, requires good lungs, calloused feet, toes with forward direction inclination and one ball for every twenty two players. That is all and then you are set to go. And how!

A fellow by the name of Braun in Nieland, Paraguay kept an eye on me so that I would not see things there that are not meant for the eyes of innocent's bleached disposition. When Braun asked me what percentage of Canadian Indians were saved, I replied that I did not know, to which he responded with authority, "Of their counterparts in Paraguay, 98% have been led to the Christian pasture by committed Mennonite hands of prayer." Amen!

That Saturday afternoon, instead of taking a brisk afternoon nap, I hiked over to watch the youth of the neighbourhood play soccer. And that, without Braun and his guiding presence. As to the pitch location? That was easily determined: there were the yelling was loudest and people were screaming like they commonly do half a minute after the Rapture.

I had arrived. The teams had started playing even without me being there; they were groaning and sweating and panting and blowing, and yes, the players were even cursing, with much snot catching on smoke and fire in the heat of ardour.

kunne see sijch biem Spell mol soo wiese auls see weare, wann see äahre tjristlijche Tjleedie aufjelajcht haude. Enn daut haude see, wiels buta Betjze, wann äwahaupt, haude de Spälasch von bowe bett unje nuscht nijch aun.

Woohnt de Menniste weare enn woohnt de Jäjnasch weare, muak mie daut Publikum dietlijch. Daut Publikum bestund measchtens ut veea ooda fief Mädtjess enn fiewennäjentijch Mejalles, enn aules Indiauna. Enn aula räde see Plautdietsch, enn measchtens auls wann see bie mienem Voda enne School jewast weare, aulso seea rejchtoo, enn ohne Tjrente-Wente, enn ohne Dreimoazharie enn ohne Oaschjetbrätjche.

Dee gaunze Loag wea mie oppe Städ dietlijch: Soo omme Hundat vom Publikum schreaje fe de Indiauna, enn eene seea läwendje Indiaunasche enn etj fe de Menniste.

Dee Indiaunamejal wea fe de mennische Maunschauft, wiels de "tjliena Sawautstje" wea "Miena" soo auls see säd. Enn dis Sawautstje wea hejchstens een Meeta dartijch lang, aulso een bät soo auls de biblischa Zächäus, waut sien Tjarpabu aunbelangt, oba dem Iewa noh wea hee derjch enn derjch een Apostel Peiwel.

Miena wea fetjs, hee rand, enn hee dreid sijch auls een Fortjs em Schneppelduak, enn hee schoot den Baul omme Atj soo's een Polietitja daut Wuat. Oba daut stund doa ver ons noch emma eent too eent. Dee Spälasch läde noch eenmol loos, enn haude nu den tweeden Wind, oba daut bleef biem Eent too Eent. Donn docht etj mie: "Daut feine Tjristentum kaun bett morje, bettem Sinndach wachte." Etj läd miene Stemm enne Pluche, enn gauf mienem Thiessesgorjel Wind von aule Siede, soo daut see mie bett Asuncion heare kunne: "Jungess, lajcht junt em Spell. Wiest dit Heidepack waut mennische Tjriste enne Been habe! Bild junt enn, dee Footbaul ess een Jeldsack, dem jie hinjeraun send, enn derjch duat Puat doahinje scheete motte. LOOS!" Daut holp.

There was so much competitive eagerness in the air because the native Indians were playing against the Mennonite team and since they normally were so much in Christian love with each other, they could, when playing Futbol, show what they were really like after having discarded their born-again vestments. And this is exactly what they did, because, aside from short pants, the players wore nothing at all. Bare of feet and of chest all around.

As to who the Mennonites were, and who the Indians, became clear from the cheering ways of the audience. That audience was comprised of four or five girls and ninety five brats of feminine gender, and all of them Indians. They all spoke Low German of the variety, had they attended school under the tutelage of my father, mainly with shortcuts, and without cute niceties or much ostentatious wiggling of affected tongue or posteriors.

I understood the entire make-up of things in a split second.

About one hundred of the audience cheered for the Indians while a lively lass and I screamed encouragement for our people.

The Indian girl was in favour of the Anabaptist persuasion because "Tiny Sawatzky" was her "Bonny" as she claimed. This Sawatzky kid was all of one meter and thirty centimeters in height, similar to Zacchaeus of Biblical tax collector fame, named in Luke, as I proudly remembered, but when it came to zeal and ambition he was a raving St. Paul all the way.

Bonny was quick, he ran and he twisted and turned like the proverbial fart in a hanky, and he dribbled the ball around corners much like politicians twist the word. The score of the barefoot battle before us was one to one and had been of such equal status for a good while. Obviously the players had just caught their second wind but the score remained tied. Seeing that, I thought to myself, "That Christianity in all its niceties can wait for a bit until Sunday." And so I switched my voice

Daut gauf uck dee Indieauna Mejall vom "Miena" Moot, enn see stund opp, enn läd loos auls eene himmlische Trompeete: "Miena, schitz ahm op! Enn wann Du fuats oppe Städ den Baul derjch daut Dooah doa hinje scheete woascht, dann loht etj die vondoag zeowents bie junt hinjrem Schwienstaul unjre Bananestud bie."

Waut dann pessead, weete blooß soohne Mensche, woohne entweda oppem TV, ooda perseenlijch eenen Windstorm mett Trejchta toop jeseehne habe. "Miena Sewautstje" läd mett Baul toop enn siene O-Been loos, enn eena sach bloos noch een Boschtje Kurrei mett Stoff enn Schwoats enn Grauss enn Bläda äwre Ead rolle enn dreie enn fäaje, enn daut aulatoop sad je dann uck mau een bett twee mol jieden Kilomeeta opp. Miena haud Sood jefoht, enn hee dreid enn tjrieseld noh jane Sied ääh Dooah auls oppjetrocke, enn daut Wundawoatj leeht nijch eea noh, bett de Footbaul em indieaunaschet Dooah fluag.

"The rest," sajcht de Enjlenda "is history."

Etj gauf nohäa dem tjlienen Sawautstje twee Dohla, enn hee gauf mie den Baul. Enn daut ess je dann uck dee Eenstja woohnen mett'e Tiet bie ons dee Pust noch emma nijch utjegohne ess.

into volume mucho grande and let it sound forth unto all the corners of creation so that it resounded all the way to Asuncion and beyond. My voice said, "Boys get into the game. Show this miserable bunch of heathen kids what kind of stuff Mennonite Christians are made of. Imagine, for a second that the futbol is a money bag to be shot through the goal at the other end. LOOS!" That worked.

My gentle encouragement also inspired the Indian girl, part-time owner of Bonny, who held forth like a heavenly trumpet: "Bonny, switch on your after burner! And if you will right away shoot that ball through the heathen goal then you can have your way with me tonight under the banana palm right behind your pig barn."

What then happened can only be comprehended who have watched a tornado, funnel and all on TV or on the Great Plains of the Midwest. "Bonny" Sawatzky took off with the ball and his O-legs and all you could see was something akin to a tumbleweed rolling and sweeping across the Prairie, touching ground twice every kilometre or so. "Bonny" was all traction as he turned and circled to the opponent's goal like a spring fully wound and this little whirlwind of wonder did not let up until the ball was unleashed past Indian goalie and past all resistance in-between.

"The rest" as they say "is history."

I gave Bonny Sawatzky two dollars for the game winning ball. And that is pretty well the only item of my trip to Paraguay which has retained a full set of lungs of hot air to this day.

De Heazhgrul

Joakob Panna wea een ellra Wätmaun, enn de Doft Henritjsche wea eene ellre Wätfru. Vleijcht jefft daut soowaut dartijch Mol den Dach enne Welt, oba daut see Nohbasch weare, soohnt pesseat nijch aule Dach. Panna wea een ziepauagja Jietsbiedel, oolt enn eitel, enn siene Uage spälde Rejchta, je noh dem sien aun Onjerajchtijchtjeite gewahnded Hoat ahm daut väasäd. Enn de Henritjsche? See haud dem Predja enn dem Diakoon jesajcht, see sulle ahr nijch mett Paulus kohme, hee wea nijch befried jewast, enn tjand vleijcht välet, vleijcht sogoa aules, oba enn eene Fru äah Hoat haud hee noch nijch nennjetjitjt, enn auls hee daut vleijcht eenmol deed, haud hee doa noch lang nijch aules jeseehne. "Enn daut ess dann fe vondoag uck aules," haud see jesajcht. Enn see fuahre auf.

Enn daut wea dann uck de Dach auls see toohm easchten Mol sijch lange Betjze äwre Lenjd streepd, enn auls see eene Wäatj lohta noch emma tjeene beese Folj erfoahre haud, schneet see sijch de Lempe auf. Eascht bette Wohde, dann een poa Doag lohta meist bett aune Tjnees. Joh, de Doft Henritjsche stald sijch mett ähre wiet äwa zäwentijch Joah verrem Speajel enn lacht enn weppad sogoa een bät, enn jintj em Goade oabeide enn besorjd ähre tjliene Wirtschauft noh de latzte Mood.

Panna wea, soo's jesajcht, nijch blooß ziepauagijch, hee wea uck ernoa kortsejchtijch, enn toom sijch eene niee Brell too tjeepe, wea hee too jietzijch. Oba kratjcht eendoohnt, hee kunn uck mett siene oole Brell meea auls jenuag seehne, enn

184

The Scarecrow

Jakob Penner was an aged widower and Mrs David Heinrichs an older widow. Similar couples may well occur thirty times a day around the globe, but that they happened to be across the fence neighbours is a rare occurrence.

Penner was a squinty-eyed tightwad, old and vain, but his eyes played judge according to the dictates of his heart, a heart much oriented towards resolving the injustices of this world. As for Mrs Heinrichs? She had told the church minister and the deacon that they ought not to preach St. Paul's moral admonitions to her since Paul had never been married, and while he may well have been knowledgeable in many areas, he had never looked into a woman's heart, and even if he had done so, he had by no means captured the entire picture. "And that is all for today," she had said. And then they knew and took off.

That was also the day when Annie Heinrichs, for the first time in her life, pulled a pair of jeans over her sturdy yet supple legs. When after a week's trial basis, she had not experienced any of the threatened, dire consequences, she cut off her pant legs. First she shortened them half way between heels and knees, and a few days later right up to the knees proper. First off, Old Annie pranced straight up to a full length mirror, posed while giggling, and even wiggled a bit at an age exceeding three score and ten. She then went to work in the garden and tended to whatever her small yard and farm required doing.

As mentioned, Penner was squinty-eyed, and also short sighted, but he was much too cheap to buy himself useful glasses. And yet, even with his old glasses, he could see more

waut hee sach auls hee mol wada, soo auls nu aul meist twalw Joah Tuntjitja späld, jefoll ahm goanijch. Joh, de oola Joakob klackad mett dem Jebiss, enn entschlooht sijch Missjoon opp siene Oat too driewe.

"Etj woa woll nijch meea bie die de Rebbeoabeit doohne tjenne," säd hee fuats auls hee de Henritjsche enn ähre niee Mondua sach, "wiels de Schreft enn etj habe doch uck hanenwada een bätje bie Die mett too rede. Enn uck ohne ons enntoomische."

"Waut fe Warm satte Die dann nu too?" fruag ahm de Henritjsche.

"Diene Oat Tjleedie wudd Dienem Obraum nijch mol em Grauf jefaule," säd Panna.

"Hee haft bett nutoo noch nuscht nijch jesajcht," gauf de Henritjsche ahm too Auntwuat.

"Eena sull nijch mett de Jnohd späle," säd Panna, enn dreid sijch haustijch wajch, foohdad siene Heehna, gauf sien Schwien vonne Dranktonn, enn veboot siene Uage wiedahans spezeare too gohne. "Waut too wiet jeiht, jeiht too wiet," docht hee bie sijch, enn speajch sogoa ut. "Enn etj haud noch em stellen jedocht, vleijcht mett ahr toop oolt too woare, enn nu tjitjt sijch dit mol eena aun!"

Daut jintj Wäatjelang soo wieda: Panna plock eascht de Eadschocketjniepasch vonne Stieda em Goade auf, enn auls hee daut doch nijch nohkaum, musst hee Priesajreen tjeepe,—daut foll ahm schwoa—enn streie. De Bocklezhane musste jejietzt woare, enn morje de Eadschocke wada jehiept woare, enn weede musst hee sowesoo, oba de Lost wea ahm veschorrt, wiels de Sind soo groot enn soo dijcht bie ahm verrem Schafott lach. Enn de Henritjsche? See deed opp ähre Oat kratjcht dautselwje, oba wann see Panna enne Ead pultjre sach, sung see "Clamentein" enn "Yü are mai Sonshein" enn "Gott ist die Liebe." Panna stald sijch schwoahearijch, enn haud nuscht too saje, oba oajre? Soo seea auls daut mott.

than enough and what he did see, and had seen in the last twelve years as a well exercised snooper, displeased him in the extreme. He clacked his dentures and decided to conduct a bit of overdue mission work in his immediate neighbourhood.

"I don't think I'll be available to do any of the heavy lifting around you're place for a while," Jakob suggested to his neighbour, when he first spied her new outfit, "because Scripture also has a say in your walk of life. And that without meddling in the least."

"What kind of worms are pestering your innards now?" asked neighbour Annie Heinrichs.

"Your manner of dress would displease your Abraham, even in his grave." answered Penner.

"Up to now he has not said a single word about it," she responded.

"One ought not to fool around with God's grace," Penner countered, then hurriedly turned around and away, gave his chickens some grain, fed his pigs from the slop barrel and instructed his eyes not to go visiting across the fence from now on. "What goes too far, simply goes much too far" he thought to himself and even spat out his disapproval in a wide arc. "And I had even entertained the possibility of getting old together with her," he thought to himself, "but now just imagine the mess she so blatantly creates.

Things went on like this for weeks on end. Penner picked potato beetles from the spud plants, but then when they gained an upper hand on him, he had to buy Paris Green poison and dust them to death; this was yet another distasteful matter, it cost money! Also he had to prune the tomato plants, and hilling the potato plants was yet another chore to be done, quite aside from all the hoeing of the garden; but he had lost all will to do much of anything, since the mountain of sin was simply too great and too close by, right before his very porch. As for Annie Heinrichs? She laboured away on her own plot in similar manner, but when she saw Penner poking around on his yard and garden, she blithely sang, "Clementine" and "Yü are mai Sonshein" with

Soo jintj daut meist dree Wäatj, bett de Henritjsche äah Hund äah Mooda eenes Morjess mol wada hinjeraun wea, enn ahr ditmol de eene Sied ohpjeflerrt haud. See wudd daut Schohp schlachte motte; see schluad nijch lang. Oba doatoo musst see enne Schien een Baultje äwre Dräajasch laje, omm den Moohda opptootritze enn uttoonehme. Enn de Baultje wea ahr too schwoa. Aulsoo: "Joakob, etj woa vondoag noch Schohpsborsch moake, enn Du tjrijchst uck eene Kommvoll, oba eascht motst Du mie biem schlachte too Haund gohne, joh?"

"Daut dooh etj, oba bloß wann..." säd Panna, oba de Henritjsche wisst je aul waut kaum.

"Du enn Diene, leewa jesajcht, miene Betjze. Waut hast Du enn Dienem Ella noch väl too vesteatje? Oba etj weet je, woa Du mol wada hanwest enn woa mie toom schlachte, mol wada eenen Rock auntratje. Tjemmst?"

"Joh."

Beid hilde se Wuat, enn boold wea de Mooda enne Jläsa, em Frostschaup, enn em Borsch.

Von nu aun jintj daut bediedend bäta tweschen dee Nohbasch, enn Panna fung sijch enn siene Phantasie daut aulwada mett de Henritjsche enn sienem Ella macklijch too moake.

Bett aum dredden August. Panna haud siene Uage wada Erlaubnis jejäwt bie de Nohbasche een bestje too nieschiere. Enn waut hee doa jäjen Owend aun dem Dach sach, wea dochwoll daut aula Latzte. Bie de Henritjsche stund hinje aum Goadetun jelehnt, een bunta Tjeadel, een strauma Maunsmensch!

Panna jintj fuats nenn, enn drunk vom Schleef Wota, soo dreajch wea ahm daut Mul enn de Seel jeworde. Hee tjitjcht noch eemol von sien Schlopstowefensta, enn wann sien Bletj uck muzhrijch wea, sach hee doa noch emma den Tjeadel

188

"Gott is die Liebe" in-between, for good measure. Penner pretended to be hard of hearing, and had nothing to say, but get steaming mad? As much as the occasion demanded.

Things went on like this for three weeks until Annie Heinrich's dog, one fine morning was hounding her ewe yet again, ripping a chunk out of one side of the sheep. She had to execute a mercy killing in a hurry but to that end she needed to place a heavy cross beam in her barn to hang up the ewe in order to eviscerate it. Lifting such a heavy load across the supports was simply too hard for her, so: "Jakob, I intend to cook up some sheep's borscht today and I will give you a good bowl full but first you'll have to lend me a hand in butchering, won't you."

"I'll do that, but only if…" said Penner, with Annie Heinrichs knowing full well what was yet to come.

"Oh you, and your, I mean, my pants, what is it that they are meant to hide at our age? But I know the thoughts you entertain, and so I'll be wearing a skirt for the occasion, are you coming over to give me a hand?"

"Na, okay."

Both kept their promise, and soon the ewe was butchered and in sealers, in the deepfreeze and in the borscht.

From now on things improved noticeably between the neighbours and Penner, in his imagination again resumed plans to cosy up to Mrs Penner a bit, if and when old age were to strike.

This truce lasted until August third of the year. Penner had again granted his eyes permission to go for brief visits to his neighbour and to snoop, if necessary. But what they were to behold towards evening of the day was the absolute and final straw. Towards the back of Mrs Heinrich's garden there stood a male gendered fellow in a gaudy suit!

Penner hurried inside and drank long and hard from the ladle at his water barrel in the kitchen.

He took another good look from his bedroom window, and even though his eyesight was hazy and murky, he still saw that damn stranger lurking behind the greens of the garden, and

hinjrem Jreens stohne, enn waut hee sach, jefoll ahm kratjcht soo schlajcht aus de Baundiete en Rußlaund feftijch Joah tridj. Panna wisst sijch meist nijch Roht, enn hee schleep schlajcht. De Welt wea mol wada too seea toonijcht. "Enn wann daut nijch bett morje aundasch woat, dann mott etj dochwoll..." säd hee, enn läd sijch dohl.

"Dentjcht junt daut doch bloß mol ut... eascht lange Betjze, dann dee aufschniede, dann wada een bätje tjristlijch biem Moodaschlachte, enn nu haft see doa sogoa bie sijch eenen jnerjen Bädel em Goade gaunz sonda Sorj stohne. Eena haud je aum Nippa bliewe kunnt, schlemma ess daut doa uck nijch jeworde," meend Panna, enn schleep langsom enn. Oba nijch eea hee sijch siene Schrootflint väähold, enn dee aum Footenenj enn sien Bad hanläd.

Aum näjchsten Dach jäjen Owent wudd Panna Rosmack hoole. "Eent fe aulemol, wann de Bädel doa wada steiht enn jniesat."

Dee Bädel stund aulwada doa, soo wiet auls de ziepauagja Panna seehne kunn. Panna muak sijch siene Brell rein, schoof een poah Patroone enn sienen Tweeloopa, enn sad loos. Wiet rundomm, oba emma dijchta nohm Ziel.

"Waut hast Du hiea bie miene Nohbasche veloare? du lestja Scherniesel. Schämst die nijch mol, Du goaschtaja Biekrupa, heh? Na, wacht mau. Enn wann Du mie nijch fuats sajchst, waut Du hiea too seatje hast, woa etj Die mett miene Schroot-flint de Betjze utneie," kommendead Panna, enn schlitjcht sijch nohda.

Panna wea aul tjeene dartijch Schooh auf, haud de Flint aul haulf bette Schulla, enn de Scherniesel haud noch emma tjeene Auntwuat jejäwt.

"Dit ess Diene latzte Jeläajenheit Diene Sind too betjanne," roopt Panna. Oba dann, joh oba donn kaum de Auntwuat von dijcht hinja ahm. "Joakob, Du wursct Die doch nijch aun miene Heazhgrul vejriepe?"

this lamentable scene displeased him every bit as much as the bandits had in Russia fifty and more years ago.

Penner was beside himself and he slept poorly. His world was far too much out of order. "And if things don't altogether improve by tomorrow, then I might just have to…" he said, and went to bed.

"Can you imagine the state of things… first her long pants, then cutting them off in unseemly fashion, and then a spell of Christian behaviour at butchering time, while now she has a sneering scoundrel standing around shamelessly in her own garden. I might just as well have stayed behind on the Dnieper…things surely could not have become any worse," thought Penner and gradually dozed off. But not before fetching his shotgun and placing it at the foot end of his bed.

The next day at twilight Penner would restore law and moral order, Christian-Mennonite style.

The scoundrel was still there the next morning to the extent that squinty-eyed Penner could make him out. Late that afternoon Jakob Penner cleaned his glasses, slipped a few shells into his gun and took off, choosing a wide, stalking arc but inching closer to his aim and destination.

"What kind of business are you conducting with my neighbour? You crafty trouble maker? Have you no shame, you naughty meddler, you? Well, you just wait a second or two. And if you won't explain yourself in a big hurry I might just embroider your pantaloons with my shotgun," Penner commanded, sneaking ever closer.

Penner was no more than thirty feet off and already had his gun half to the shoulder but the rascal had yet to respond.

"This is your very last chance to come clean and confess your sins," Penner yelled with throaty righteousness. But then, yes then, an answer came from very close at hand, right behind him. "Jakob, surely you wouldn't get involved with my scarecrow, would you?"

Sasquatch, endlijch

Joh, daut stemmt, etj sie noch niemols opp'em Calgary Stampede jewast, oba daut bediet noch lang nijch, daut etj nijch weet, woo daut sijch doa aulatoop vehelt, ooda waut doa väajeiht, enn sijch aufspält. De Fantasie ess toovelessja auls de soojenannde Wertjlijchtjeit, enn wann jie mie daut uck aul mol wada nijch jleewe welle, dann froagt doch bitte den leewen Gott. Dann weet jie, enn etj sowesoo.

Oba eent weete sogoa aul de krommbeenje Cowboys mett ährem grooten Datjsel oppem Kopp, woohne se doa eenen fiefgelloonjen Hoot (ruhm twintijch Lieta), aulso eenen omjestelpten Drankamma, leijcht oppjeweppt, nanne. De Cowgirls doa sitt'et nijch väl aundasch, bloos daut see doa mett eene hejchre Stemm "Yippie!" dach enn nacht schriee, uck wann ahn tjeena nijch tjniepe deit.

Sesst ess daut doa soo meea äwareen: den gaunzen Dach äwa riede see, ooda säle sijch em Stoff, enn zeowends drintjche se biem Faut Calgary Redeye, waut soo väl ess, auls Beea mett Bocklezhanesauft. Daut saul den Kota, aulso daut Ruzhe emm Kopp von toovät Beea supe, vedriewe.

Noh Calgary toom Stampede kohme uck väl, seea väl Texauna, enn dee ertjant eena doaraun, daut see daut Scheetiesa benne enne Betjze droage, enn niemols nijch von Beea eenen Kohta em Kopp tjriee, wiels see measchtens eenen ladjen Bähn habe. Enn daut mott soo, wiels see doa bowe aulejemeen seea väl Domms spitjre.

192

Sasquatch, you betcha

Yep, it's true. I have never been to the Calgary Stampede but that doesn't for a minute mean that I don't know what goes on there. The human imagination is generally more reliable than so-called reality and if you choose not to believe me, then just ask our Father who is, and then you'll know.

There is something which all the bow-legged legged cowboys, the ones with five gallon (twenty litre slop pails with a furry feel to them) hats there know how to do, as do the cowgirls who yip: "Yippie!" around the clock, even if no one is around to pinch their curvy butts.

Aside from yipping, things are pretty well the same with both genders: during the day they ride, rope and shoot and come evening, they drink Calgary red-eye, meaning beer with tomato juice. This cocktail is meant to ward off potential marinading of the brain, and cure hangovers, known to those who actually possess grey matter in the third storey.

Many Texans congregate at the Stampede as well and bring along whatever shooting equipment they can get away with. Very few Texans are prone to hangovers for reasons stated.

But all this is a mere aside, an introduction to the sermon, proper.

In 2013 I intend to launch my debut at the Stampede and do it big time. At the concluding evening, at the gloaming of the Stampede, my company and I have been invited to entertain. This entertainment has a long and hallowed tradition from the Mennonite *Jugendverein* at which conclusion there was

Oba daut aules mau soo bieaun, soo auls de Einleitung too de Predijcht proper.

Woa etj oba hanwell, ess dit: nääjchstet Joah woa etj enn Calgary oppducke, enn daut fuats een bät em Grooten, wann aules nohm Plon jeiht. Wiels? Joh, wiels etj hab mien Auftrett doa von lange Haund jeplohnt, enn daut heet, eene Grupp enn etj welle doa, sootoosaje, mett een Stetjch toom Frei- williges opptrede.

Miene Poatnasch enn etj habe tweschen Kaumplaups enn Shushwap Lake, enn een bät ooste doavon, endlijch een Sasquatch Nast jefunge, woohnt'et soo meea noh eene Kolonie von disse Sort litjend. Daut finje diead ons lang, seea lang, enn wie musste väl Opfa brinje. Oba wie tjreaje vonne Mormone aulnoch jehearijch Jeld fe onse Expeditsjoon, dee wie seea jeheem den Code Nohme Klatsch enn Quatsch gauwe. Enn Opfa musst wie uck brinje, wiels wie musste je Wääj enn Meddel finje omm de Sasquatch noh ons too locke enn too taubre, aunstautt, soo's auls aule aundre, dee wille gruselje, buzhaja, zulltaje Donnasch Joahrelang hinjeraun too ranne, omm ahn psychologisch bietookohme.

Enn eenem Stetjch wea wie onse mennische Missjoons- Konkurrenz wiet veropp: wie jinje mett Beea auls Lockmeddel nijch spoasom omm, enn wie rede je, emm Jäjensautz too de George Bush-Jinja Mennoniete, aula Plautdietsch, aulso eene Uasproak, woohne sijch, soo auls sijch daut rutstalle sull, de Sasquatch väl bekaunda enn uck vetrulijcha auls Texas Englisch ess. (Wann jie enn dissem Stetjch meea Informats- joon habe welle, dann froagt enn Nuadamerikau bitte bie Al Reima ooda Reuben App noh, enn enn Europa bie Peeta Pota Wiens, enn enn Asien Karl Peetasch; dee weete; see send em Bild, soo's eena sajcht.) Oba waut ons aum measchten too Good kaum wea seea eenfach; wie jinje bieblisch vää. Ons Motto? "Eene Staudt oppem Boaj watjcht den Janka"; enn soo wohnd wie doa opp eenem Anboajch een haulwet Joah, rede

opportunity for talent to go on stage, without planning, coercion, fear or favour. This is known as *Freiwilliges,* which translates, if at all, as talent urging for release, similar to spontaneous delivery at a church in which the spirit is encouraged to speak up, sing out, or witness to creativity, urges no longer containable. This tradition is identical to artistic potluck.

Reference was made to company and such is explicit in purpose. My partners and I have, after long and arduous research, managed to locate a Sasquatch nest between Kam-loops and Shushwap Lake, deep in the bush where game is plenty and the climate forgiving. In numerous waterways, fish of every variety float and wiggle in line to be caught and induce culinary orgasms to the human palate.

Finding these elusive long lost remote relatives was no easy matter but our persistence has paid off. First we applied and received substantial research seed money from the Mormon Inc. which intends to get to the bottom of things to prove the Bible right. We had similar purpose in mind.

Since my team and I had conducted our research well and proper, we knew that spiritual expeditions are generally undertaken with chase and catch tactics in mind; then bring home the trophies for public display, including the altar. Bearing this in mind, we early on decided that instead of employing aggressive policies ala George Bush, we would simply set up an attractive model camp on a knoll, hoist a flag proclaiming benevolence, with the wording City on a Hill emblazoned on it in both Low German and English, and let them come to us, labouring, heavy laden, shaggy of coat or demeanor, or otherwise.

Since we were convinced that all things primordial appeal to people indigenous, the originals of homo sapiens lineage, we had very few but basic rules to which we adhered religiously in attempting to establish contact with the Bigfoot, one

bloos Plautdietsch, bleewe bie de mennische Manneare, trocke ons ooltkolniesch aun, enn schmeatjte entweda goanijch, ooda Piep. Hanenwada leet etj eene Piep oode de aundre toop mett Baby's Bottom, Parson's Pleasure, ooda uck Barnyard Pleasure Tobak bute äwanacht lidje. Enn boold nauhm mien Tobak auf enn mien Erfoljch too. Enn, soo's auls jesajcht, kunn de Sasquatch-Jemeend emma bie ons aum Beeafaut schwalje. Enn daut deede se je dann uck schmock noh de mennische Oat: eascht han enn wada de Nacht een Schluckstje ute Buddel fippse, enn boold ernoa utem Faut supe. Jeseehne hab wie daut nijch, oba wann een Ammavoll Schum noch oppem Deiw em Graus tieidjch zemorjess bruddelt, dann weet je eena, daut entweda een Steinbacha, eena ut Bayern, ooda een Sasquatch Eltesta aum Woatjch jewast ess.

O joh, enn onse Frulied druage blooß Ratjch, enn niemols nijch Betjze ooda Jeans, wiels Sasquatch, soo docht etj mie, habe weinijch Vestendnis fe bedajchte Fruesbeen. Woaromm wudd ahn daut aundasch gohne auls mie, ooda dem leewen Gott? Etj sull mol wada enn dissem Stetjch Rajcht habe.

Na oba, oba etj hab daut mett disse Jeschijcht vetalle too drock, omm mie mett Nebensejchlijchtjeite opptoohoole. Etj bedd omm Vestendnis.

Dee Red wea von Opfa brinje. Enn doamett ess daut uck mol wada soo: een jieda weet waut daut meent, oba meist tjeena weet nijch waut daut eajentlijch bediet. Bie ons wea daut soo, enn daut vetall etj uck mau bloos, wiels de Missjoonare, woohne noh ons bie de Dusende manke Sasquatch aunkohme woare, sijch väl Meaj enn Jeld spoare tjenne, wann se schmock tooheare woare.

Aulsoo: Wann Mensche too Menschefrätasch woare tjenne (enn daut hab etj selwst opp Sulawesi erläwt; etj kaum uck mau mett Tjniepameaj mett mien Läwe doavon, enn doawäjen sie etj Experte, enn earnst too nehme), dann tjenn

synonym of many, whom our aim and intention was to domesticate. Assuming that our forebears were vegetarians before the Fall, we, likewise, set a vegetarian example. Secondly, our language was exclusively Low German, a dialect, hoary with age, but alive with yeast like potential. Thirdly, our womenfolk wore only skirts. While ankle length, they did reveal a strip of leg, enough to arouse temptation. Our reasoning was simple but persuasive: if God would have wanted jeans and designer wares on women, He would have said so. He did not, meaning He prefers commodious apparel, if at all. So did we. We got it right as the story will reveal. Our children, three in number, wore Lederhosen and good manners.

Meat was forbidden in our research facility although we stocked a bit or Mennonite style spare ribs and a cut or two of osso buco in a modest refrigerator, should our financiers, the Mormons, surface to inspect progress; these people of steadfast persuasion like a taste of meat now and then, even if they rarely came to visit.

Also, we placed a few bottles of beer, Alexander Keith to be explicit, at random points around camp should the occasional Sasquatch roam of nights and be thirsty after a chase, meaning a hunt.

Obviously, in a research team consisting of academics who are more prone to intelligent arguing than to brotherly resolutions, we had slight dissensions, meaning two of the women in our ranks gave word to the speculation that some Sasquatch of our proselytizing intent might have strayed from the faith of the fathers and had become roundhouse cannibals. Even if argumentative, these women were on the right track, or path, more apt, for our haunt.

As occasionally happens, there is the odd misadventure to flawless ventures. We had in our ranks an American kid who answered to, but rarely listened to his name, Bubba Janz; he

jie junt dentjche, waut de Sasquatch soo aules väa habe, wann see zeowends mol aum Raund von eenem Darp spezeare gohne.

Een poah Universitäte habe dree Milljoon Dolah enn tien Joah Tiet jeopfat, om uttoofinje, wem de Sasquatch emm Mieagrope nennschmiete enn goah brohde, enn mett Hoot, Hut enn Hoah oppfräte, enn wem nijch. Enn ditmol habe see sogoa rajcht: De Sasquatch fräte aum leewsten fleeschfrätende Mensche opp, oba dee woohne sijch meea mett Jreens enn Jetjätjs bejneaje, lohte se jeweehnlijch mett eenen Dentjzadel ranne. Aulso haft toom Biespell een Texas Missjoonoa, woohna sijch emma fein rund enn saut aum B.B.Q. frat, doa tjeen Chance. Dee veschwinjt fuats mett den Buckvoll Beef, mett Steewle, Jeans enn eene grooten Smile em Mieagrope, enn woat oppjegnaubat. Dee Survival Rate mank disse ess bett nutoo .005%, enn doawäajen hab jie niemols nijch jeheat, waut doa emm kenaudschen Bosch enne Sasquatch-Provinz pesseat.

Aulso säd etj fuats too meine Forschungsgrupp: "Wäa nijch reed ess Vegetarier too woare, kaum fuats noh Hus gohne. De Alternative ess Fooda fe den Sasquatch Mieagrope. "Aulso: Joh ooda Nä?" Enn dann wea Fräd. Bett opp een Bubba Jaunz, een tjliena Vada vom Jaunz Team, läw wie aula; Bubba schmenjd foaken hinjaridjsch Schwiensfleesch, enn nu ess hee manke Jreewe. Wie funge emm Zelt eenes Morjess sien ladjet Bad, oba ons Tjeelschaup wea noch ohp; dee Sasquatch haude ahm beluaht, ahm jeleewat jenohme, enn ahm eenfach emm Miagrope unjajeduckt. Wiels dem Bubba daut Jeld emma soo wijchtijch wea, de Sasquatch oba nijch wisste, waut see doamett doohne sulle, haude see zemorjess bie ons oppe Oppfoaht sien Tjnippsbiedel mett äwa fiefdusend amerikaunsche Dohla Boajeld doabenne hanjelajcht, enn uck een Kommtje Jreewe, dee ons bekaunt ritjchte. Aulso een

was a son to prominent missionaries; Bubba wore cowboy style attire and entitlement in bearing. Initially we ignored the evidence but Bubba proved to be a habitual nosher of carnal cuts, meaning meats; in short, this punk was a delinquent of the Old School.

Bubba became living proof that the Sasquatch roamed around of nights and that they were accomplished hunters. One early morning we responded to a slight commotion in our kitchen and found Bubba AWOL. His fate was a mystery, he had disappeared without a trace; the fridge door stood agape, and his cot was empty. Early the next morning the Bubba enigma was resolved. We found a Jewel jar of cracklings some hundred meters down our path to civilization. One whiff of the contents revealed that Bubba had been canned. Within a few centimeters from Bubba's sealed fate, our relatives, as we preferred to name them, had left Bubba's wallet with some five thousand in cash currency behind. It was obvious that the Sasquatch had not yet been contaminated by mammon. Bubba, on the other hand, loved money and meat until his disobedience and his preference for things material had fashioned him an early epitaph.

Since we had reason to believe that our roving forebears had indeed imbibed brew of beer since the beginning of civilization, we purchased a sizeable keg of draft from the Bubba estate, and placed it in a hollow by the wildwood. A few days later and two mornings running, we witnessed a bucket of barley scented froth bubbling in the dewy grass of the early morning and concluded, that a Steinbacher, a back sliding Holdeman, a Bavarian, or a Sasquatch bishop had made the rounds and that we were inching closer to success in domesticating the noble savage.

Our program of research became routine; to that end we abided by all house rules encouraging patience to prevail. We were a surprisingly happy lot and hoped that our accord

Kommtje Dank enn Aunertjanung, woohnt wie feierlijch emm Frostschaup bett vondoag oppbewoaht habe.

Aulsoo, nu weet jie mien Jeheemnis, nu goht schmock han enn tut dasgleiche.

Jenuag, de lange Tiet von onsem jewaultjen Missjoonsenn haft sijch jeloohnt. Aulsoo: Näajchstet Joah, aum latzten Dach vonne Calgary Stampede, soo jäjen Owend, wann de Mensche sijch aul aunfange too freie, waut'et näajchstet Joah vleijcht aules jäwe woat, enn aundre sijch aul ve luta Langewiel aunfange too schobbe, enn endlijch Tiet habe Frindschauft noh too fädme, dann woa wie dree Menniste mett eene Famielje Sasquatch opptrede.

Heete woat de Tabun Obraum, Joakob enn Isaak, enn dee twee Oolasch Saulmoon enn Eadmaun.

De Fruees Sort, woohne wie mett korte Ratjch enn eenen rooden Hoot, aum Raund uck een bät noh de latzte Mood oppjeweppt, utstraume woare, heete: Sarah (ooda uck Susch), Mitsch, Rebecca, enn Trien.

Twee tjliene Sasquatch, woohne sijch noch, sootoosaje, enne Broodstatsjoon befinje, selle dann Nooah enn Mooah heete. See woare mett rutjche Schaldeatja, oba uck boaft, romm-zauble.

Dee Bood, enn dee wie dee Kolonie rommfeahre woare, woat gaunz eenfach: Elloaga-Nippaenja heete.

Na joh, oba soo's de fraunzeesische Mejalles nu aul dusend Joah saje: Eene Maun ohne Schnurrboat ess soo auls eene Supp ohne Solt, enn soo, sootoosaje, hab wie uck eene Schnurr reed, nämlijch: etj woa mie mett Obraum fohte, aulso rautze. Wie woare beid eenen Pojas äwre Schlaubbetjze droage, enn ons veseatje too schmiete, ooda sogoa unja too nehme. Daut wie dit Proowstetjch aul tweenhundat Mol, wann nijch foakna, je-eewt habe, brucke de hundatdusend Mensche doa nijch weete. (Enn jie eajentlijch uck nijch, oba daut endat aune Sach weinijch, wiels de Resslasch oppem TV,

would be a living testimony in attracting a rare species to our fold, and who knows, possibly leading to a Mennonite congregation; I, for one, could not suppress the gentle but persuasive urge to spread my faith.

Like all people right with God, we had as common endeavour, the Indian Summer as a chronological aim during which we would make the first but grand gesture to bring home those drifting far from the shores of civilization and to provide them with a haven of solace and welcome. Indian Summer induces in mankind a homing instinct to return.

Since the song is our common Mennonite DNA and every bit as assertive as is a beard to a billy goat, we, as a *Gemeinschaft* on many levels, applied some of our Mormon funds, supplemented by a grant pending from the Plett Foundation to hire one Dr Al Reimer and coax him out of retirement to sing and to choir conduct. To that end, Mennonite volunteers literally came out of the many woods, to join in singing loud and long, with heart and fervor competing in gaining the ear of those roaming but inching closer to a happier future.

The second evening after a round of German folksongs was concluded, with a divine rendition *Ich weiß einen Strom,* and with Al then suddenly bringing the choir to a dead halt, we heard by way of an echo on that mild Indian Summer night a warbling coloratura of both wolves and one human, and our inner delight was similar to a response from a thousand spectators offering thunderous applause to a Verdi opera in Milano, or Nozze de Figaro at the Salzburger Festspiele in Austria.

The next night proved better still, with Al singing one verse of *Ich bete an die Macht der Liebe* by Bordjansky in Russian, with our choir rousing all of nature while singing the song to completion with God Himself joining the venture in a fine tenor voice, just to prove that He was on our side.

doohne je daut selwje, enn uck dee, jleewt tjeena nijch, mau Sposs em Groffen eewe.)

Na joh, oba Obraum enn etj woare enn een Drohtklotje mett acht Atje, dartijch Schooh em Derjchmäta, ons hinjeraun satte bett Fall, Schweet enn Schnodda fleaje woare. Wie woare doabie uck soo's de Grunzkujels schindeare, wiels sesst kohme de Amerikauna nijch.

Etj wudd seea jearn wieda vetalle, woo dee Schluss utfaule woat, oba daut dooh etj nijch, wiels sesst kohm jie nijch too de jratzte Show on Earth. Oba eent kaun etj junt aul nu verohde: toom Schluss woa wie aulatoop daut Leed:

"Hab oft im Kreisen der Lieben
Im duftigen Grase geruht"

sinje, mett besondre Betoonung opp Duft. Wann disse noch emma een bät wille Bonsch doabie aunfangt de Hacke enne Loft too tjriesle, daunze aulsoo, dann hoolt ons daut bitte too good; see send noch emma nijch gaunz mennisch. Daut tjemmt noch.

N. B. Brinjt ruhijch jun Frindschauft mett. Bett'em näajchsten Stampede hab wie de Willasch sowiet, enn dann kaun de Tabun aul schriewe. De easchte fief Dusend Jast tjriee von Saulmoon Sasquatch een Autogram. Omsonst. Oba loht bitte de Worscht enn uck daut sesstje Fleesch Tus; etj kaun Backsliders nijch vedroage. Butadem: Eena saul Freschbetjeade nijch enne Versuchung brinje.

But it was the third evening that all of our decade long efforts came to fruition. Our choir, reinforced by several dozen children of the wider neighbourhood, and all of purity of provenance sang *"Wenn der Heiland, als König erscheint"* when, suddenly, a sprightly bunch of Sasquatch children jumped out of the woods and joined in the refrain. Their virgin voices compensated for knowledge of ways of the world and the word.

Our womenfolk, intuitive as only women can be when their walk is pure decency of intent and purpose, had obviously reckoned with a response akin to an altar call, if you will, and waitressed around with platters of tofu and egg salad, aka cackle berry sandwiches, which the cute little Sasquatch devils devoured with more hunger driven purpose than etiquette.

We had not yet contained our excitement at the home coming when we already witnessed lively activity around our beer keg. It became obvious to everyone irrespective of denomination that beer was invented for a noble purpose.

The rest is history, as we say, but there are reams of success yet waiting to be revealed, so please stay tuned.

Dankscheen

Jasch Niefeld enn Peeta Bruhn—eajentlijch Niefelds Jasch enn Bruhne Peeta wiels see eentletsijch weare—weare twee mennische Foarmasch. Foarmasch? Na, eajentlijch noch een bätje meea auls Foarmasch, wiels see weare sogoa Ranchers enn Siedsaskatchewan.

See foarmde, nä, etj meen rannde eene Ransch toop, haude eene Häad von sasshundat Tjeaj enn nochmal haulf soo väl Jungveeh, enn eene Tabun feine Pead.

Emm Läwe intressead ahn buta daut ranche enn Jeldmoake measchtens noch een bät Rodeos emm Somma enn Wilf Carter emm Winta. Enn wann Wilf Carter sinje sull, mußt Jasch den Grammaphoon emma jenietsch opptratje enn Peeta späld dann uck Jetoa enn jodeld mett. Joh, Peeta sung en jodeld, daut de Cojotes wiet rundomm de Näse noh de Mond zielde enn mettjulde. Lied vetalle, daut dee Präriewilw sogoa hielde wann Peeta enn Wilf "Miene tjliene schmocke Buschtje wiet emm Bosch", sunge enn jodelde, oba etj jleew, daut ess een bät äwadräwe. Enn nijch doawäjen, wiels dee Präriewilw daut nijch seea scheen heat, nä wiels Cojotes daut mett Hose jriepe emm Winta too drock habe, soo daut see sijch nijch foaken leeste tjenne, sentimental too woare. Oba musikalisch selle see senne auls bille een Väasenja, enn daut jleew etj uck jearn.

Na joh, soo wea daut mett Jasch enn Peeta enn äähre Ranch, daut Grammaphoon-Opptratje enn Jetoaspäle enn Sinje enn Jodle enn Jeldvedeene enn emm Somma Heimoake enn aum

Thanks, Jake

Jake Neufeld and Peter Braun (actually Neufeld's Jake and Braun's Peter because in Mennonite nomenclature bachelors assume more formalized attire of name only after marrying), were two Mennonite farmers. Actually, they were more than just farmers, they were ranchers in southeastern Saskatchewan.

Together they operated a ranch with some six hundred head of cattle, as many again of heifers and calves and a herd of beautiful horses.

Life was treating them pretty well. Aside from making money, their interests lay in visiting rodeos in the summer and the yodeling cowboy, Wilf Carter, come winter time. When Wilf Carter was on the agenda, Jake had to wind up the gramophone while Peter accompanied the great cowboy singer on his guitar and yodeled with the best of them. Indeed, Peter sang and yodeled in such fine voice that the coyotes all around punched their noses towards the moon and howled along for the musical ride. People claimed that these Prairie wolves literally wept when Peter got into his favourite "My little grey haired mother in the West" but I believe this is a slight exaggeration, and not because the coyotes do not appreciate such music, but because they are simply too busy catching rabbits in winter to engage in over sentimentality. But they are as musical as any precentor; this is widely known.

Weekend dolle Bolles mack riede enn wille Pead enn Broncos oppteeme enn sijch selwst fierijch riede.

De twee Jungess weare eajentlijch goot too liede; Jasch wea vleijcht een bätje tjniepaja auls Peeta enn maunjchmol sogoa een bät hinjaridjsch, oba Peeta wea doafäa een Straight-Shooter, soo's de Lied doa tweschen Swift Current enn de Montana-Jrenz opp dietsch saje.

Dee Twee kaume aulnoch goot ut enn weare emm grooten enn gaunzen jleie Tjeadels, wiels etj ahn eenmol emm Currentschen Shopping Center biem Koffedrintjche troff, enn dee jefolle mie. Jasch siene Uage kullade een bät dolla wann hee een poa läwendje Panty-Hose sach, während eena Peeta aunsach, daut hee leewa oppem Pead auls oppem Stool sette deed.

Daut wea aune Eenefeftijch loht emm Oktoba, enn onse Cowboys haude wiet emm Waste eenem Frind jeholpe Tjeaj enn dem Wintatun tooptojoage. Noh dree Doag Oabeid jintj'et aul tiedijch zemorjes noh Hus. See reede enn reede, foodade äähre Pead unjawäajess Howa, enn vebeete sijch selwst een bätje, enn reede wieda äwre groote, walje Prärie-Stap noh Hus. Enn haulf veea pessead'et dann uck. Eascht word de Himmel greiw, dann dunkel enn boold kaume uck aul de easchte Duhne rauf, enn boold schnied daut enn word kolt. Klock fief wear'et soo wiet: entweda ooda.

"Daut well woll toowintre, waut meenst, Peeta?" säd Jasch. "Kratjcht waut du, well'we ons de easchte baste Krupunja seatje." Enn daut deede see dann uck. Enn soo kaum daut, daut see omm haulf sass ut opp eenem Hoff noppreede, enn fruage, auls see enn de Pead hiea Schulinj finje durwe.

See tjannde sijch nijch. Eascht wull de Lady ahn goanijch soo rajcht oppnehme, oba auls see sach, waut bute loos wea, säd see opp Enjlisch: "Kohmt nenn, enn moakt de Dääh too!" See worde sijch boold eenijch: De Pead worde emm Staul

206

Well, that is the way life played out in those part with Jake and Peter on their ranch and their winding the gramophone and playing the guitar and singing and yodeling and earning money and making hay in summertime, then riding angry bulls into submission on weekends, and then bridling broncos and riding themselves fiery all in one sweep.

These two fellows were an agreeable pair; Jake was a trifle more miserly than Peter, and sometime even slightly devious, but Peter was a straight shooter as the people between Swift Current and Montana called him in the going German lingo.

They got along well and, all told, they were more than tolerable fellows because I met them occasionally at the Current shopping mall for coffee and we enjoyed mutual amiable company, even if Jake gave walking panty hose undue attention, while Peter preferred a saddle to a coffee house chair.

It was late in October in the year fifty one when our cowboy friends had helped out a friend move his stock to winter lots on his ranch way out west just northeast of Maple Creek. After three days work they set out for their return at the crack of dawn. They rode back for hours on end, stopped to feed their steeds oats now and then, and took their own brief lunch snacks before resuming their ride over the great waving Prairie towards home. Then at three thirty of the afternoon it happened. First the sky turned grey, then dark, and soon the first downy snowflakes of the season wafted down on the riders of the plains. Soon the snowfall got serious and the weather turned cold. By five o'clock either or had struck.

"Well, Pete, what's your opinion on the matter? Winter for real?" said Jake. "Let's look around for the first best shelter for the night." And that's what they did. It happened that at five thirty they rode onto a yard and asked if they could shelter their horses for the night.

nennjeleit, enn jefoodat, enn Jasch enn Peeta funge uck Obdach.

Biem Owendkost vetallde see sijch äwa Wind enn Wada, enn äwa Sodeltiet enn Eiwste, enn Pead enn Tjeaj enn äwa Priese enn Oppjoah. Daut stald sijch rut, daut de Lady Wätfru wea—enne baste Joahre—äah Maun wea vom Bronco enne Sandhills raufjebockt worde, enn wea boold doarophan jestorwe. Enn see bleef auleen oppe Foarm, äahre feine, groote Foarm. Woa sull see uck bliewe? Woa sull see uck han? Eea see schlope jinje, nauhm Peeta de Jetoa von'ne Waund, stemmd de enn, enn sung noch een poah Leeda, enn donn word de Laump utjepust.

Peeta enn Jasch schleepe oppe Lidjbeintj enn Schlopbeintj, enn de Wätfru jintj noh bowe oppem Bän schlope.

Aum näajchsten Morje lach dee Schnee soo wiet auls daut Uag mau seehne kunn, oba daut Sonntje schiend frindlijch. "Mol han!" "Mol wada!" enn wajch weare Jasch enn Peeta...

Schnorrijch, oba von dem Dach aun wea de Eentracht tweschen onse mennische Cowboys een bät jesteat. Wäa weet waut doa wea, oba de Jungess weare eenfach een bät emp-findlijch jeworde, enn see weare sijch nu mett eenmol emma enn aulewäje emm Stijch. Oba see beete de Tähne toop enn proowde wieda toop too betschlere, oba daut wull aulatoop nuscht nijch meea woare, enn soo entschloote see sijch em Farjoah noh de Sodeltiet utenaunda too haundle. Enn woo word'et dann uck...

Aum feftienden Aprel tjreajch Peeta Bruhn von eenem Audwekoht metteenst eenen Breef. Enn doa stund jeschräwe: "Wiels Du soo leeftolijch too mie weascht auls Du emm Oktoba bie mie emm Onwada äwanacht bleefst, hab etj Die miene Foarm vemoakt. Etj sie seea krank, enn wann Du dit Testament lese woascht, sie etj aul doot." Peeta flautade de Henj, enn sien Mul wea dreajch, enn hee kaum daut mett'em

When they knocked at the door, a lady appeared, slightly apprehensive, but once she took in the impending weather picture she let them stable their horses in her barn and invited them in. "Come in and shut the door!" The horses were fed and bedded and Jake and Peter were made welcome.

During supper they talked about wind and weather and about seeding and harvest, about horses and cattle and prices and next year. It turned out that the lady was a widow in her best years; her husband had been bucked off a bronco in the Sandhills and had died shortly thereafter. She remained alone on her sprawling ranch, a beautiful place it was. What was she to do? Her kids were not interested in the spread and so she made do and hung on as best she could, which was obviously considerable. Before they turned in for the night, Peter took a guitar from the wall, tuned it and sang a few songs before they all called it a day. Outside the blizzard bucked and bellowed while inside it was as cosy as only a wood burning stove can deliver; then the lady of the house suggested bed time had come.

Peter and Jake slept on a futon and a window bed while the lady of the house repaired to her room upstairs.

The next morning a blanket of snow lay as far as the eye could see but the sun shone bright and friendly. Morning had broken to pristine beauty with post blizzard activity and distance beckoning.

"Thanks for a lovely night and a better breakfast" which the widow served with copious grace, coffee, eggs, bacon and croissants, freshly baked. "It was an unexpected pleasure," said the widow. "And now, God speed and thanks for the company and the fine songs." Then, within minutes Jake and Peter were homeward bound.

Strange it was, but as of that day the accord of collegiality built by time and a common shoulder put to many occasions of effort was a bit disjointed. Who knows how fate plays its

Tjwiel moake meist nijch noh. Waut ess dit bloß aulatoop? Waut jeiht hiea eajentlijch väa?

Peeta reet mett Breef toop noh Hus, enn langsom jintj ahm een Lijcht opp…"Du, Jasch, auls wie emm Oktoba bie de Wätfru äwanacht bleewe, schlitjchst du die Nacht noh bowe enn spälsd du doa Treesta, enn sädst du ahr noch bowenenn, du heetst Peeta Bruhn?"

"Daut jeiht die weinijch waut aun, oba daut kunn senne."

"Dankscheen fe ähre Foarm, Jasch! Dankscheen!"

hand when it comes to relationships, but the two friends now found each getting in each other's way, more often than not. But they gritted their teeth in common endeavour and tried their best to surmount the hill of unnamed discord and kept on bacheloring together as best they could. However, a leak had sprung in their relationship and it could not be contained, and so they decided to go their own ways after seeding time of next spring. And that is what happened.

On the 15th of April there was a surprise letter from a lawyer for Peter in the mail. That letter read, "Since you were so kind and understanding when you stayed overnight at my ranch last October, I decided to will you my farm. I am very ill and by the time you receive this communiqué and testament I will be dead." Peter was thunderstruck. He looked utterly perplexed, and just kept shaking his head. Finally he headed slowly for home. And by the time he got there, he'd had enough time to think it all through, and now the questions he needed to ask were at least clear to him. At home, Jake was pitching the last bales from the stable loft.

"Listen, Jake, do you remember when we stayed overnight at the widow's place close to Maple Creek last October?"

Jake seemed to remember the occasion.

"Did you by any chance slink up to her room in the middle of the night and play the grand comforter and tell her that your name was Peter Braun?"

"That is hardly your business, Peter, but it might have happened."

"Thanks for her ranch, Jake! Thanks a lot!"

Trua

Daut wea aum säwenden Juni aune vearentachtenijch, aune Tweedusend auls mien Frind Viktor Peetasch enn etj enn Israel rommdwaulde. Daut de Jude noch meea Helljedoag habe auls wie mol haude wisst wie, oba daut wie aun dissem Dach diretjcht enn eenen grooten Heljedach meist soo onverhoffts auls enn eenen Koohplautz nenn stiee wudde, wisst wie nijch.

Oba daut deed wie.

Soo's jesajcht, de Jude habe meea Helljedoag auls een Eatjekohta Nät enne Tjeewe, enn dee eensja Grund woarom see sijch soo väl Tiet toom sijch offiziel Zanke enn Rommsette leiste tjenne ess wiels ähre Nobach enn Frindschauft, dee Wetjeltjapp aulso, dee Meddasatjeit noch earnsta nehme auls see.

Enn soo auls daut bie de Jude mott, send de measchte von äähre Helljedoag vonne earnste, joh vonne truje Sort. Enn dann hiele see noch dolla auls mennische Mumtjess wann see vom Triebsaul enn Russland vetalle.

Etj docht emma, Mensche hiele bloos wann see opp earnst trurijch send, oba dauts goanijch soo, weit gefehlt! Nä, see hiele uck toom Scheengohne, enn habe daut A Capella-Hiele rut auls een mennischa Chooa bie K. H. Niefeld daut Sinje. See hiele dree ooda uck veeastemmijch, enn hoole doabie schmock Wies. Enn wann see dann veea bett fief Stroophe vom selwjen Leed jehielt habe, dann lohte see noh om Wota, Pepperminttee ooda uck Arbuseslurpies too drintjche, sonst rannt ahn de Trohneborm dreajch. Enn dann jeiht daut Leed

212

Sorrow

It was the seventh of June in 1984 of the twentieth century when my friend Victor Peters and I idled around in Israel. The fact that Jews celebrate more than we do was known to us, but what we did not know is that we stepped right into a big one on this day; this came as much of a surprise to us as stepping into a cow pie back home.

But that's exactly what happened. As I said earlier, the Jews have more holydays than squirrels have nuts in their jowls, and the only reason they can afford to take so much time to quarrel and fight, and then sit around and talk about King David is that their neighbours, relatives and adversaries, the Turbanites, take their Days of Treachery and then of Leisure just as seriously as they do.

The Jews practice celebrating their holydays reflectively, indeed sorrowfully.

At such times they cry more mournfully than Mennonite women do when telling of the tribulations in Russia.

I always thought that people cry only when they are genuinely sorrowful but that is not true, by a long stretch; by no means, Jews in the Holy Land cry a lot just for the fun of it, and are as expert in wailing and weeping *a capella* as Mennonite choirs did singing under K. H. Neufeld's baton in his day. They weep in three- and four-part harmony and in perfect tune. And after wailing four to five verses of the same song, they let up a bit to drink water, peppermint tea or watermelon slurpees, for otherwise their tear well runs dry. And then they start the same song from the beginning until

von Väahre loos, daut sogoa de Meistasch em Jule, de Wilw, sijch hansatte enn opp niee Hieljedanke kohme.

Oba tridj noh Israel: Eenjefäah dartijch Kilomeeta nuadoost von Beer Sheba, de Obraumstaudt aulso (Beer Sheba ess äwajens soohn schatajet Darp, daut daut tjeen Wunda ess, daut Voda Obraum emma rommrannd enn met siene Fru enn äah Aunhenjsel aulewäje jieden Dach dree bett veea mol Koffe drunk), doa lijcht mol wada een strauma Tjoatjhoff, enn dissa ess woll fiefdusend Joah oolt oba stendijch em Jebruck, wiels daut Voltj Israel emma von Gott Ordasch tjrijcht dissem ooda janen mett siene gaunze Famielje toop de Tjapp auf too säble, enn dann säble dee Wetjeltjapp tridjaun, enn schlohne uck de Jude han enn wada de Feet bett hinjre Uahre auf, enn dann jeiht daut Trualeed von Väare loos. Soo auls vondoag.

Oh joh, enn wiels daut uck Jude jefft, woohne daut Hiele nijch besondasch goot jeiht, oba see doch hiele motte, haft daut aul emma Kloagwiewa jejäwt, dee fe goodet Jeld reed send een Unjaspaun ooda uck twee too hiele enn sijch doabie aune Lunze too pletjche, enn trurijch too senne, soo lang auls Mensche ahn doabie tootjitjche enn bewundre.

Etj tohld soo meea ut Sposs een noch tjlanderet Mädtje aun dissem Dach, noch verr Klock Tien zemorjess tien Dohla— mett Gott auls Troost doabowe—wiels etj docht, daut daut Mejaltje ut Sibirien ver kortem jekohme wea, enn mie daut om ahr jaumad. Oba see docht, etj meend daut earnst, enn dann sung see, etj meend, hield see loos, soo auls oppjetrocke. See hield soo meea Tchaikovsky Melodiee, enn doawäjen kaum etj opp Russlaund too räde.

Joh, enn disse Mejall juhld soo schratjlijch loos, daut fuats dartijch Hunj enn noch meea sijch om ahr hansade, de Näs noh dee Stearns puschte, de Poote verre Uage hilde, enn uck looshielde. Dis Chooa word mienen aul emma spendoblen Frind Vietja dann doch too väl, enn hee gauf daut Mädtje fuats fief Dohla, daut see oppheare sull. Oba see haud mett

the masters in howling, the desert wolves, sit down to likewise engage in mournful weeping.

But back to Israel. Some thirty kilometers from Beer Sheba, the city of Abraham and a bit of a shitty town (so much so that it is small wonder that Father Abraham and his entourage constantly kept on the lookout for a better brew of coffee and some new stories, including improbable yarns to stretch and tell posterity), there lies yet another well-kept cemetery. This one was five thousand years old and constantly in demand because the people of Israel are always getting orders from God to saber off this family or the other, and then the Turbanites eke out revenge and cut off Jewish feet at the throat with Songs of Tribulation ensuing like today.

And, yes, because there are Jews who simply do not enjoy crying, weeping and wailing all that much, but are required by the prophets to tribulate, there have always been weeping women handy who, for good money, are prepared to weep for a shift or even two, and while they are at it, pluck and pick at their dresses and tresses and do a good job of it all as long as the audience is right, and gratuities and attendance ample.

More or less just for the fun of it, I gave a sprightly girl apprenticing in teenaging ten dollars .

Because it struck me that this little girl had probably arrived from Siberia recently and I felt sorry for her. But she thought I was serious and then she started singing, I mean crying, as if wound up. Her crying had a Tchaikovsky lilt to it and that is why I assumed she came from Russia.

This girl got off to such a howling start that right away some thirty dogs, or even more and ever about in those parts since the days of Lazarus, punched their noses in common accord and endeavour to the stars of Bethlehem, placed their paws before their eyes and started weeping mournfully, like so many prayers for their dad and dead. This choir in full voice proved too much for my friend Victor, and he whipped out

ähre Stemm Väs jefoht, enn hield nochmol gaunz Sibierjen voll.

Wie leehte den aunjeschnädnen Chooa stohne enn toom Deel uck lidje enn muake ons oppe Socke, wiels vondoag musst wie je eenen Huagen Helljedach fieahre.

Oppe rajchte Sied vom Wajch, dijcht biem Tjoatjhoff, stunde jewaultje Trocks mett hundade Dusende Näjeltjess ooda uck Roose doabowe, enn eena kunn sijch von dee soväl omsonst nehme auls eena wull, omm de fresche Bloome oppe Jräwa too laje. Enn daut deed wie dann uck. Wie sochte ons jieda een Grauf ut, enn daut ess je nijch wieda schwoa, wiels de measchte Graufsteehna doa een Photo habe, daut eena weet, wem eena Blooma ritjchwirtjend hanlaje well. Daut oppem Tjoatjhoff enn Israel veraun too kohme ess je nijch soo leijcht wiels eena sijch emma tweschne Maschienejewehre derjchbuchle mott, enn uck aune Bajonette vebie, mett dee see eenem egol enne Rebbe poakre.

Wie weare aunjekohme. Doa word jekloagt enn jehielt auls wann de measchte daut mettem Truajeschrejch enn mett dem Trohnevejeete daut noh de mennische Oat drock haude. Oh mai!

Enn eena steiht doa, enn weet nijch rajcht auls eena metthiele saul ooda sijch wundre saul. Eent woat je eenem opp Städ dietlijch: wann Menniste toopkohme, dann sinje see fuats ähre Leedaspitjasch ladijch, oba Jude hiele sijch saut. Han enn wada sinjt dann uck noch een Cantor, oba daut kunn etj too eena Tiet uck. Eena mott sijch dann bloos dijcht bie eene Bieeromp opphoole, enn wann dee dann loosprätjle, woat eena stauntepee too eenem utjewossnen Cantor.

Bie aul de groote Trua aun dissem Dach, aun dem de haulwe Welt toopkaum omm ähre väle Doodes too bekloage, foll Frind Viktor enn mie oba doch eenem soo een bätje aum Raund vom Tjoatjhoff opp, wiels dis Mensch, enn straum aunjetrockna Tjeadel, omsonst hield enn Trohne utem Hoat

five dollars for the girl from Tashkent to stop. However, her voice had caught traction and she kept on weeping until all of Siberia was full of her lament, the wind to that end was right.

We then left the choir behind and set out since we were meant to celebrate a high holiday today.

On the right side of the road, close to the cemetery stood huge trucks with hundreds of thousands of carnations or also roses, and we were allowed, even encouraged, to take as many fresh flowers as one[we?] wanted, gratis, and to place them on the graves of our choice. And that is what we did. Victor and I each searched out a grave, which is not difficult since most gravestones comes with a photo, making it all the easier to place flowers on the grave of choice and to honor the interred retrospectfully, so to speak. It is not all that easy to make your way through a Jewish cemetery, since you have to elbow your way through machine pistols and sub-machine guns, and also bayonets which soldiers poke in your ribs with practiced, indeed smirking, routine.

We had arrived. There was much groaning of lamentations and genuine weeping of real tears, almost as if most mourners were following the Mennonite model of being very busy in their sorrow.

And there we were, not really knowing whether we were meant to join in the chorus of crying, or simply express surprise at the scene of real in your face *Oy Weh* Old Testament grief. There is one common element to it all which immediately struck Victor and me: when Mennonites get together they sing to depletion their portable granaries of song, while the Jews likewise weep their repertoire to a congenial ending. Now and then, and then far and near, a cantor gets into the act of vocal hover and I know all about it because at one phase of my earlier life I also managed to cantor. I once accidentally hung around a bee hive in my early youth back home and once they started prickling me by the

vegoot. Eena woat ajchte Trua nijch soo schwind loos, enn soo trock ons dee Eensaumtjeit von siene deepe Trua dochwoll nohda.

Dee Tjeadel word ons jewoah. Hee wescht sijch de Uage enn säd: "Bitte haben Sie Verständnis: ich bin zwar Jude, und sogar gebildet, aber ich spreche nicht zehn Wörter Hebräisch, und nicht viel mehr Englisch, aber einmal im Jahr komme ich aus Berlin an diesem Tag meine tiefe Trauer kund zu tun." Enn dann hield hee noch eenmol twee Schneppeldeatja voll.

Wie weare deep jereaht. Viktor dretjcht ahm de Haund mett Mettlied, enn etj uck. Dann säd Viktor: "Das tut uns aufrichtig leid; Sie haben Ihren doch durchaus ansehnlichen Freund—" enn wees doabie opp daut Photo oppem Graufsteen "—offensichtlich sehr geliebt."

"Es liegt anders, lieber Freund!" säd dis jinjra Einstein. "Ich habe ihn nie gekannt. Der Grund meiner ungeheueren Traurigkeit ist: Dieser Mann, Moische Gerstein, da auf dem Bild, ist leider viel zu früh gestorben. Er war nämlich der erste Mann meiner Frau."

dozen, I metamorphosed into a fully blown professional cantor within seconds.

During all the great sadness of the day at which half the world assembled to mourn their many dead, my friend Victor and I noticed a respectable, well-dressed gentleman at the edge of things whose weeping was quiet and dignified; he shed heartfelt tears of grief. Genuine grief gets to you; it was his lonely sorrow that probably attracted him to us.

This fellow took note of us. While wiping his eyes, he softly said, "Please bear with me. Although I am Jewish and swell-educated, I do not know more than ten words of Hebrew and not much more of English but once a year I travel all the way from Berlin on this day to express my deep sorrow." And then he proceeded to fill two more handkerchiefs with tears.

We were deeply moved. Victor shook his hand with compassionate sympathy as did I. Then Victor said, "We are genuinely sorry; obviously you must have loved your friend—" and while saying so he pointed at the photograph on the gravestone "—very deeply."

"Things are very different from your assumption, my dear friend!" replied the grieving younger pilgrim.

"I never met him. The reason for my abject grief is the following: This man, Moische Gerstein, there depicted on the photo, died much, far, too early. He was the first husband of my wife."

Mangosteen

Auls daut Schmeatje noch nijch een Kilo Tjräft enn jieda Zigarett haud, vedeend Tjleppensteens Tjnals sijch mett Chesterfields schmeatje ernoa Jeld. Hee sad sijch eenfach oppem Kunta enopp dem Imperial Tobacco verhäa eenen Sodel oppjelajcht haud, enn dann stetjcht hee sijch eent aun enn tjitjcht nohm Wieden Waste enn säd doabie:
"Hallelujah, leewe Lied
Etj schmeatjch aum leewsten Chesterfield."
Enn dann opp Enjlisch hinjeraun: "Lucky Strike on a Chesterfield", enn donn plintjad hee eene Langhoaje mett korte Betjze too. Doafäa tjreajch Tjnals een Peat, een poah Ladasteewle, een Soofa, enn een Hoot, enn dree Japps Paparossie, enn twee Fuppe voll Boajeld. Dee Paparossie vekofft Tjnals, aulso stockt hee siene Erspoarnisse noch dijchtijch opp.

Enn dit wea aulatoop aune Fiewefetijch, (1955 aulso) auls Tjnals, seea restijch, fiewenzäwentijch Joah oolt word. Etj haud, soos se opp Jantsied sajen, vääje Wäatjch dit aules em Dentjch.

Enn jistre fuah etj Tjnals mol endlijch wada beseatje, wiels etj enne Carillon News jelest haud, daut'et nu wada eenen Eewijchtjeitsborrem jeft, enn dee sogoa hiea dijcht verre Däah, enn dissa heet Mangosteen. Etj kofft fuats eene tjliene Papsiebuddel voll fe feftijch Dolah, enn fuah loos noh Tjnals opptoo. Mol seehne, auls hee doa noch emma tweschen Burwool enn Roosegoad oppem Hempel wiet auf vom Onjezeffa, Germs enn sestje Jefährlijchtjeite wohnt. Enn auls hee äwahaupt noch läwd, enn auls hee noch emma goot too liede

Mangosteen

When smoking not yet contained a kilogram of cancer in every puff, Klippenstein's Corny earned a goodly amount of money by smoking Chesterfields. He simply sat himself down on his gelding which Imperial Tobacco had gifted him together with a western saddle and then he lit up; then putting on his Wild West gaze over many horizons, he recited: "Lucky Strike on a Chesterfield" while winking at one of those ever handy ladies, long of hair and of leg, and tight of shorts. For such commercial slogan Cornie received a horse, a pair of cowboy boots, a sofa and a cowboy hat, and three hands full of cigarettes, and two pockets full of cash. Cornie sold the smokes, stocking up his bank account.

All this transpired in 1955 when Cornie, in mighty fine shape, turned seventy five. Cornie and his world came to mind and memory last week.

Yesterday I finally paid Cornie a visit after I read in the local Carillon News that a new Fountain of Eternal Wellness had been located and that right in front of my door, so to speak; this Well of Wonder is called Mangosteen. I immediately purchased a small Pepsi-Cola bottle full of this panacea for fifty dollars in cash, and took off to visit Cornie. Just to see if he still lived between Rosengard and Burwalde on a knoll in the bush far away from insects and germs and related dangers to health and aging. Also, I wanted to determine whether he was still alive and represented tolerable company. And if he had indeed and finally started to fail, then I would serve him a tablespoon of Mangosteen and disperse the stiffness out of his members, restoring him to accustomed vim and vigor.

ess. Enn wann'a aunjefonge haft too tjwieme, wudd etj ahm mett eenem grooten Läpelvoll Mangosteen wada de Jlieda dee Strufheit utdriewe, soo docht etj mie.

Etj kaum biem Tjnals aun, enn musst mie wundre. Eena kaun von eenem hundatennfiewentwintijchjoaschen Mauns-mensch nijch velange, daut hee soo auls een Fallem oppe Weid mett de Hinjabeen utschleiht. Ooda daut hee oppem Jugendverein emma mett een nieet Jedijcht tjemmt, ooda vonne Steinbach Post waut Tachentijjoaschet oppwoamt. Enn eena kaun je dochwoll uck nijch meea vom Tjnals velange, daut hee soo auls enn siene baste Joahre, dee zastijch Joahlang aunhilde, enne Barjchtholsche Tjoatje aulewäje mett eene Soag enn eenen Boage Evanjeliumsleeda späle wudd.

Joh, oba jie send woll uck kratjcht soo nieschierijch auls etj, woo'rett Tjnals, dee enn Dreejoahhundade Tus ess, woll sitt.

Nijch schlajcht. Eletrischet Lijcht haft'a nijch, enn rannendet Wota hafta, em Farjoah wann daut vom Dack biem Deiwe rauftjemmt. Joh, enn hee haft een Hiestje em Bosch, enn auls Papiea deend ahm de Zionskunde, dee mol enn Steinbach jedretjcht word, enn nohm Utspetze vom Tjnals fe twee Dolah oppjekofft word.

Enn daut Äte enn Sesstjet? Wann Tjnals eenmol enn twee Wäatjch waut fehlt, dann phoont hee (joh, hee haft een Phoon), eene jeheeme Numma, enn dee brinje ahm dann waut Tjnals habe well, enn dann noch meea. Auls wann jie daut nijch fuats jerohde habe, Tjnals ess dann doch uck een bät een lestja Scherniesel jeworde, oba wann hee Imperial Tobacco weete lat: "Daut wea je woll uck nijch aules gaunz woah, waut wie donn enn donn de Lied oppschmäde…" dann lohte de groote Jungess biem Imperial Tobacco aules stohne enn lidje, enn brinje Tjnals Howajreet, Eia, Spatjch, Zujbotta, Zocka, Mehl enn aules waut'a well, soolang auls hee nijch vetalt, waut sienatiet aune Woahrheitstonn aules vebie jejleppt wea.

I arrived at Cornie's abode and was surprised. One cannot very well expect that a fellow aged one hundred and twenty five will kick and frolic on the pasture like a frisky colt. Or that he will surface at various *Jugendvereins* equipped with a memorized poem and recite it for all to share, of that he will read an excerpt from the Steinbach Post, and serve it up like so much re-fried literary fare. Or, for that matter, expect him to still play a series of evangelical songs on a saw as he did in the fullness of youth in the Bergthaler Church, lasting a rounded three score and counting.

Obviously you are interested or even curious to know how Cornie, a man who was at home in three centuries, has fared.

Not badly. He has no electricity but he has running water in the spring of the year when the snow leaks from his roof. Also, he has a biffy in the bush and a generous supply of toilet tissue; this source of somewhat toughened Softly and Tender wipe, Cornie managed to buy en gros for two dollars after the Messenger of Zion, printed in Steinbach, went belly up at the turn of whatever century.

As for his victuals and other essentials of life? Whenever Cornie is in short supply of this or that once a week, Cornie phones (yes, he has a phone) by dialling an unlisted number and his supplies of need and desire are personally delivered to his house and home. As if you have not guessed it, Cornie has in the course of time become a bit of a sneaky scoundrel and so, whenever he informs Imperial Tobacco these days that "not everything we, meaning you and I, claimed in our yester-year of commonality, was the truth, the whole truth and nothing but..." then the big boys at Imperial Tobacco quickly get the message and they drop everything and deliver to Cornie oatmeal, eggs, bacon, pig butter (grey or crackling lard), sugar, flour and whatever else he has need of with dispatch, as long as he makes no public mention of what slopped over the Barrel of Truth when they negotiated the deal of nicotine truth in a former day.

Säd etj uck Eia? Mau selden, wiels Tjnals haft twee Schlop-
stowe enn sienem Hus—mett Pappelholt jehett—enn enn
eene von disse Stowe haft hee sass Heehna enn een Hohn
unjajebrocht. Sien Schwien, Putj jenannt, mott oba emm
Schwienshock, aulso bute, sijch derjchfräte.

Soo's auls daut je dann uck mott: Tjnals siene Heehna habe
aula Nohmes, oba dee woa etj nijch oppreaje; dee Hohn heet
Stauntepee.

Tjnals siene oole Kobbel heet Maschka enn sien Kohta, dee
sijch noch aun Gorbachew dentjche (ooda soo se opp Jantsied
sajen: "Gorbachew em Dentjch haft") kaun, heet Iesbraund
enn ahm sitt'et uck doanoh.

Tjleppesteens Tjnals helt nijch seea oppe latzte Mood, aulso
haft hee een, soo auls erwähnt, Lucky Strike Chesterfield
Soofa, enn sesst bloos eene Reaj Heiwtjlatz mett Schopsfall
betrocke rommstohne. Sien Heat haft kruggelje Been, oba
reatjat noch meastens noh bowe Joh, enn siene Schlopstow?
Dee sitt'et seea onnbefriet; Tjnals sien Bad henjt derjch, enn
de Datjche kohme measchtens vom easchten Weltjrijch, aulso
Army enn Navy Surplus. Oba hee haft eenen seea gooden,
grooten Tjalla mett aulahaund doabenne, enn noch eenen
bätren Goade. Enn Enjemoaktet enne Jläsa bie de tien Dutz.

Joh, oba jie welle nu doch drinjend weete, woarom
utjereatjend diss Tjleppesteens Wellem soo oolt jeworde ess,
enn woarom hee enn sienem boold ooltestmentlijchen Ella
weda Brell noch Jebiss bruckt? Dauts seea eenfach. Mangosteen ess mau de latste von väle Sorte Eewijchtjeitsborrems,
woohne de Menniste aul emma uzhend fe sijch haude. Enne
Ukraine wea daut Nippawota woohnt grootet Ella vespruak.
Enne Stäts haude de Menniste Schlagenöl, enn enn Kanada
haud wie eascht Alpentjreita, enn dann Peadsdokta Pettja sien
Bocklezhanesauft, enn noch een poah aundre Sorte, soo's
Shakley's Vitamien Pelle, ooda soo's Methuselah Dreppe. Joh,
enn aul disse Meddel haft Tjleppensteens Tjnals sien gaunzen

Did I mention eggs? He rarely orders these because Cornie has two bedrooms in his house, heated by poplar wood, and in one of these bedrooms he keeps six laying hens and a lusty rooster. His pig, called Putj, has to make do with a sty located in free roaming style under the open sky.

Just as things and names ought to be, all Cornie's chickens have names; his rooster even answers to a fancy Latin one, namely *Stauntepee,* meaning On the Spot.

Cornie's old grey mare goes by the name of Maschka and his tomcat, who still remembers Gorbatchow well, is called Icebrand and looks his name.

Klippenstein's Cornie is not up to things modern and for this reason he has an old fashioned leather Lucky Strike Chesterfield, and aside from this well worn hammock, he has a series of chopping blocks covered with sheep furs standing around randomly. His kitchen range has short clawed feet but does smoke mainly to the top and as for his bedroom? It looks unmarried; his bed swings low while most of his covers and spreads are of the Army and Navy Surplus variety. Cornie maintains a well stocked cellar with a variety of canned and sealer topped vegetables and wild fruit; these can be counted by the dozen.

Obviously, you are lining up wondering what makes Klippenstein's Cornie such a marvel of old age and why he at his almost Old Testament chronology, enjoys perfect hearing, impeccable eyesight and has no need of dentures? The reason is simple. Mangosteen is only the latest of many Eternal Wellsprings which Mennonites have always laid exclusive claim to. In Ukraine it was Dnieper Water which guaranteed great age. In the States Mennonites had snake oil, while in Canada every household had a steady and ready supply of Alpenkräuter, and then came along a horse doctor named Poetker with his panaceanic enriched tomato juice, and a few other varieties of this and that, as well as Shakley's Vitamin Pills and also some Methuselah drops. And, yes indeed, Klippenstein's Cornie was a steady imbiber and ingester of

Läwelang enjenohme. Enn hee ess je dann uck seea, seea oolt jeworde. Enn trotzdem haft uck hee een Probleem, een grootet Probleem, wiels? Joh, wiels nu well Tjnals aul seea jearn stoawe, oba daut woat nuscht nijch, daut jletjcht ahm nijch, hee mott wieda läwe wiels hee soo jesund ess.

Leewe Lied enn Lesasch (emmahan ruhm dreedusend), etj musst junt disse Jeschijcht eenfach vetalle doamet jie weete woo'ret eenem gohne kaun, wann eena too deep enn too lang aum Eewijchtjeitsborrem mett'em Schleef jedrunke haft. Daut Scheen-Jesundsenne ess aulso nijch gaunz onjefährlijch.

Joh, enn daut woat junt dann woll uck nijch besondasch wundre wann etj junt saj, daut auls Tjleppensteens Tjnals mien Jeschentj aun ahm, aulso de Mangosteen Buddel sach, hee soo schratjlijch doll word, daut etj mie bloos wajch, bloos wajch muak, sesst haud hee opplatzt noch eenen Hoatschlach jetjreaje, enn wann hee dann noch weens veea By-passes brucke wudd? Daut wull etj ahm je dann doch nijch aundoohne; etj tjann disse Prozedua aum eajnen Lief, enn Tjnals ess mie dann doch too schod fe soohne Prunarie.

Oh joh, wann mie irjendeena fiewentwintijch Dolah fe miene gaunz niee Buddel Mangosteen jefft, dann sie etj reed dee fe billjet Jeld auftoojäwe. COD.

Enn wann nijch, dann mott etj den Mangosteen auleen utsupe, enn dann hab jie mie aunstaut feftien Joah noch weens dartijch Joah eea etj em Modesack nennkrup. Enn wea well daut?

each and everyone of these miracle cures and panaceas which withered every onslaught of ailment, affliction or age. And, obviously, he has managed to attain great age. Cornie is literally a walking antique of the Old School. And yet, Cornie now is beset by a problem, a huge problem in his opinion. What gives? you ask. Cornie now dearly wants to die but no such luck, he can't manage dying and has to go on living because he is simply far too healthy to call it quits.

Dear pilgrims and readers all (three thousand and counting), I have no recourse but to tell you this story in exacting detail and to report how and what happens when you have spent all your years sitting by the Well of Eternity and drinking copiously thereof with a sturdy ladle. In short being healthy as a horse is not without danger in the very long run.

And so you might not be all that surprised when I now inform you that when Klippenstein's Cornie saw my present to him, meaning a modest bottle of Mangosteen, he became so explosively enraged, so dreadfully mad that I took to my heels as never before for otherwise he might well have suffered a heart attack, and if he then would have had need of four heart by-passes? I have personal experience of exactly such a surgical procedure and I would certainly not inflict such messing of the inner man on a favourite and long time friend like Cornie.

And one other matter: if there is anyone out there who is prepared to pay me twenty five dollars for a completely new and unused bottle of Mangosteen, I am prepared to sell it a steeply reduced price. COD.

If no deal can be struck, I am left with no alternative but to drink the Mangosteen on my own, and then it might well be another thirty years or more before I finally slip into my very own maggot bag aka coffin. And who would want that?

Be careful what you pray for

Auls wie aum Friedach Owend biem Schemmawoare aum 23 Septamba, aune 1953 verre Jebädstund enne MCI heade, daut Hugo Unruh, de jinjsta Sähn von Prädja enn Eltesta Nikolai Unruh ute Ste. Elisabeth Lichtenauer-Jemeend, von nu aun aum United College Theologie studeare wull, ooda sogoa aul deed, donn sad wie ons oppe Flooa han, enn wißte daut wie seea, oba seea bäde sulle enn musste.

Hiea ess von "sade ons han" dee Red. Bäd wie emma biem Sette? Measchtens, joh. Oba auls wie de schratjelje Kunde heade, daut een Sähn von een beriehmden Eltesta, enn doatoo uck noch Molotschna, sich manke United Churchla vebiestad haud, foll wie vonne Beintj enn vonne Steehla, enn kaume oppe Flooa too sette, enn too lidje. Soo schlemm wea daut! Joh, aun dem Dach auls Hugo ons velohte haud, jintj de Sonn eene goode Stund verrem Himmelsplohn unja. Daut word tiedja diesta; soo earnst nauhm uck de Voda em Himmel daut, wann eent von siene Schoptjes äwrem Sälestrang sprung enn sich enne Wille Hundat manke sindje Schops—enn Kozzebatj vebiestad haud!

Niedarps Peeta ut Jnodenthol, Sähn von dem breedaje-meendschen Peeta Niedarp, red enn bed foaken enn schmiedijch, enn wann dee "Gebetsgegenstand" een earnsta wea, soo's vondoag, musst hee sich aulnoch foaken den Jeiwa vonne Tjeewe wesche enn de Trohne vonne Uage enn Backe.

Dee Ense-Jungess von Rivers haude aul jebet, enn uck fe ähren Voda, dee doabie wea een haulwa Russeliet too woare. Dann wea Netjels Obraum von Stuartburn aune Reaj.

And may the doves...

It was towards twilight on a Friday evening on September 23, 1953 just as we prepared for our customary weekly Prayer Meeting at the MCI when breaking news struck to the effect that Hugo Unruh, the youngest son of the Reverend and Bishop Nikolai Unruh from the Lichtenauer Congregation of Ste. Elisabeth was about to study theology at the United College; worse still, he might even be at it, as we spoke. Urgency was of the essence since we knew it was time for high supplication, and we were meant to pray long and hard to prevent such disaster with dispatch.

Generally Prayer Meetings were held by sitting in a circle, unbroken and discussing urgencies with Our Father. However, in the light of such calamity, we fell to our knees of common accord when hearing that the son of a famous bishop, one who even came from the Molotschna elite was now seriously lost. Hugo had wandered too far from shore. This matter was so pressing and so urgent that heaven itself took note and darkness set in a full hour before schedule. This meant that God himself was involved in this tragedy and we knew it. A precious lamb had erred and was now part of the sinful black sheep and naughty goat congregation.

Neudorf's Peter from Gnadenthal, son of the M. B. Peter Neudorf Sr., prayed often and arduously, being well versed in supplication, and if the object of prayer was of a serious nature like tonight, he frequently got so involved in setting things straight at the Eternal Throne, that he often had to

229

Obraum bleef biem Bede measchtens em easchten *Gear,* wiels sien Plautdietsch enn dem Gang tusijch wea, enn nich ennet Huagdietsch nennjleppe wull.

Bie Leahra Schäfa, dee Eppaschta, Starschie enn School-diretjta aules enn eene Persoon, wea daut mette Sproak äwaroasch. Kluag soos'a uck wea, enn sogoa enn Bessarabien utjebilt, dee oola Donna bleef biem Huagdietsch, enn sien Plautdietsch haud emma Holidays, Urlaub aulsoo...

Dee Näjchsta, woohna foaken enn pienijch bäde deed enn wull wea Pätkaus Peeta ute Lowe Foarm-Sperling Jäjend. Diss Peeta, den se uck Extension Pete nannde, wea een iewaja Benjel, enn litjend eenen doffen Deffat mett wietleftje Fadre oppen Kopp. Hee wea een haulwa Sommafelda enn een haulwa Rudnaweida enn ahm sach'et uck doanoh. Sondaboa, oba dis Peeta wea äwabrestijch enn hollbuckijch toojlitj. Tus bie Pätkaus haude de Stintjkaute emm Heehnastaul Rosmack jehoole, enn nu wea daut Eiajeld knaup. Peeta vetald daut dem leewen Gott, enn meend, de leewa Gott sull doch endlich mol aul de hasselje Stintjkohtasch läwendijch aufwarje. Amen.

Oba noch mol tridj vom Heehnastaul noh de Flooa enne MCI, woa dee Jebedstund noch lang nich too Enj wea. Dann wea daut aun mie de Reaj.

Wiels etj den Eltesta Unruh een bät tjannd, enn fe ahm Hochachtung haud, enn wiels mie daut mett dem leewen Gott uck kratjt soo jintj, pausst etj opp, waut etj säd. Etj wull mie daut mett dee Twee Groote Jungess, eajentlich meea Manna, nich vedoawe.

Oba etj wea mett mien väsejchtjet Jestucka noch nich mol gaunz too Enj, auls dee erwähnde Niedarps Peeta loos-schnautad auls een Brommtjriesel:

"Vater im Himmel, schon wieder hat sich ein traier Bruder mang die schwarzen Schafe Dainer Waide verirrt und ist jefährlich verbiestert. Diese Sache, traier Herr, ist soo

230

wipe spittle from his trembling lips or even wipe tears from his eyes and cheeks.

The Ens Boys from Rivers had already stepped to the plate of prayer and even prayed for their father who had recently flirted with the J. W.'s. Then it was Nickel's Abram's, from Stuartburn, turn. Abram prayed mainly in the first gear since his Low German was stuck in this part of his prayer transmission, and refused to slip into the gear of High German.

With Teacher Schäfer, the head honcho, the CEO and school principal and all three in one person, the matter of language took on a reverse angle. As clever as he was, and even educated in Bessarabia, this sturdy serious heavyweight stuck strictly to High German; his Low German was awol.

The next fellow who prayed often and eagerly was Petkau's Peter from the Lowe Farm-Sperling area. This Peter, who went by the nickname of Extension Pete, was a lively chap who resembled a cock pigeon with sparse foliage on his receding hairline. He was half Sommerfelder, half Rudna-weida and looked the part. Strange, but Peter was hollow of girth and barrel chested, all in one piece.

At home, at the Petkaus, the skunks had exercised serious mischief in the hen house and now their egg money ran low. Peter reported all this to God and asked the Higher Authority to put an end to all the misery by choking the living daylights out of the skunk family, bare-handed, if possible.

But back from the hen house to the prayer floor of the MCI with the business at Hand; it was my turn to have a word with God.

Since I knew Bishop Unruh somewhat and respected him and had similar arrangement with our loving Father, I watched my words. I had no intention of spoiling my relationship with either and did not intend to get on the

231

bedenklich, daß wir ihn beim Namen nennen müssen: es handelt sich hier um Hugo Unruh, Sohn des Ältesten Nikolai Unruh, und wenn sie auch allzumal nicht zur Brieder- jemainde jejieren, soo sind sie vleijcht doch allzu Hauf Daine Kinder, und jetzt wird hier auf Erden aber auch im Himmel viel gebetet und noch mehr gewaint.

Vater, bitte vertraib diesen jungen Bruder von der United Church Waide zurick auf die Wiese der Gerechtijkait und des echten Mennonitentums. Bewege ihn zur Umkehr. Laß ihn zum Handlanger der Wahrhaftigkait werden, und wenn er dann den Weg nach Hause findet und ein richtiger Prediger des Evangeliums wird, dann laß Deinen hailigen Gaist loos, und laß tausend waisse Tauben sich auf den Gesegneten als Zaichen Dainer Gnade und Fiehrung aufs Haupt setzen!

Amen!"

Wie stunde langsom vom Jebed opp, stritjte ons den Mell vonne Tjnees, enn etj tjitjt dann doch een Uagenbletj nohm Himmel hinjre Pempenboaj: wäaweet, vleijcht wea dee himmlischa Voda vondoag doabie Overtime too oabeide, enn dem Hugo derjch dee Kukkeruzzstap dijcht bie de School diretjt derjche MCI noh Hus too hohle!

Soo's bie de measchte Bedarie enn uck Bäderie äwa meist een gaunzet Läwe, haud etj uck dissen Owend biem Schemmawoare em Läwe meist gaunz vejäte.

Wie MCI Absolvente jinja aulatoop doahan woa dee himmlischa Voda ons hanschetjt, jeweehnlich oba woa daut measchte Jeld too talle wea, enn Hugo word bie de United Churchla Predja enn Seelsorja.

Ältesta Nikolai Unruh storf emm biblischen Ella mett meist hundat Joah enn druag eenen weetenden Schmusta oppem Jesejcht em Soatj. Wäaweet, vleijcht docht hee biem Auf- scheed aun sien Sähn Hugo.

wrong side of these big boys, or Big and Tall Men, as the case may be.

However, I was not yet through with my careful meanderings when the already named Peter Neudorf swung into verbal action like a well honed spinning top.

"Our Father in heaven, and yet again a dear brother has lost his way among the black sheep of your pasture. This matter, dear Lord, is so serious that I cannot but name the boy so sadly lost and fallen. He is Hugo Unruh, son of Bishop Nikolai Unruh and even if not one of them belongs to the Mennonite Brethren, they still may well be part of your circle, who knows? and now much prayer is spoken and more tears are shed on their behalf both here on earth as it is in heaven.

Father, please drive this young brother from the United Church pastures back to the meadows of salvation of true Mennonitism. Change and turn his ways and intentions. Let him become the arm of proper direction, and if and when he finds his way home and he becomes a true minister of the word of faith, then release your Holy Spirit and let a thousand white doves descend on the blessed as a sign of your grace and direction on the head of all involved and concerned!

Amen!"

We rose from our supplication, stroked the dust from our knees and I briefly directed a fleeting, hopeful glance towards the western heaven behind the Pembina Hills; who knows, maybe the Good Lord was working overtime tonight and would send Hugo directly through the corn field close to the school, and straight through the MCI on his way home.

As with most prayers over a life span I had almost forgotten this one but now that the twilight of my own life is approaching, I have become reflective.

We MCI graduates went wherever the God Lord wanted us to go in life and if such station involved a bit extra in cash, so

Wann Jie meene, disse Jeschijcht ess nu too Enj, enn haft een Happy Ending, dann saj et Junt: Weit gefehlt, liebe Geschwister!

Väje Wäatj looht de Scheenwäsajemeend, woa Hugo sien Onkel, Dr honoris causa, Ohmtje enn Eltesta Johaun Enns feftijch Joah Seelsorja enn Schäfa wea, noh aul de lange, lange Joahre toom easchten Mol The Reverend Hugo Unruh, Accredited Minister of the United Church of Canada, too eene Predijcht enn.

Etj wea doabie. Tjeene fief Minute lohta jintj daut loos: Oppe veaschte Tjoatjebeintj saut Ältesta Enns enn siene goode Fru Taunte Agath, enn dann Ältesta Nikolai Unruh enn siene feine Fru "Mama".

Meist vejäte…"Wea de Tjoatj voll?" "Joh, dee wea soo voll auls een mennischa Buck nohm Schwienschlachte!"

Enn Hugo Unruh stund hinjre Kaunzel enn predijcht loos soo auls een Salomoon mett eene Gabrielstemm. Donn fonge een poah Hundat Ennse "Großer Gott, wir loben Dich!" aun too sinje, mett Ernst Enns auls Dirijent.

Daut Leed wea noch nich too Enj auls dusend witte Duwe von de Notre Dame Rejchtung derjche Däare nennjefloage kaume, enn sich bie jiedem oppem Kopp hansade mett een Olivenblaut emm Schnoweltje.

Niedarps Peeta sien Jebäd vom 23 Septamba, 1953, wea zasstijch Joah lohta enn Erfellung jegohne.

much the better. While Hugo indeed became a minister and shepherd among the United Church lot.

When Bishop Nikolai Unruh passed on at the biblical age of almost one hundred years, he wore a knowing smile in the coffin, discernible for those in the know. Who knows? Maybe his last thought en route was of his son Hugo?

There is more. Last week the Schönwieser Congregation aka First Mennonite Church of Winnipeg in which Hugo's uncle Bishop Johann Enns, Doctor *honoris causa*, has shepherded a fine flock for all of fifty years invited The Reverend Hugo Unruh, accredited minister of The United Church of Canada, to a first guest sermon after all those many, many years.

I was present. In the front pew sat Bishop Johann Enns and his good wife Agatha, and next to him Bishop Nikolai Unruh and his "Mama" resided, smiling happily. Behind them sat a hundred and more family. Ernie Enns, choir and song director for half a century and more directed *"Großer Gott, wir loben Dich!"*

When Hugo Unruh commenced his sermon, a hush fell over the congregation as a thousand doves and more descended on as many congregationists, with each dove bearing an olive leaf of peace as they softly fluttered in from the direction of Notre Dame.

Bie Kloßes oppe Berstaund

Aune 1936 emm Somma wea daut soo grulijch heet enn uck soo schratjlijch dreajch, daut väle Mensche dochte, daut groote Triebsaul haud nu doch toojeschloage, wiels de Mensche so haßlijch weare. Em Staul gaupte de Tjitjel mett op'nem Schnowel noh Loft enn Wota, enn de Ente freide sijch wann eena han enn wada een bät uttjwield. De Pogge enne Ritsch sunge aula Baus, enn bie Peeta Schallenboajs haude de Tjeaj soo weinijch too supe, daut de Schallenboajsche biem Maltje reine Bottatjliesta manke Finjasch tjreajch. Sogoa de Tjoatje mußte sijch omstalle, soo dreajch wea daut, enn boold fong de Breedajemeend aun mett eenem Schmaundkauntje too deepe, enn de Tjoatjeltje gauwe Rain-Checks.

Enn enn Winnipeg wear'et noch väl schlemma; doa bleewe de Koare maua grohdsoo emm koakenden Pavement steatje, enn woar'a nijch koakt, schluage de Lied Heehnaeia op enn brutzelde de oppem Pavement goa. De Ope em City Park gaupte enn funge aun tweestemmijch daut Leed vonn'e Sons of the Pioneers, "Water, cool, clear water" too sinje, wann'et schemma word.

"Yes, Lied daut ess heet," säd Pankrautz, kreiweld sijch manke denne Wonse oppem Kopp, dee nijchj rejchtijch schosse wulle, enn jintjch nenn. Dee Tjinja wulle nijch meea boaft gohne, nijch wäajne Heehna em Graus; nä, dee weare see jewant, oba de Steena enn de Saund weare soo heet, soo heet auls de feurige Ofen ute Sinndachschool. Lange Hiebat veseffst enn säd: "Toom Schinda mett disse Mestwirtchauft,"

236

Klassen's Melon-patch

When in 1936 it was so hot and as dry as in any Sahara, many people claimed that the Great Travail had come to visit and mainly because the human lot was evil to the core. In the barn, the chickens were gaping with open beaks, while the ducks were happy if you spat in their direction every once in a while. In the ditches, the frogs all sang basso profundo, while at the Peter Schellenberg's place, the cows were so needy of water that Mrs Schellenberg claimed that, while milking, she had wads of butter sticking to her fingers. Even the churches had to make adjustments, it was that dry, and in short order the Mennonite Brethren, those eternal Dunkards, started baptizing with a cream jug, while Mennonites of other persuasion issued rain checks.

And in Winnipeg things were even more dire, cars got stuck in the boiling pavement, and where the pavement did not froth, people cracked eggs on the streets and cooked them to perfection. Monkeys at the Assiniboine Park gaped for moisture and started singing in two part harmony the song of the Sons of the Pioneers "Water, cool, clear water" at the gloaming.

"Yes, folks, it is hot," said Pankratz, while scratching his waning patch on his crown which refused to hatch, and went inside. Farm children were reluctant to walk barefoot on the yard and not on account of getting chicken shit between their toes; this they were used to, but the stones on every yard were as hot as the fiery furnaces in the Book of Daniel taught at Sunday School. Old Longjohn Hiebert moaned and said, "To the devil with this misery," when his church inclined wife was

auls siene Oole nijch doabie wea enn säd, hee haud uck enn Rußlaund manke Roode bliewe kunnt.

Oba soohne Hett haft twee Siede, säd Taunte Kloßsche emma; daut jeft jewaultje Arbuse, säd Kloße. Enn soo wear'et dann uck; boold vekofft Kloße eenen Entjelbaks voll Arbuse fe dree Dohla. Lied muake Arbusezieropp enn bie de Tonn, Taunte Ungasche backt Bruschtje auls en Rußlaund, enn de Lied trocke äahre Tjinja noaktijch ut, enn leehte ahn aune Arbuseklompes sijch saut äte, tweemol den Dach. Väle Mensche muake Arbuse emm Steentopp enn; aundre dreajde Soht, enn enn gaunz Siedmanitoba ritjt'et noh Rollkuake. Joh, enn bie Kloßes kaume de Lied enn jinje, oba aula haude see Arbuse em Foatijch.

De Russe oba, dijcht bie Kloßes, haude wada eascht emm Juni Goade jemoakt, enn waut de Cutworm nijch nauhm, daut nauhm de Moltworm. Oba uck de Russe wißte von Kloße siene Berstaund enn jinje doa de Nacht tjnippse. Enn de wißte aulnoch schnorrijch woohne riep weare; de riepe Arbuse barschte see eent mett'e Fust enn fraute dee mett Tjäna toop opp.

Donn säd Kloße toom Russenoba Tofan: "Diene Jungess vebiestre de Nacht enn gohne dann bie mie manke Arbuse! Hool diene Balj wiedahans Tus sonst woa etj de opplatzt noch de Reaj delenjd jehearijch de Zarakoasch voll heiwe!" Tofan word blauß enn säd opp dietsch: "To heck mett Junt, miene Jungess schlope de Nacht. Bie die fräte dietsche Schnodda-näse de Arbuse opp. Moak mie nijch bossijch," enn jintjch nenn. Kloße roopt hinjreaun: "Wann etj eenem mett'e Schrootflint eent aum Zint bullre woa, woat daut nijch dien Jung senne?" "Fe shure nijch," säd Tofan.

Kloße jintjch nenn, dreid sijch eenen Old Chum, trand sijch eene Arbus op enn läpeld dee ut. De easchte Nacht bleef hee Tus, oba de tweede? Joh, horjcht mau wieda, waut Oohmtje Kloße de tweede Nacht deed. Nohm Äte puhld hee daut Blie

238

beyond earshot; he might just as well have stayed in Russia among the Reds, he lamented.

"Such heat has two sides to it," said Mrs Klassen, the know-it-all; "We'll have a dandy crop of watermelons this year," said her husband. And that is just how things came to be; soon Klassens sold a trailer full of watermelons for three dollars. Other families boiled watermelon syrup like in the Old Country, while Mrs Henry Unger baked watermelon sweetened dark short cake like on the banks of the Dnieper. Most every family allowed their children to go naked and have their fill at giant heaps of watermelons twice a day. Still other families pickled melons in stone crocks; while most dried the seeds, and all of southern Manitoba smelled of fritters, the obligatory Mennonite accompaniment to watermelons. At the Klassens, already named, people came and went, but all left with a load of watermelons on their various crafts.

The Russians, neighbours to the Klassens, had, as usual, only made their gardens in late June and whatever the cutworms did not eat, the mole worms did. However, they, too, knew of Klassen's fabled melon patch and they sneaked to that field of plenty and commenced thumping for ripeness of the fruit. Somehow they knew which melons were ready for the eating and these they smashed open with their fists and ate them, seeds and all.

Then Klassen said to his neighbour Tofan, "Your boys get lost at night and stray straight into my melon patch. From now on you had better keep them at home for otherwise I might be tempted to give them one hell of a licking on their bare arses." Tofan reddened and replied, "To hell with you, my boys sleep at home and that every night. It's the German Mennonite snot nosed kids who devour your fruit. Don't get me mad!" and went inside. Klassen called after him, "So if I shoot someone in the ass with my shotgun it won't be your kids?" "For sure not," said Tofan.

ute Schrootflintkugel rut enn schedd doa growet Solt nenn. Dee stoppd hee enne Loop nenn, enn auls'et diesta wea, läd hee sijch enne Berstaund dohl enn wacht.

De Mond jintjch soo schmock opp, de Schirtje piepade, de Wilw fonge aun too jule, een Schop metjad, meist aules schleep, aules gaupt meed noh fresche Loft. Bloß Kloße lach doa enne Berstaund oppe woame Ead, docht aun Frind-schauft enne Welt vestreit, docht aun sienen schmocken Hoff enn Rußlaund, docht aune schataje Steena hiea enn siene Schopsfenz, dreid sijch eenen Old Chum, enn wacht manke Arbuseranke. De Mond tjitjcht soo nieschierijch too, dretjcht een Uag aum Himmel too auls'a sach, daut de Mensche hiea enn doa een bät goastrijch weare, enn freid sijch besondasch auls'a mett eenst Kloße enn siene Loop manke Arbusebläda sach.

"Na wacht mau," docht Kloße, "Du jniesaja Himmel-stjarps," enn freid sijch, daut de Mond ahm soo scheen dache deed. Mett eenmol head Kloße waut enn hee vestuak sienen Old Chum. "Youbetscherleif, doa kohme see, de rusche Tjräte," docht hee sijch enn wacht. "Enn doch," säd Kloße sijch, "eena meent, eena ess Tus aum Nippa; disse Loft, disse Ead, disse Arbuse, de Mond enn de Chochole!"

Tofans Peeta betjcht sijch, tjnippst, plock enn aut, eenmol, tweemol, dreemol. "Daut's O. K." docht Kloße, "loht ahm mau, wie habe jenuach." Oba waut meen Jie, Lied, de Jung haud eenen Sack, eenen Biedel, enn een Pinjel mett enn auls'a nu saut wea, fung hee aun dee volltooprommle. "Bozhe, pomozhe," säd Kloße, "da wallt dem Deutschen doch…" docht aun Uhland enn tjneep een Uag too, enn hoof de Loop opp auls Tofans ääh Jratzta sijch betjcht enn tjnippst. Kloße zield noch eenmol, poakad han enn häa, de Loop lach nu stell; opp'em aundren Enj twalw Schräd auf sach Kloße eene dobbelde schwoate Mond… "Pascholl!" schreajch'a, enn trock den Trigga… Tofans Peeta—soo maut Kloße aum nääjchsten

Klassen went inside, rolled himself an Old Chum, split a watermelon and spooned it into submission. That night Klassen remained at home, but this story will shortly reveal what Klassen was up to the next night. After dinner he removed the lead shot from a shotgun shell and replaced it with coarse salt. He slipped the load into his gun and when it was dark, he laid down in the patch and waited.

The moon rose cozily, crickets chirped, coyotes howled all around, and a sheep bleated, but otherwise everyone slept, with all gaping for the fresh air of the night. Only Klassen lay in his watermelon patch on the arm earth and reflected on his relatives, scattered all over the globe; he remembered fondly his wonderful yard in Ukraine, thought of all the damn stones in his sheep fence right here in the Promised Land, rolled himself another Old Chum and waited among the melon vines. The moon regarded the entirety of the scene with an amused demeanor, shut an eye when it saw that some youngsters were feeling their oats here and there, and happily observed Klassen with his barrel of salt potential among the melon leaves.

"You just wait a bit," said Klassen, "you gloating heavenly pumpkin," and was rather happy that the moon shone so brightly just for him and his intentions. Suddenly Klassen heard something and he doused his Old Chum. "You betcherlife, here they come, these Russian scoundrels," he thought to himself and waited. "And yet," he reflected, "one imagines being at home on the Dnieper; the air, the earth, the watermelons, the moon and the Ukrainians."

Tofan's Peter bent down, thumped a melon, picked, smashed it agape, and ate, once, twice, three times. "That's okay," Klassen thought to himself, "let him be, we have enough of God's fruit." But can you imagine? That boy had along a bag, a sack and a cardboard box, and when he had had his fill, he started filling them up. "Bozhe pomozhe," said Klassen, "this is too much for any enterprising farmer, Christian, or pending

Dach ut—wea mett eenem Sautz vom Deadstart vearend-
artijch Schooh wiet jesprunge, enn haud biem tweeden
Sprung noch twee Schooh Loft tweschen sijch enn de
achtschooje Schopsfenz jelohte. "Postoj!" roopt Kloße, oba
Peeta haud'et bosijch, enn rannd enn schreajch "Tschorrt!"
enn brelld "Tschorrt!" enn rannd.

Kloße jintjch noh Hus, dreid sijch eenen Old Chum,
schmustad auls de Kloßche säd, de Stauldäah wea oppeenst
lud toojeschloage, enn meend, hee wull noch een bät
Daumbratt mett'em oolen Tofan späle. Hee jintjch noh
Tofans, enn späld Daumbratt, heiwd den oolen Tofan
dreemol ut enn fruach dem Oolen: "Du Petro Wasiljewitsch,
woa ess Peeta? Mett dem jankat mie uck mol too späle."
"Don't know," säd Tofan. "Dann well wie dem mol seatjche
gohne," säd Onkel Kloße.

Enne Schien, doa saut'a! Haud de Betjze raufjetrocke enn
saut enne Bett mett woamet Wota enn leet sijch daut Solt
utem Hinjarenj tratje. Saut doa enn tjitjcht rauf, enn schämd
sijch: wea mack auls'ne doodje Pogg, haud noch Arbusetjäna
manke Hoah enn red waut, daut hee von nu aun doch een
bätje aum Diewel jleewe wull. "Waut ess dem?" wull Kloße
weete. "Dee haft Gnautz," säd Tofan. "Mett Solt ennriewe,
dann jeiht dee wajch!" säd Kloße, enn schmustad polietsch,
enn piepad, enn jintj noh Hus.

in the faith" and then, reflecting on what the German poet he had in mind would do, raised his gun, closed one eye while aimingly zeroing in on Tofan's biggest boy's zarako. Some twelve paces distance was the thiefing double moon of his gun's intent and then… "Pascholl!" he screamed, and pulled the trigger… Tofan's Peter—so Klassen measured the next day, had jumped twenty four feet from a dead start, and in his second leap he had cleared the eight foot high sheep fence by a good two feet. "Postoj, Stop!" Klassen called, but Peter was too busy to pay much attention as he galloped and yelled, "Tschorrt!" meaning devil in every language and then repeated "Tschorrt!' while motoring on every cylinder.

Klassen walked home, rolled himself an Old Chum, smirked knowingly when his Frau claimed that the barn door had banged loudly when the wind blew it shut, and suggested that he would walk over to the Tofans to play a game of checkers with the head of the house. He trounced his neighbour three times at the game and then asked: "Petro Wasiljevitsch, where is your Peter? I would like to play with him a little as well." "Don't know, ja ne znaju," replied Tofan. "Let's go and look for him," suggested Ohmtje Klassen.

In the barn is where Peter sat. He had his pants pulled down and sat in a tub of warm water and let the water draw the salt out of his ass. Peter just sat there, ashamed; as docile as a dead frog, still had watermelon seeds in his hair and on his shoes, and talked about believing more fervently in the devil from now on.

"What's with him?" Klassen wanted to know.

"He suffers from poison ivy," replied Tofan.

"Rub salt in it and it will go away," Klassen recommended. "And, by the way, I found a sack, a bag and a cardboard box in my melon patch. Here they are, maybe you have use for them." Then Klassen rolled himself a final Old Chum before departing for home, whistling all the way.

www.ingramcontent.com/pod-product-compliance
Lightning Source LLC
Chambersburg PA
CBHW031122030726
47496CB00002BA/641